What others are saying...

Paradise may not be all that it seems. Like the sunken wreck on the ocean floor, everyone seems to be hiding dark and dangerous secrets. The Bimini Road's End Resort in Bahamas survived a recent hurricane, but will Jayna survive the brewing storm threatening her and the lives of people she cares about? Kristen Hogrefe Parnell will have you holding your breath as you wait to find out.

Sara Davison, Carol-Award winning author of Lost Down Deep and Driven

Kristen Hogrefe Parnell always weaves a tight story of suspense mixed with just enough romance to keep readers turning the pages. Hold Your Breath is a delicious, thrilling story you don't want to miss!

Shannon Redmon, Publisher's Weekly Best-Selling Author

Kristen Hogrefe Parnell rips back the curtain on paradise in her intriguing romantic suspense, Hold Your Breath. The Bahamas locale hides sinister secrets that threaten to do more than derail heroine Jayna's idyllic vacation--it might cost her life. Kristen weaves in different threads to create a fast-paced story destined to make you forget to breathe.

Sarah Hamaker, author of The Dark Guest, 2023 Selah Fiction Book of the Year

With an idyllic tropical setting, a deranged drug dealer, and a perilous engagement, Hold Your Breath will have you doing exactly that—right to the end of the book!

Jayna Scott is an ex-model and travel blogger with more than a mere suitcase of life-baggage she carries around… why does she have to find love in all the wrong places?

Private Investigator Liam Bracken is protective of his broken heart and neck-deep in a narcotics investigation—until Jayna catches his eye and renders him smitten.

Crisp dialogue, flawed characters, and an intricate plot are perfect ingredients for this delicious page-turner, and although I also thoroughly recommend the first book in the series, this one can absolutely be read as a stand-alone title.

A hiking retreat, an unlikely love-match, and a fight to stay alive in paradise—this action-packed adventure has everything for avid fans of Christian romantic suspense.

Laura Thomas, author of "Flight to Freedom" Christian romantic suspense series

HOLD YOUR BREATH

CROSSROADS SUSPENSE

Take My Hand—Book One
Hold Your Breath—Book Two

HOLD YOUR BREATH

CROSSROADS SUSPENSE: BOOK TWO

BY

KRISTEN HOGREFE PARNELL

Hold Your Breath
Published by Mountain Brook Ink
White Salmon, WA U.S.A.

The website addresses shown in this book are not intended in any way to be or imply an endorsement on the part of Mountain Brook Ink, nor do we vouch for their content.

This story is a work of fiction. All characters and events are the product of the author's imagination. Any resemblance to any person, living or dead, is coincidental.

Scripture quotations are taken from the New King James Version of the Bible. Public domain.
ISBN 978-1-953957-38-2
© 2023 Kristen Hogrefe Parnell

The Team: Miralee Ferrell, Tim Pietz, Kristen Johnson, and Cindy Jackson
Cover Design: Indie Cover Design, Lynnette Bonner Designer

Mountain Brook Ink is an inspirational publisher offering fiction you can believe in.
Printed in the United States of America

Dedication

To all the *Jaynas* who read this book,
May you know God's overwhelming, pursuing love for you.

Acknowledgments

Hold Your Breath is my eighth published novel, and I do not take for granted the privilege of sharing a story in print. I have so many people to thank for making this project possible, but here is the short list.

Thank you, Miralee Ferrell and the team at Mountain Brook Ink, for inviting me to be part of your publishing family. What a joy it has been to partner with you in my Crossroads Suspense series! Thank you, Kristen Johnson, for fielding so many emails and questions and always being gracious when people mix up the "Kristens." Thank you, Tim Pietz, for being such a helpful publicist. Thank you also, Fay Lamb, for your editing insights.

Thank you to my lovely agent Stephanie Alton for representing me and coaching me in the publishing journey. I have learned so much from you and am truly grateful to be part of the Blythe Daniel Agency. Blythe, you are a blessing to me as well!

Thank you, James, for being such a wonderful husband and daddy. The way you encourage me to write and cheer me on never ceases to fill me with gratitude. Thank you for watching and caring for our baby boy so I could attend Zoom meetings and meet my deadlines.

Thank you, Mom and Dad, for always believing in my writing. Thank you, Mom Fran, for being an encourager.

Thank you, Ashley and Amberlyn, for being both best friends and writing buddies. You are the only two people I know who can follow my tangent conversations from writing to motherhood and back again. You help keep me sane, laugh with me, cry with me—I am forever grateful for you both.

Thank you to so many—too many—dear friends to name here! You know who you are. I count your friendship among life's richest blessings. Thank you for being so faithful and praying for me—and buying a book or leaving a review even if romantic suspense isn't your genre of choice!

Thank you, dear reader, for joining me on this adventure. I pray Liam and Jayna's story transports you and inspires you in ways I might not even have imagined.

Thank you, Jesus, for saving me and giving me stories to tell. May I always write stories that please You, and may You show me how to use my time and words wisely in this beautiful, messy season of new motherhood.

Prologue

Bimini, Bahamas

"You know what they say lies at the end of the Bimini Road?" Mario Delgado lifted his cocktail glass to the barely sober couple across from him. The sun had long since set on his resort's beachfront, and if he didn't clear the lingering guests soon, Kevon would have choice words for him later.

The cozy flame in the firepit had died out several hours earlier, and everyone but this couple had taken the hint and hit the sacks. It had to be almost one in the morning.

"Is it a pot o' gold?" The woman laughed at her Irish accent imitation and reached for her glass again.

"No, dear, that's at the end of the rainbow." Her slightly less drunk companion rolled his eyes. "It's this Bimini Road's End Resort, Maggie."

Mario rose. This pair was impossible to corral to their suite. "I don't mean our resort, though we are named after the Bimini Road. I mean the lost city of Atlantis itself."

The last of her margarita spewed from the woman's mouth, missing Mario by inches. "That's crazy talk."

He stepped back to increase the distance between them. "Maybe, but you can see for yourself on the snorkeling excursion tomorrow. But man, look at the time. We leave at nine sharp, so if you want to join, I suggest getting some shut eye."

"Nah, who needs sleep?"

"You do, Maggie." Her partner stood. "Let's get to bed."

She crossed her arms and slouched in the wicker chair. "I don't wanna."

Mario felt the heat rushing to his face and had to remind himself for the hundredth time why he did what he did.

Swallowing a crass comment, he forced an even tone to his voice. "Sand fleas get awful bad this late at night."

The woman shrieked and bolted from her chair. "Sand fleas?"

"Bed time for you, Maggie." The man wrapped an arm around her waist, raised his empty glass toward Mario, then staggered toward their room.

Relief seeped through his core, and Mario collapsed onto his adjacent seat, facing the water. He had so much to do. Process payroll. Do laundry. Respond to that travel blogger and decline her request about hosting her so she could bring awareness to his community. Her idea to show Bimini's strength in recovery from the last hurricane season as this summer's season started wasn't a bad idea, and the truth was, she intrigued him. He loved a good philanthropist effort, but right now, the last thing he needed was a nosy writer poking around his resort.

He could deal with her and everything else in the morning, and get at least seven hours before his excursion, but Kevon wanted to see him. Which usually spelled trouble.

Why couldn't the man be content that Mario kept his end of their agreement? He cleared the beach by one-thirty every morning. He cordoned off sections of his damaged resort for Kevon's purposes and didn't ask questions. He didn't need the details on Kevon's deliveries or what other activities went on offshore at night.

He just needed that paycheck.

A light flashed twice offshore. The signal. Forcing his weary body to rise, Mario rolled up his pant legs and strode toward the shore's edge where he'd left his inflatable boat tender waiting. At least after this meeting was over, he could ride to his yacht and sleep there until morning.

The engine purred to life, and Mario guided the tender toward the flickering light. Kevon's fishing boat had anchored at the edge of the rocky point, invisible in the night's inky blackness except for the occasional signal. In minutes, Mario reached the vessel and slowly brought his tender alongside it. Kevon's crew made quick work of helping him tie on, and a rough hand welcomed him aboard.

"Kevon is in the cabin waiting for you." The man motioned him toward a doorway.

Mario didn't need the guidance but said nothing. He'd already been on Kevon's boat more times than he deemed necessary. His stomach knotted at what the man wanted this time.

Straightening his linen shirt but not bothering to uncuff his pants, Mario smoothed back his hair and stepped inside the dank stairwell. Yellow can lights guided the way. Lopsided frames displayed Kevon's licenses and hung on jagged fishing hooks, jutting from the wall.

Mario shook his head. What kind of man decorated with fishing hooks? But then, the rusty, ugly edges matched Kevon's cover as the meanest Bahamian fisherman. It wasn't surprising this fishing vessel should complete the look without hinting what activities filled the man's deep pockets.

The scarcity of the place struck Mario as it always did. At the base of the stairs, one crusty table with bench seats filled the space. Beyond them were a simple kitchenette and a bunk bed. That was it.

But a man like Kevon didn't need much when others always gave him what he wanted.

The lanky Bahamian drug runner uncurled his frame from the bench and rose. Mario matched him in height, but that's where their similarities ended. Kevon was faster than an eel, meaner than a bull shark, and swifter to sting than a provoked manta.

His tight goatee framed a mouth Mario had never seen smile. "It took a while to empty the beach tonight."

Not this again.

Mario cleared his throat. "All my guests were in their rooms before one-thirty as per our agreement."

"Try not to cut it so close, eh?"

He would not apologize this time. "You wanted to see me?"

Kevon motioned to the table, and Mario reluctantly sat. Somehow, being in any position other than ready to run seemed unsafe in this man's presence.

"We're getting too much heat. As the storm debris clears, our cover gets thinner. The Coast Guard is upping their game again.

3

They caught one of our men."

"Does that mean—"

"No. We got him back, and he won't be talking, but we have to be more careful. I want you to build a bulletproof cover for your resort. Put forward a stronger front about making the community better for tourism. With your sterling reputation, the Coasties will look less closely into what goes on around here."

Mario's toes curled. What did this man think he'd been doing since Hurricane Darby nearly blew away everything his family had built? When his parents immigrated from Cuba, they had worked hard to build a new life and broken even with this resort. Since Mario had taken over, though, he'd taken one hard hit after another—and Hurricane Darby had pushed him into Kevon's path.

The man seemed to be his only chance for replenishing his family's hope fund.

Mario leaned back and met Kevon's gaze. "There's a travel blogger who reached out to me. She wants to bring awareness to the Bahamas and encourage tourists that it's safe to return. I'll invite her to the resort, and she'll give us a roots-focused face. How does that sound?"

"I like it." Kevon drummed his fingers on the table. "But I need you to do three things."

"Yes?"

"One. Don't let her get any idea there's something else going on offshore. Two. Give yourself an hour buffer for any events on the schedule I text you. Three. Temporarily store something for me."

The hair on Mario's neck stood on end. Something was off here. "Store what?"

"It's already in your dinghy. I suggest putting it in the freezer you keep on your yacht for fishing. I'll get it from you in the next few weeks."

A dozen alarms sounded in Mario's head. Storing something for Kevon could easily make him a scapegoat.

Kevon's stare suggested he didn't have a choice. "I'll wire you triple for your trouble."

Mario swallowed the bad taste in his mouth. "Anything

:lse?"

"Pay closer attention to your schedule—and I want my)uffer."

"You got it." Mario rose and showed himself out. Sure :nough, there was a black bag in his tender. It looked like a body)ag, but half the size.

It smelled rancid.

Willing himself not to look at it, he steered for his yacht noored offshore of the resort. After tying in, he sucked a deep)reath and then grabbed the bag's handles. Ugh, heavy. Too heavy.

At least the freezer would help with the smell.

When he finally managed to get it inside the boat and down o the freezer below deck, part of the zipper had come undone. 3iting his lip, he reached to seal it.

A bloodied finger popped out.

Everything he'd had for dinner came up.

An hour later, the bag was in the freezer, his floor was clean, ind he had showered twice. Lying in bed, though, sleep evaded lim.

Would he get caught? Was Kevon incriminating him? Or was <evon just testing that he would do what he was told?

How far was he willing to go? Freezing a dismembered body lad never been part of their agreement.

But the money was good, more than good, and he owed it to lis family. He had promised. The means might not be pretty, but he end would make it right.

He was one day closer to setting Gabriel and Camilo free.

Chapter One

Jayna Scott winced and pulled her cell phone farther away from her ear. With her free hand, she tugged her rolling suitcase and inched closer to the front of the Silver Airways boarding line.

Even with her phone volume on low, her sister's shrill voice came through the speaker loud and clear. "You shouldn't have. Mom is going to freak."

Well, Jayna 'shouldn't have' a lot of things, but there was no going back now. "Calm down, sis. You're overreacting."

"Overreacting? You promised you were going to settle down after your last traveling fiasco in Jamaica."

Jayna balanced the phone between her shoulder and ear so she could dig out her ID from her Calvin Klein bag. She chose to ignore the glare of the passenger behind her. "Lots of people get bit by wildlife every year."

"Not a venomous forty leg," Beatriz blurted.

The flight attendant quirked an eyebrow at her cell phone, but when his gaze met her face, his features transformed into a vibrant, interested smile. She'd seen that look a hundred times and didn't want the attention. Instead, Jayna pressed her passport and boarding pass into his extended hand, offered a tight smile, and marched forward in line the moment he returned her ID.

She followed the guest in front of her out the door toward the thirty-four-passenger airplane. Florida's Memorial Day sunshine made her squint, but she needed a third hand to pull her suitcase, hold her phone, and find her sunglasses. The sunglasses would have to wait. "Listen, Bea—"

"I didn't even know what a forty leg was—had to look it up—I can't believe centipedes could be so large and terrifying."

Jayna joined the line at the ramp stairs bridging the gap between the pavement and the plane. She squinted and slammed her luggage handle down. "I'm fine, you're fine, Mom and Dad are fine—"

"They won't be when I tell them you're heading to another Caribbean Island. What dangerous wildlife does this one have? Sixty legs?"

"There's no such thing." The guest ahead of her on the stairs might as well have been a snail. But then, this conversation with her sister wasn't going much faster.

"What about the men? You need a guard dog with the way they chase you."

Jayna flipped her thick braid out of the way and hefted her bag. "Can't say I'm not to blame as much as they are."

Her sister seemed to ignore that idea. "What about that nice, safe condo in Tampa your friend said you could stay in? Wouldn't that be the most—"

"The most boring place for a travel blogger to live? Yes, you're absolutely right. It would be." The door was within reach, and a whiff of AC fingered its way toward her face. So close.

Beatriz huffed. "That's not what I was going to say."

"But it's the truth. A travel blogger, by definition, must travel. Besides, the condo wasn't even in Tampa but some suburb called *Lutz*, which is one letter off from *klutz*, so there you go."

Her sister paused her argument. "I can't visit you in the Bahamas with my babies. Is it wrong to want a sister you can visit?"

Jayna ducked into the plane and almost knocked the knees of the front row passenger with her bag. The man frowned and gave her a look that said *stop yacking and pay attention.* This plane was too small for this conversation.

"Listen, sis, it's only a thirty-minute flight to Bimini, so you could totally visit for a day. Hey, I have to go. Love you lots, and I'll call you when I get there." Jayna didn't wait for Beatriz to reply before ending the call so she could stow her carry-on and set her handbag under her seat.

Glad she had the window seat, she let out the breath she didn't know she'd been holding. Tropical blue waters, beaches, and a sexy landlord were exactly what she needed.

Not that she'd ever met Mario Delgado, but he didn't sound old by any means. He had the most delicious timbre to his voice–the perfect mix of huskiness, humor, and pure masculinity.

Better hope he was married and she could save her poor heart one more heartbreak.

Jayna popped in her earbuds as soon as she buckled her seat. Whether she listened to her beach playlist was irrelevant. The buds served as her best deterrent to unwanted conversation. The last time a guy chatted her up on a plane had sent her on a whirlwind romance that ended with another chip on her heart.

Serial bad luck with men seemed to run in her DNA, and Jayna's heart needed a break.

Or a hot Bimini landlord.

Someone's bag collided with her shoulder, and she cast an annoyed glance to her left. What about "earbuds in" did this guy not understand?

No, it was an older woman. Well, she wasn't old, maybe early sixties, but she had an overstuffed purse and was wearing an overly sweet vanilla scent that made Jayna want to gag. Subtle, this woman was not.

"Sorry, dear." Bright red lips pursed into a smile.

Jayna nodded and turned to look back out the window.

"Is this your first time to Bimini?"

Maybe she could pretend she didn't hear the woman, but Jayna was a horrible faker. Instead, she exaggerated pulling out an earbud. "What's that?"

The woman removed her wide brim straw hat and placed it on her lap. "This your first time to Bimini?"

"Yes, ma'am."

"I'm Cindy. It's such a shame about the hurricane damage, but I'm glad they're opening things up again."

"Definitely."

Cindy tapped bright teal fingernails on her thigh. "I hope the Hilton wasn't damaged too badly. Is that where you're staying?"

With a sigh, Jayna removed her other earbud. There was only

one hope to end this conversation. "No. I'm staying at a smaller resort. The reason I'm going is to bring awareness to the island through my travel blog and encourage other tourists, like yourself, to start traveling there again. I'm working on my first post concept during this flight, so don't mind me with my earbuds. Just working."

"Oh." Cindy blinked as if collecting her thoughts, and Jayna used the opportunity to plug back in.

It wasn't that she didn't like people. She didn't like uninteresting ones, nor did she need any other well-meaning female prying into her personal life. Her mom and sister were more than enough.

Minutes later, they were in the air. Jayna felt her body relaxing against the seat as the water progressively became bluer and brighter.

At only thirty minutes long, the flight soon moved into its descent. Her stomach churned at the first view of Bimini and debris that still littered parts of the island. She could only imagine how much progress had been made and how far the resilient Bahama Islands still had to go.

She would help. One post at a time.

Thanks to Mario Delgado who had agreed to host her at fifty-percent his regular rate. His was the most generous offer. Even though some of the other hotels she'd contacted were on larger islands, his resort included excursions around the island and transportation to neighboring islands for additional exposure.

Okay, his offer was also the only response she'd received. Probably because the larger hotels were too busy to respond or because she was a budding travel blogger and philanthropist still building her portfolio.

Whatever. She only needed one *yes*.

It was a win-win all around. For her. For Mario Delgado. For Bimini.

Chapter Two

The turquoise blue waters and white sandy beaches gave way to pavement—and Jayna's plane landed with series of jolting bounces that Beatriz would call an omen.

As the plane taxied to a stop, Jayna uncurled her fingers from the armrest. Rough landing behind her, she was here. The small plane soon disembarked, and she stepped into the sunshine and tropical air.

From the air, Bimini was nothing short of paradise. From the ground, it only got better.

A dark-haired man with flawless olive skin about the same shade as her own strode toward her. Perhaps he shared her Puerto Rican roots or had ties to some other Caribbean island. His light gray suit and pressed white shirt made him look like a cover model for a fashion magazine, but it was his smiling mouth that captured her attention.

"Ms. Scott?"

She had memorized that voice.

"Yes?" She smoothed her emerald skirt and white blouse while peeking at his left hand. Empty. "And you are—?" Better to pretend she hadn't guessed.

"Mario Delgado, your host." He flashed another smile. "Welcome to Bimini."

Not two minutes on the island and her heart was already in trouble.

"I didn't expect you to meet me," she said.

"I make a point of meeting all special guests in person." He pointed to her suitcase. "May I?"

"Of course." She smothered the smug grin threatening to break through as she passed the handle of her luggage to him. Her writing might not have impressed the other hotels, but it had certainly impressed him.

His dark eyes sparked with interest and led the way to a parked white sedan. "Let me get your door, Ms. Scott."

"Please, just Jayna is fine."

He slid her suitcase in the back seat and popped open the passenger door for her. "There is no such thing as *just* Jayna. Your writing is exceptional, and quite frankly, so are you."

He was laying the flattery on thick, but maybe he treated all his guests this way. Beatriz would tell her to be careful, guard her heart, focus on the job.

"Well, thank you. I look forward to promoting your resort and the island." There, her sister would approve of that answer.

"And I—" Mario's phone buzzed in the car's console. The screen flashed the name *Kevon*.

Had she imagined it, or had he stiffened? With a swift swipe of his finger, Mario sent the call to voicemail. "Sorry about that. What were—"

The phone again buzzed, and *Kevon* once more flashed on the screen.

"It's fine." Jayna buckled herself in. "I don't mind if you take the call. I'll enjoy the view."

Mario started the engine. "I was hoping to enjoy the view myself." He winked. "Be right back."

Before she could protest, he swiveled out of the car and strode away. What was so private about the call that he couldn't discuss it in front her? She glanced his way. While pressing the phone against his ear, he had his other hand on his hip.

Maybe Kevon was a creditor. The Bahamas had been hit so hard by Darby. Whatever she could do to help attract business, she would do it.

A smile tugged at her lips. *While enjoying the view.*

The minute she closed the door of her room behind her, Jayna flung her suitcase onto a chair and yanked the zipper open. She would take in the beauty of the suite later. Right now, she needed to sink her toes into the white beachy sand outside her window and the too-good-to-be-true reality that Bimini was her home for the next two months.

Mario's comment about needing to tend to something on the beach might also have something to do with her haste.

He had been more subdued after his phone call, though no less attentive to her. When she had asked if everything was all right, he'd waived off the caller as nothing for her to worry about.

After a quick change into her swimsuit, she grabbed her cell phone, sunscreen, and straw hat before slipping back into the hallway. A door at the hallway's end promised a shortcut to the beach, and she took it.

Once past a concrete slab, she slid out of her sandals and pressed her toes against the soft, manicured sand that someone had raked earlier that day. A dozen or more guests milled about the main beach area, but she needed to make a quick call, so she turned toward the more remote stretch. It wasn't fair to leave Bea worrying about her safety.

In a place like this, her sister had no reason to fret.

At the far end of the beach was a rocky point that capped off the small bay. Someone had loosely cordoned off a section of it, though she could see no reason why. Maybe there was a turtle nest or debris she couldn't see.

After scanning the beach and coming up short for any sighting of her host, Jayna speed dialed Bea and sauntered toward the point.

On the fifth ring, the call went to voicemail. "Hey, sis, just didn't want to leave you hanging. I landed safely here, and let me tell you, this place is amazing. I wish you could see this beach—"

A revving engine made her finger slip to disconnect the call. Seconds later, an ATV surged onto the beach from just beyond the point ahead.

It headed straight for her.

Jayna picked up her pace and moved toward the shoreline, closer to the handful of lopsided barricades and tape. The driver adjusted his course to intersect her.

The darkening scowl on his face did nothing to calm her

acing heart.

A wave splashed against her legs, and her feet sank in the wet and that slowed her steps. What could he want with her?

What so many men had already wanted—and taken.

No, she was being paranoid. This was all some mistake.

The driver jerked to a stop mere feet away and jumped out, he force of his bare feet spraying her with tiny clumps of prickly and.

"What are you doing here?" He towered over her, his dark nuscled arms waving with animation. "It's not safe."

Jayna swallowed to ease the dryness in her throat. "I—I'm orry? I just got here."

His anger faded to a glowering smirk as his eyes raked over ner swimsuit. "I can take you somewhere—safe."

She teetered as another wave sucked the sand from beneath ner feet. Any place with this man promised to be anything but safe.

"Got you." He grabbed her elbow and pulled her toward him. His black wife beater reeked of sweat and a substance that probably wasn't legal in either the U.S. or the Bahamas.

Jayna pulled away. "I'm fine. I'll just head back to my room now."

"Nah, you can come with me." Once more, he wrapped a hand around her arm. "We'll have a good time."

Her gaze darted to the ATV and more barricades in the back. "You're busy. I should go."

His lips cracked open, revealing a gold filling. "My friend will take care of this. We'll go back to my boat. I'll show you around. No charge."

Her heart hammered. She had to get out of here. "Please—"

"Kevon!" A man's sharp voice snapped her attention to the beach behind her. Jayna's knees wobbled as Mario raced across he sand toward her.

Kevon dropped her arm and crossed his. "Your barricade needs work."

Mario ignored him and splashed to her side. "You're all ight? I'm afraid there's been a misunderstanding."

"I—I'm fine." Jayna accepted the hand he offered her. With

Mario beside her, the tightness in her chest began to subside.

He squeezed her hand before releasing it and spun toward Kevon. "You can't be scaring my guests. I know some areas are still—dangerous for swimming—but there's no reason to cause alarm."

Jayna hugged herself to hide a tremor. "What's wrong with the water?"

"There's debris from the storm in some snorkeling spots, so we have to cordon those areas off until we're able to clean it up," Mario said. "Kevon's been helping me do that."

Kevon stared hard at Mario before climbing back into his ATV. "Until I'm done, you need to focus on keeping your guests safe." He tossed half a dozen larger barricades off the back of the vehicle. "Didn't mean to scare you." Kevon's words jolted her from her thoughts. His tone held no apology, but he saved her the awkwardness of a response by speeding away.

Mario put his back toward the barricades that littered the sand. "I'm sorry about that. Kevon is rough around the edges, but he is helping my resort in more ways than one. Let's forget him. I've got an itinerary for you I think you're going to love."

How dangerous was the water? It appeared much less dangerous than Kevon himself, but Jayna dismissed the thought. She hadn't come here to focus on Bimini's flaws but reveal its potential to tourists.

Her host offered her an arm. "How about we talk over dinner? Then, I hope you'll join some of our other guests and me for our evening beach bonfire."

His dark brown eyes and reassuring smile melted her worries. Here was a man wanting to give her a chance to make a difference and the means to do so. He had guarded her from Kevon, and she would have to trust his reasons for working with the man.

She wrapped her arm around his and nodded. "I'd like that very much."

Chapter Three

Bimini, seven weeks later

Sunlight streamed through the palm-print curtains she'd forgotten to close last night, coating her canopy queen bed with a heavenly glow.

This was paradise down to the rich mahogany wood furnishings, the plush coral comforter—and the owner who had stolen her heart.

Was a week shy of two months too soon to fall in love?

Jayna's lips arched upward at the memory of Mario's lingering kiss. Every memory of the past several weeks seemed straight from a fairy tale. He had taken her on every excursion from snorkeling the *Sapona* shipwreck to swimming with stingrays at Honeymoon Beach. He had shown her every courtesy, though his "perfect host" act had soon vanished as they dropped their professional barriers and transitioned to friends and then something more.

It didn't seem possible that she had just met this man. Her heart told her they belonged together. He even shared her philanthropic vision and talked about how they could make a difference in the world together.

The care he showed his guests and attention he lavished on her could mean only one thing—she had finally found the perfect partner for her life.

A giggle surged up her throat. Yesterday, he told her he had a special surprise for her tonight. He was clearing his schedule this evening and delegating all guest relation activities to his manager.

When was the last time a man had made her feel this special? No, she wouldn't answer that. Most of her relationships started with flare and fizzled with unmet expectations.

But Mario was different. Now, she only had to convince Beatriz, who was the world's biggest skeptic when it came to Jayna's choice in men.

She would save the phone call with her sister for later. Her blog post was overdue, and Mario was tied up this morning anyway.

A knock sounded on the door.

Or was he?

She placed a hand on her hair. He couldn't see her with bedhead. She snapped the hair tie off her wrist and twirled her thick waves into a top bun. "Come in."

It was only one of the maids carrying a tray, complete with a red Hibiscus flower. "Mr. Delgado ordered you room service. I'll set it here for you."

"Thanks, Rose." Jayna smiled, but it felt like disappointment. "Has Mr. Delgado already left for the day?"

"Yes, ma'am. He had that early snorkeling excursion this morning, but he said not to deliver your breakfast until after nine to make sure you had time to rest."

Could this man get any more thoughtful?

"He sent a note."

Rose slipped out as quietly as she'd entered, and the moment the door closed, Jayna flung off the comforter and skipped toward the tray. The scent of Belgian waffles—her favorite—made her stomach rumble, but she reached first for the sealed envelope adjacent to the coffee mug.

Morning, dear, I hope you slept well and enjoy breakfast. I'll meet you on the beach at six o'clock sharp. Love, Mario.

A tingling sensation spread from her fingers to her toes. She would have Mario all to herself tonight. What did he have planned on the beach? Was he going to take her on his private yacht? She'd seen the *Seaduction* moored offshore, but so far, she'd only been on the catamaran he used for guest excursions.

She read the note twice more, hoping for a clue she'd missed, but Mario was being secretive. She didn't even know what to wear.

Then again, she did. Something feminine and flirty. Something her sister wouldn't approve of.

She shoved Beatriz's chiding voice from her thoughts. Jayna hadn't slept with all her boyfriends, but this certainly wouldn't be her first rodeo, and Mario was going to last forever. Her gut told her so.

First things first. Enjoy breakfast and pull out her laptop. That post wouldn't write itself. She also needed to update her socials. Affiliate marketing made up a good portion of her income, and without fail, when she posted outfits, she always made money. Guess all those years in modeling weren't a waste after all.

The memories still made her lips pinch though. Those years had left deep scars and made her grow up faster than a teenager should have to. She didn't want to think about her past now, not when her future was inviting her into the arms of happily ever after.

The hours passed more quickly than she'd expected. She published her post, scheduled a second, updated her social media, and checked her metrics. Her last post was outperforming anything she'd posted so far, and a glance at her affiliate earnings boasted strong numbers.

Plus, she felt good about herself. Making money was a mercenary part of life, but if she could do it while bringing awareness to an economy that desperately needed to recover, all the better.

Her stomach rumbled again, and she glanced at the time. It was already past one o'clock. If only she had a kitchenette and supplies, she could whip up something for herself. Cooking was one of the few joys in her life that she missed while traveling.

Oh, well. Guess it was time to put on some real clothes and head to the dining room.

She slipped on a teal sundress that showed off her curves. On the chance Mario was back from his excursion, she didn't want to look anything less than alluring.

The silent hallways suggested most guests were spending the day in the sunshine, and she didn't blame them. But she would have her fill of fun tonight. Already, she could visualize a picture-perfect sunset on the horizon.

The hallway opened to the hotel's lobby and dining room off to the side. Mario had done wonders with the place, and she adored his vintage Caribbean theme. Palm-tree upholstered dining chairs offset rich teakwood tables. A wall of glass windows overlooked the resort's beach front where bright blue umbrellas dotted the pristine white sand.

"Good afternoon, Miss Jayna." A Bahamian man bobbed his head from behind the lunch buffet where he was replenishing the salad bar.

Jayna helped herself to a salad bowl. "Hi, William."

"It's another day in paradise."

"You're right about that." She eyed the fresh pasta bar but instead heaped more salad into her bowl. She couldn't splurge on carbs and risk a food baby. Instead, she piled her salad high with fresh veggies and allowed herself half a dozen croutons.

The dining room was empty except for a young couple who seemed completely lost in each other's eyes and a lone man in the far corner.

Kevon.

She shivered and picked a seat on the opposite end of the room, next to one of the sparkling windows. After her initial encounter with him, she had tried to avoid him when he appeared on the beach. The few times she'd been unsuccessful, he had been civil enough, but he always gave her a vibe that somehow felt off.

Mario had later explained that Kevon was a respected fisherman who stepped up to help several resorts identify and clear debris fields concealed beneath the water's surface, but the man didn't look like a fisherman. His hands were far too smooth, and there was something in the way he looked at her. Maybe it was because his eyes wandered everywhere but her face.

She wouldn't let Kevon spoil her lunch. Not when she had a front seat to paradise.

She speared her salad. Outside the window, Mario's dog, Cabana, rested in the shade. It was the friendliest dog she'd ever met. What had he called it? A Sheba Inu? Anyway, the breed looked as though it had a perpetual smile on its face, so what was not to love about that? Its honey-colored coat and fluffy, cork-screw tail completed the package that most guests found a charming addition to the resort.

A few children rubbed its fur before running after their parents to the beach where couples and other families strolled or played in the surf. Her gaze wandered to the far right of the private beach and the reminder that even paradise had its scars.

She hadn't ventured to that section of beach since her first day, and the swimming area remained cordoned off due to debris that still needed to be cleared.

As hardworking as Mario was, he'd probably have even that evidence of the storm cleared in the next few weeks.

"Hey, Jayna."

She choked on her salad and jerked her head up to where Kevon now stood inches from her.

Grabbing for her water, she took a gulp and swallowed. "Kevon."

His eyes glinted, but his smile seemed more like a work of plaster than a sincere reflex. "You're wasting the day inside?"

Recovering, she set down her glass and forced a smile. "Work."

"All work and no play makes Jane a sad girl."

She tried to chuckle, but it came out more like a cough. "Oh, I'll get in my playtime later. How's the fishing?"

"Good. I'll be back out there tonight, but I could take you on the boat now."

Her toes curled in her flipflops. No way could she step on his boat without getting hooked by him. She hadn't wanted to go on his boat seven weeks ago, and a personal tour was the last thing she wanted today.

"Thanks, but I still have work to do. Enjoy the day though."

But he still stood there. She dared to take another bite of her salad, hoping he'd take the hint.

"Offer stands if you change your mind." His hand reached for her bare shoulder and squeezed. "See ya around."

His touch sent chills racing down her arm, but she had to play cool. "Yeah, thanks."

Maybe the low-cut sundress was a bad idea after all. Kevon finally released his hand but let his finger trail down her arm before walking away.

She shuddered but took a steadying breath. Once Mario finished clearing the debris, Kevon would have no reason to darken her piece of paradise any longer.

Her appetite gone, she dumped her salad in the trash and grabbed a bottled water before retreating to her room. She'd just stay there. Six o'clock was only a handful of hours away anyway.

Her work might actually be done, but a good beauty nap, luxurious bath, and primping would fill the time nicely.

At least in her room, she wouldn't have to worry about unwelcome advances from a creepy fisherman.

Chapter Four

Liam Bracken released his grip on the power boat's wheel to pull his buff higher around his neck. Another bead of sweat slipped from beneath his mesh Panama Jack hat and raced down his rash guard. Mid-July in Florida would bake his Irish skin faster than he could blink, so covering up was the only solution.

The wicking clothing still felt oppressive on his skin.

Another boat passed through the Anclote channel. The driver ignored the idle speed sign and kicked up waves that rocked his craft where he waited on the side of the channel.

Where was the Florida Wildlife Commission officer when he needed him? But careless boaters weren't the reason he was posing as a fisherman while on the clock today.

Not that he minded a reason to be on the water, but he preferred fishing when the sun wasn't blazing overhead.

His radio crackled with his partner's voice. "*Yankee Dog* left the dock."

Finally, he could get out of this channel. "Roger that."

Liam steered away from the river's edge where he'd been idling and into the main channel. Once he got through the no-wake zone, he'd continue toward the Gulf of Mexico where the suspected craft would likely head for scalloping. The short window Pinellas County offered for open scallop season ensured that the waters would be packed with other vessels, allowing him to get fairly close without causing suspicion.

Just in case, his partner Drew was on a jet ski and would be coming in from behind *Yankee Dog*, the suspected pontoon boat.

More sweat ran down his spine. Maybe the heat wasn't solely responsible. This was the first tip on the otherwise dead-end Russo case, and it was a lucky tip. Someone at the Anclote Marina had reported a half-torn brick of coke while cleaning one of the boats.

The cocaine brick had the same black, purple, and green coloration as the ones they had discovered hidden in Valentina Russo's yacht which they had confiscated during the Gasparilla boat parade. Aside from the kidnapping and attempted murder charges they held against her, Russo also sat in prison on illegal drug running charges. None of their best interrogators could pull even a shred of helpful information from her tight lips.

Not that he blamed her. If Russo reported to Big Eddie, the suspected head of Tampa's no-longer extinct underworld, she would be much safer rotting in prison than leaking evidence that would get her killed. That's how her former colleague Casale had found himself hanging from a rope.

But Avery Reynolds, the lead detective on that case, had made no attempt to conceal her frustration when the trail went cold. Even the flash drive his friend Kaley had helped them recover offered no hint at Big Eddie's identity, though it supplied evidence against Russo and some of her associates, all of whom proved equally tight-lipped.

For some reason, this case seemed personal to Reynolds, though he didn't know why.

Only a month after they had captured Russo, Reynolds had left on good terms with the Hillsborough County Sherriff's Department to start her own private investigator business. Many of her contracts came from the department itself, for cases the force didn't have the time or manpower to pursue.

When she offered Liam a job, he had hesitated for only a moment. The pay was tempting enough, as was her promise for a change of pace. Undercover narcotics work had taken a toll on his personal life.

After they rescued Kaley, she had chosen to start a relationship with his best friend Reef instead of him, and though she had let him down in the nicest way possible, the rejection still burned.

He needed a job that would give him space to focus more on his personal life but still provide the purpose he found in his work.

So, he had accepted the offer, become an associate with Reynolds Investigations—and ironically, found himself working on the same case that had connected him with Reynolds in the first place. This new lead could help bring Casale's killers and the underworld mastermind to justice.

The radio crackled again. "*Yankee Dog* is heading your way." Liam grabbed it and responded. "I'll let you know when I have eyes on her."

Once he passed the no-wake zone and was well into open water, the breeze offered some relief to the otherwise oppressive heat. It fanned at his beard and hairline, turning the sweat into Florida's version of natural air conditioning.

Just ahead, the cluster of boaters signaled a good scalloping spot. He glanced over his shoulder. Sure enough, *Yankee Dog* was coming up behind him. He slowed slightly, and the boat veered to his right.

Perfect, he'd let them take the lead and then follow at a distance. Maybe he'd even hook a tarpon and enjoy his sport once he came to a stop.

Yankee Dog anchored well beyond the boat cluster, which fit with their suspicions. If there was something going on underwater, the boat would want to stay away from crowds and prime scalloping grass beds but still blend in.

Liam chose a spot in clear view, but not too close. He'd leave the close-up for Drew and his jet ski. They agreed that Drew would put up his dive flag and snorkel nearby to get an underwater scope of the area while Liam maintained a casual watch while fishing. After setting his anchor, Liam went to work with his fishing poles. Drew checked in once more on the radio to let him know he was getting in the water. He spotted Drew's ski and would keep an eye out for him. Though more than capable, Drew and every good undercover agent relied on his partner.

Now that he was stationary again, the day's heat began once more to burn down on him. The boat's shade helped, but the heat, silence, and stillness grated on him more than usual.

Waiting had always been his weakness. Maybe that was why God asked him to practice it so much on the job and in his personal life.

He gulped remembering his hopes for a future with Kaley. She really was a catch of a girl. He was happy for Reef and her, but still, it was hard not feeling sorry for himself.

Everyone told him he was a great guy. Was that his problem? Was he too nice? Did girls really dig dangerous guys?

Not that Reef was dangerous, but he was rugged, adventurous, and a bit of a daredevil.

Liam sighed. It was pointless comparing himself to his friend. He would never find the right girl pretending to be someone he wasn't.

But then, he had never expected to be in his early thirties and still single. He had stood by his friends' sides in their weddings more times than he could count. Thankfully, he only had to rent the tuxes, but the privately owned tux shop most of his friends used knew him on a first-name basis.

After setting the last hook and baiting it, Liam cast it and let the wait begin. Then, he dug his binoculars out of the glove compartment and surveyed *Yankee Dog*.

Several divers were milling about on deck.

Donning full-body wet suits.

Liam frowned. He had been fishing and scalloping in these waters since he was old enough to crawl on his dad's power boat. Most Floridians didn't use full body wetsuits in July. Most wore barely enough swim attire to be considered decent. Most also just snorkeled in the shallow waters, but all the divers from this boat used scuba tanks.

There was nothing to do but wait now. Wait for the fish to bite. Wait for Drew to surface. Wait for one of these divers to show their hand.

If he were to guess, they might have an underwater cache where they transferred bricks like the one discovered on the pontoon. Perhaps that would account for the wetsuits. They could possibly hide them on their bodies.

Hopefully, Drew could get close enough to observe them.

Minutes ticked by. Movement to his left alerted him someone was out of the water.

It was one of the divers who held up a scallop bag, half full, and swam toward the back of the yacht to dump his catch in coolers.

Liam frowned. The boat was positioned so that he couldn't see the diver when he bent down. Moments later, the man was back in the water, and another diver switched places with him to unload his catch.

The pattern seemed innocent enough, but Liam wished he could see exactly what the divers did when they bent down to unload their catch. Were they unzipping their wetsuits? Did they look any skinnier or thicker when they returned to the boat than when they had entered the water?

It was impossible to tell at this distance.

Drew's voice came over the radio.

Liam snatched to answer. "How's the viz?" To his right, one of the poles dipped down.

"Not bad," Drew said, "but not great."

"Can you tell if they're loading or unloading anything in their suits?"

"No, man. There's a dozen or so crab traps—empty—but there's nothing else that looks suspicious."

Interesting. Scallops were in season but crabs weren't.

Liam sighed. Reynolds wasn't interested in off-season crabbing, even if it was illegal. She was going to be disappointed if this day turned into a dead end. His boss was borderline obsessed with getting a fresh lead on Big Eddie, but the man left no footprints to follow. Didn't he ever get sloppy?

"I'm going to circle around to the other side of the pontoon and see if there's anything unusual under the water."

"Roger that."

"On the bright side, we can have scallop scampi for dinner."

Liam chuckled. "I'll cook if you clean 'em."

"Deal."

Liam smiled. His partner and friend was as single as he was, and the poor man really couldn't cook. Liam had learned from his dad, and it was a skill that served him well. Even if his cooking didn't impress the girls, hospitality had been a way to show many

25

of his work friends God's love and introduce them to the community of young professionals his age at church.

His first pole jerked harder, and he tucked the radio into his belt to grab it. Maybe he'd catch something to contribute to dinner as well.

The fish put up a good fight, but after a minute, the line sagged. Sure enough, it had snapped the line.

Moments later, all the divers surfaced and climbed aboard *Yankee Dog*. Liam re-hooked his line while watching. The pontoon engine purred to life as one of the divers pulled up anchor.

Leaving already? They had been here only an hour. Most scallopers took half a day to get their limit. Maybe they were moving to a new spot.

No, *Yankee Dog* turned around and started back in the direction of the channel. The divers were done for the day.

His heart dropped. At least Drew could look around more freely, but his gut told him there was nothing here to find.

Maybe there never had been. Either that or Big Eddie's men had once again slipped right under their noses.

It was too much of the same story of his last few months. First Kaley. Then the leads from her kidnapping case. Now this lead was going cold fast.

He pulled in his lines. Maybe someday, he would have something to show, something to replace the one that got away.

Just not today.

Chapter Five

Bimini

Golden hour had never glowed this way for him before. He had spent his whole life working for his parents at their resort—now his resort—and watched honeymooning couple after couple lose themselves in each other's arms during the sunset.

Mario ran a hand through his hair and paced the shoreline in front of his anchored tender. Would tonight be his night? Sure, he'd had women before, but none of them sent his pulse and heart racing like Jayna Scott.

She was different. She was gorgeous and intelligent and big-hearted. She wanted to make a difference and so did he. She wasn't like girls he'd dated before that only wanted to crawl into his bed. She had self-respect, but she also had it bad for him.

He smirked. The last several weeks had gone fast, but they were the best weeks of his life. If she said yes, they'd be only the beginning.

His gut clenched. What if this was too soon? But if he waited, she'd leave for the States, and then he'd be too late.

Movement to his right made him jerk his head. Jayna promised to meet him at six sharp, but it wasn't Jayna.

It was Kevon.

He wanted to growl at the man to go away. What was he doing here in daylight anyway? Beyond him, he glimpsed a woman's dress flowing in the breeze. Jayna. She would be here any minute.

Kevon removed the long cigar from between his lips. "You're welcome."

"Come again?"

"Aren't you glad I suggested a grass-roots effort?" Kevon

cracked a sly grin and nodded over his shoulder to where the world's most beautiful woman sashayed toward him.

"I'm busy tonight, Kevon."

The fisherman whistled. "I'm sure you are." But the mock smile vanished a moment later. "I've been busy too. Just don't let her go below deck to the freezers."

Bile climbed up his throat. Mario had spent hours preparing his yacht for a sunset dinner and romance, but he hadn't gone downstairs. He hadn't needed to.

"You told me you cleared out your mess weeks ago—"

"I got busy. I'll take care of it tomorrow." Kevon cast one long, lingering stare at Jayna and then sauntered away.

Could she hear his pounding heart? Everything was perfect, ready. She wouldn't have any reason to go below to the freezer. It would be fine.

Still, a part of him wanted to kill Kevon for casting doubt over his evening.

"Everything okay?" Her voice was unsteady, unsure.

Mario turned to give her his full attention. She wore an ankle length semi-sheer rose dress with a revealing slit up her right leg. She'd curled her thick, long hair, which fell below her bare shoulders.

He reached for her hand and kissed it. "My dear, you look radiant."

"Thanks, you look pretty great yourself." She nibbled her glossy lips.

"You ready?" He motioned toward the tender. "I've got a surprise for you back on my yacht."

Her eyes sparkled. Everything about her sparkled. "You're the only surprise I need."

Oh, she was perfect.

He gave her his hand while she tugged her dress above her knees to keep from getting it wet while stepping into his tender. Part of him wished to see what a wave would do to her sheer dress.

Patience. She'd be taking it off for him if his night went as planned.

He pulled up his small anchor, hopped inside, and started the engine for their short cruise to his yacht. "How was writing today?"

"Productive. I got a lot done." She hesitated. "I can't believe it's almost time for me to leave. You've been the most amazing host."

Amazing host? Was that what she thought about him? No, she was being shy, waiting for him. A woman didn't dress like this—look like this—for a stiff dinner with her host.

"You've made my job an absolute pleasure," he said. "I love the awareness you're bringing to my community. I'm booked out through next month already, thanks to you."

Oh, that smile.

He cleared his throat as they neared the *Seaduction*. "It's more than your gift for words—for caring for people. Do you make it this easy for all your hosts to fall in love with you?"

A blush crept from her neck to her cheeks. "Most people don't really notice me."

"Ha!" He tied the tender off to a cleat on the edge of his yacht. Then he jumped on board and spun to help her. "Now that, my dear, is perhaps the first fib I've heard you tell."

He gripped her hand, pulled her up beside him, and tugged her body against his. She trembled but leaned in closer.

"Not notice you?" he whispered and wiped a wavy strand of hair from her face. "Even a blind man would notice you."

Jayna's breath hitched. She hadn't been standing on Mario's yacht two seconds, and she was already in his arms.

Which was exactly where she wanted to be.

Melting against him, she lifted her gaze to meet his eyes. They were hungry, but respectful. He was waiting for her.

She tilted her chin and caressed his cheek—inviting him to dip his lips to meet hers.

Oh, his kiss! It was both sweet and hard, gentle and intense. When he pulled back—probably to make sure she was still breathing—she didn't know if she was.

He kept her hand clasped in his. "Come on. Let me show you around."

It was a good thing he held her hand, or she might have fallen head over her bare feet.

Never mind. She already had fallen for the man himself.

His yacht was immaculate. The deck was a rich auburn color and felt smooth to her feet. Mario had strung white lights from the cabin to the far end of the deck. Centered beneath them was a table for two complete with candles, a rose, and a champagne bottle on ice.

He pulled out a seat for her. "Please, make yourself comfortable. I have everything prepared and will be right back."

Jayna caressed the rose. "What happened to the full tour?"

Mario flashed a jagged grin. "We'll finish the tour later."

Her fingers tightened, and her thumb grazed a thorn as Mario turned and disappeared inside the cabin. She retracted her thumb and brought it to her lips. Better remember that even the most beautiful flower could hurt her.

But Mario wasn't a flower, and he was being the perfect gentleman. No, she was being a silly schoolgirl. Her nerves were having a play date at her expense.

She would enjoy this beautiful night, this perfect moment. On Monday, she'd have to fly home one way or another, but this weekend was hers to enjoy. Hopefully, Mario would enjoy it too and invite her back.

A shiver ran down her spine. What if he wanted to use her and discard her like so many others had done? What if he didn't want commitment?

A faint click brought her back to the present, and she glanced up to find Mario balancing a tray in one hand and snapping a picture on his phone with the other.

"That might be my new favorite picture." He slipped his phone into his back pocket and placed the tray before her.

The knot in her stomach relaxed. "Mmm, sushi. My favorite."

"I know." He poured them both a glass of champagne and then took a seat. "I've got key lime pie for dessert too, but I have a confession."

She searched his expression for any cause for alarm, but there was laughter in his eyes—and something else. Something that looked like love.

His bronze complexion colored. "I'm no chef, so I special ordered them."

The rest of her nerves fled away. This man cared enough about her to pay attention to what she liked and make sure he gave her the best.

Jayna reached to place her hand over his own. "That was so thoughtful of you."

"I've heard that women like men who cook, but I'm awful at it."

She laughed and curled her fingers around his. "I'm more than happy to be the cook for us both. I don't care that you didn't cook this. It looks amazing."

His face relaxed into a warm smile. "I'm glad you like it."

She took her first bite. There was a tanginess, perhaps a lemon cilantro flavor, and the sushi was crisp. But she needed to focus on the man, not her food obsession, and make the most of this opportunity to know him better.

After a sip of champagne, she set down her glass. "You seem to know me so well already, but tell me, what do you like most?"

Mario thoughtfully chewed and then wiped his mouth. "I like you."

Heat rushed to her cheeks, but she would not be deterred. "Right back at you, but I mean, what do you want most out of life?"

He glanced at her with a sly smile. "Am I not allowed to say you again?"

What a tease. "I like hearing that, but I mean what are your dreams and your plans?" She held her breath. Would his plans be something she could fit her life into?

"You're one of the first girls who has ever asked me that. Do you really want to know?"

She studied his chiseled jawline and defined, clean-shaved features. His complexion—somewhere between olive and a deep tan—hinted at a heritage that didn't originate in the Bahamas or the States. She very much wanted to know his story, what made him tick, and what he wanted out of life.

"Yes, please."

He smiled, that rare smile of someone completely at ease and sure of himself. "I'll give you the short story, because I don't want this night to be about me."

Mario reached for her hand and held it. "My parents were Balseros—rafters—and part of the mass exodus from Cuba during the 1990s. Most of our people sought refuge in the States, but some of us chose the Bahamas instead. I was a baby at the time and don't remember any of the journey. All I've known is the life they made here in Bimini."

Her mind raced. She'd seen pictures of the Balseros Crisis in her history book but hadn't thought much about it.

He cleared his throat and continued, "We were the lucky ones, but those who remained behind, not so much. My mother's sister was too pregnant, and her husband too ill to make the journey. Both have since passed away, but they left behind two sons, my cousins. More than anything, I want them to have a new life too."

"Isn't it easier to leave Cuba now that Castro is dead?"

Mario sighed. "In theory, yes, but truthfully, it's almost impossible to get a visa. There is a lottery, and I'm working hard so that I can send them money to increase their chances."

Jayna's heart swelled. He cared so much about his family to make a way for their freedom. This was a man she could follow.

"I think that's wonderful."

He took another bite of his sushi as if to consider her compliment. "There is something else that I want."

Her toes curled. "Yes?"

"I want a woman to spend my life with, to share this resort with, to travel with, to share my desire to help others."

Had this man read the textbook for melting her heart?

"Well, all I can say is she will be the luckiest woman alive."

After the meal there was dessert and then dancing. Mario played reggae music while they twirled around his deck until only the last bit of sunset remained.

Suddenly, he spun her tightly into his arms. His breathing

)ecame heavier, and his pulse nearly beat out of his wrist into hers. She pulled back slightly. "What's wrong?"

His dark eyes were pools of desire. "Wrong? Nothing is vrong. Everything is right. Perfect. You're perfect."

Mario gulped and squeezed her hands tighter. Then slowly, ıe got down on one knee.

Jayna gasped. Was he? Yes, he was. Her own eyes swelled as ıe released one of her hands to pull a ring case from his pocket.

"Jayna Scott, I've spent barely two months with you, but hat's long enough to know you're the woman I want. Will you ıtay with me? Marry me?"

Happy tears sped past her eyelashes. She had dreamed of the lay when the man she loved would ask her this question. She'd ıad plenty of men tell her they loved her, but they had never)acked up their words with a promise like Mario was offering. She ıdored this man—after such a short time. How much more would ıhe adore him for a lifetime?

"Yes!" It was all she could manage before choking on her)wn tears. He stood, wrapped her in an embrace, and gave her a ‹iss she never wanted to end.

Chapter Six

Morning sunlight streamed through the small cabin window and warmed Jayna's cheeks. They still felt hot after last night, but she had never felt more adored.

Mario was passed out on the sheets next to her, and she wouldn't wake him. He worked so hard and deserved a day off. He had treated her like a queen last night, and breakfast would be her opportunity to pay him back.

Sliding softly onto the floor, she wrapped his robe around herself and padded out of the room. There was a small separate kitchenette with a mini stove, microwave, and fridge. But the fridge was empty except for leftover key lime pie and bottled water. She helped herself to one and frowned. Surely, he would have eggs or pancake mix or something she could whip up for breakfast.

Wait, during his yacht tour, Mario had mentioned another level below deck for storage and freezing fresh catches but had said there was nothing interesting to see and hadn't shown her down those steps. Maybe there were more foodstuffs there she could use.

She slipped through the storage room door leading to the lower level and squinted in the blackness for a switch. It sure was smelly and dank down here. Flicking on the light switch revealed two large freezers. Maybe there would be bacon or fresh frozen fish she could defrost and grill up.

The first freezer was empty, and she had low hopes for the next. Maybe she would have to ask William or one of the kitchen hands for permission to use the resort kitchen sometime.

Yanking open the second door caused a large black bag to tumble to her feet.

Her stomach did a queasy flip flop. Why would Mario store

ood in a black bag? And there was red along the edges. Maybe he
iadn't had time to clean the fish? She wouldn't know. A
isherwoman she was not.

Well, she had to get it back inside the freezer anyway. Might
is well have a look.

She unzipped the bag part way and froze. It was as if someone
iad taken a life size Mr. Potato Head and dumped it inside.

This was no child's game. This was a blood-battered body. In
>ieces.

She slapped a hand over her mouth to trap the rising bile and
cream that threatened to break through. She slammed her eyelids
hut, wanting to unsee the frozen corpse.

Images like these were the reason she told Beatriz to stop
vatching those police shows. Now, she was in the epicenter of one.

But she was here, on Mario's boat. What was this—who was
ie?

Swallowing hard, she jerked the zipper in place and mustered
he courage to shove the bag back inside. Leaning against the
reezer, she made sure it had shut before darting up the stairs in
earch of a sink—of anything that would let her try to wash away
he memory of what she'd seen.

The sun was no longer warm and glowing. It was
>ppressively hot. It was now ugly and smiling on her foolish
lreams of a life with Mario.

Her gaze fell to her left finger. What had she done? Agreed
o marry a murderer?

Her body recoiled at the way she had given herself so fully to
iim. She leaned over the rail and vomited.

Perhaps he was still asleep and she might escape. But how?

A small engine buzzed nearby. She wiped her mouth and
pun to catch sight of a small motorboat speeding their way.
Vlaybe she could catch a ride away from here.

But she was wearing only Mario's bathrobe. That wouldn't
lo. She had dropped most of her clothes before they even reached
he bedroom. How could she be so foolish, so blind?

Tears stung her eyes. Now she felt cheap, used, anything but
pecial.

Rinsing her face in the kitchen sink, she dried her skin with a course hand towel and forced herself to take deep breaths. If she kept her head on straight, she could survive this. She could have her cry later. Right now, she needed to get away.

Footfalls sounded on the deck, and she spun to see who had boarded. Two broad men came into view.

Kevon was one of them.

She ducked behind the counter and hoped they hadn't seen her. What was he doing on the boat? Who was the other man?

Biting her lip, she took a risk and peered over the edge. They were gone—must have gone below deck.

The hair on her neck prickled. What if they had found her there? Were they going for the body?

The minutes ticked by impossibly slow, but then she heard a thud and then a deep voice. She risked another look.

The kitchen door swung open, and she jumped up. There stood Kevon, a smirk plastered on his face.

"K—Kevon." She smoothed the bathrobe to give her nervous energy something to do. "Wh—what are you doing here?"

"I see you spent the night." His eyes roved over her. "What were you doing hiding like that?"

Her throat tightened, but she forced herself to think. "I—I wasn't decent."

He stepped closer. "Fine by me."

She flattened herself against the countertop. "M—Mario might mind."

"Mario might mind what?" Mario slipped through the doorway and sidled up to her.

Kevon straightened and stepped backward. "Morning. I was in the area and thought I'd grab the gear I left here. I heard someone in the kitchen and was saying hello."

Mario wrapped an arm around her waist, and Jayna used every ounce of willpower not to shove away from him. "Well, you can be the first to congratulate us then." He reached for her hand and held it up to show off the ring—an oval diamond set in a classic gold band.

It was the ring she had swooned over last night. The ring she wanted to throw in his face right now.

Kevon snorted. "Congrats. Well, I gotta go." He cast one last glance at her but seemed to narrow his eyes at some part of her bath robe. Then without another word, he showed himself out.

Mario spun her to face him. "Darling, I hope he didn't bother you."

She gulped. "Oh, no. He surprised me is all."

His gaze raced over her face. "You look pale."

"I—I'll be fine. Just not feeling well this morning. Maybe you could take me back to shore? Maybe some food or hot tea would help settle it. I wanted to make us breakfast—but I couldn't find anything."

Disappointment traced across his features. "Of course, I was hoping—but we need to get you feeling better first."

She had to keep up this act long enough to catch her flight out of here. "Thanks, I'm going to use the bathroom now."

The door could not shut behind her fast enough. She pressed the lock and slid to the floor. Covering her face with her hands, she let the silent tears rack her body. No, she had to keep it together for a little longer until she was safely in the privacy of her own room.

Again, she splashed water on her face and dried it with the first towel she could find. Then, smoothing her robe, she glanced down to her hand.

And saw the red splotch on the hem.

Her chest tightened. Grabbing the towel, she wet it and scrubbed at the stain. Some of the dried blood must have gotten on Mario's robe when she was shoving the bag back into the freezer.

Had Kevon seen it? Was that why his eyes had lingered on her?

If he had collected the bag this morning, was he behind the murder too?

It didn't matter. All that mattered was that she run as far as she could from the happily ever after that was fast becoming a nightmare.

Chapter Seven

There was nothing so satisfying as a clean catamaran at the end of another perfect Bimini day.

Except for the feel of his girl in his arms.

Mario shut off the spigot and wrapped up the hose. In a few days, Jayna would be back, and they could start planning their future.

A man's shadow made him look up, and he sighed. These days, Kevon seemed to take pleasure in stalking him. Mario hadn't even heard him sidle up to the catamaran. Kevon sure had some nerve to collect the body bag while he had his sweet Jayna on board.

But she hadn't been any wiser, and he was at least rid of the awful proof that the man he worked for wasn't one he ever wanted to cross.

So, he forced a fake smile and nodded. "Good evening."

"There's nothing good about it." Kevon's scowl spread from one side of his face to the other.

Mario sighed. "I promise to have the beach cleared extra early for you tonight. It won't be a problem as I've scheduled other indoor entertainment for my guests."

"That's not the problem."

"Then what is?" Mario wiped wet hands on his board shorts. Now where had he left his sunglasses?

"She's not coming back."

Mario froze. She? He didn't mean—

"Yeah, Jayna."

He whirled to face Kevon. The man's arms remained crossed, but he could uncurl and strike if provoked. Choking down an angry retort, Mario mirrored his posture and waited for an explanation.

"She's in the States."

Mario rolled his eyes. "Of course, she is. Her flight left this norning, and she went back to tell her family our news in person."

"She isn't coming back."

Kevon's one-line statements grated on him. What was he doing poking his nose in Mario's business? How dare he presume Jayna wouldn't be back?

He forced his tone to stay level. "Listen, man, you have your business, and I have mine. Leave Jayna alone, okay?"

In a split second, Kevon uncoiled, leapt forward, and slapped him hard on the face.

Mario staggered backward into the railing. "C'mon, man—"

But Kevon grabbed his collar. "Listen good, because I'll only warn you once. You got sloppy. You let Jayna spend the night on your boat. She found the body."

He jerked out of Kevon's grip and rubbed his smarting cheek. "She was with me the whole time. That's impossible."

"I found her in the kitchen alone. There was dried blood on the bathrobe she was wearing."

Mario's mind raced. Jayna had acted funny after they returned to shore, but she had begged off on account of her time of month. Plus, she was understandably nervous about telling her family about their sudden engagement. She came from a good family that cared about her, so certainly her actions had reflected nerves and not feeling well. Nothing more.

"No, man, you're wrong. She was nervous about how to tell her parents we're getting married. Plus, she said she wasn't feeling great."

Kevon shook his head. "Man, you really are blind. First, she lied to me. Second, she was scared."

Scared? Jayna? The thought made his blood burn. He wanted to protect her from anything that could hurt her or scare her.

"Maybe you scared her."

Kevon cocked his head and snickered. "Yeah, I know I do, but this was fear on a new level. I could read it in her eyes. She found the body all right, while you were sleeping."

Mario closed his eyes and tried to remember their conversation after Kevon left. What had she said? *I wanted to make us breakfast— but I couldn't find anything.*

Had she found the body instead, and that's why she acted so distant? She hadn't let him touch her again before she left, but all her excuses seemed reasonable.

It made sense now. Oh, his dear Jayna. What did she think of him?

He covered his face with his hands. The woman he loved was terrified of him. The thought itself was torture.

Surely, she would understand when he explained he had nothing to do with the body. It wasn't his fault Kevon made him store it. He was doing what he had to do to buy his cousins' freedom. She had respected that decision, praised him for it. Yes, she would come to see things from his perspective.

"She rented a car at the Miami airport and hasn't stopped driving. Last report showed she was north of Naples."

"Her parents live in Miami. She was going to visit them—"

"Dude, she's running."

Mario ran a hand through his hair. "Then I have to go after her, to explain."

"No woman is going to listen to a murderer."

He slammed a hand onto the railing. "I'm not a murderer." *You are.*

Kevon leaned against the railing across from him. "She thinks you are. Doesn't matter though. You have no choice but to bring her back. Because if she talks, not even I could protect her."

What did Kevon mean? Who did Kevon work for? Not that Mario had ever bothered to ask, but he'd always thought of Kevon as the boss. He'd been wrong about that too.

"You'll be better off leaving Jayna to me."

Mario released the railing and straightened. "I don't trust you with Jayna."

Kevon snorted. "Now you're thinking straight. I wouldn't trust me with her either." He turned to his motorboat. "I have some business here that I might need your help with. But I'll be taking a boat to Miami no later than Saturday morning. Be ready to leave on a moment's notice. If you don't show up when I tell you, I get her without you."

Mario's throat tightened, but he nodded. "I'll be ready."

Chapter Eight

The girl in the mirror was a stranger. Bronze streaks now highlighted her dark brunette hair, chopped to her shoulder, and new tortoise frames hugged her nose. She didn't need them, but they were her best disguise.

As for Mario's ring, she had stowed it in her duffle bag. She'd figure out what to do with it later.

Jayna pushed away from the small bathroom vanity of her friends' Lutz condo. It was the last place she wanted to be, but the one place available to her with no strings attached. Meredith was thrilled with her last-minute offer to house sit, and it gave Jayna a place to collect her thoughts and figure out her next move.

She'd put off calling Beatriz for too long. Sliding the door open, she stepped onto the small third-floor balcony. At least the condo was nice and overlooked a small lake. She collapsed into a wicker chair and let her finger hover above the speed dial button for Beatriz.

What would she say? Jayna didn't even know how to begin, but she already knew her sister's response—*I told you so.*

But she couldn't put off this call any longer. Her family would be wondering why she hadn't returned when she was supposed to.

She sucked down a deep breath and pressed the button.

To her relief, after several rings, the call went to voicemail. After the beep, she started into her message. "Hey, Bea, it's Jayna. Listen, I'm not coming home right away like I had planned. Some—work stuff—has come up. Don't worry about me. I'm fine and will call again when I can. Love you."

She exhaled and slid the phone onto the patio table. It was better not to make them worry. Nothing about "I'm engaged to a murderer" would help ease their minds.

No, she'd made the right call. When she got her new footing, then she could reach out and talk more. If Mario didn't chase after her and she kept her mouth shut, maybe she'd be fine.

Liar.

The thought brought fresh tears to her eyes. Who was she fooling? She was anything but fine. Her heart was shattered. She was scared to death of who Mario and Kevon really were, and if they would figure out the truth. She had mailed a note to Mario from Miami and hoped it would pacify him, but if he at all suspected she knew about his secret life, it probably wouldn't.

There was no point feeling sorry for herself. She needed a distraction. She would run to the grocery store and then cook up a dozen delicious things to distract herself.

Wiping her cheeks with the back of her hand, she stood and strode toward her bag to find her keys. Already, she was craving shrimp scampi, stir fry veggies, and ice cream. Lots of chocolate ice cream.

Not until she unloaded her rental vehicle did Jayna consider she might be using food as an escape outlet. This was way too much food for one person. Holding her keys between her teeth, she filled both hands with plastic bags and kicked her car door shut.

Well, there would be plenty of leftovers. The paper handle on one of the bags tore, sending a package of frozen shrimp and three ice cream tubs tumbling onto the ground.

She needed another hand but managed to corral two of the ice cream tubs. The third tumbled across the condo's parking lot as if competing in an elementary school model car race.

A jogger appeared in her peripheral and darted for the runaway. The woman's light brown hair flowed from a high ponytail, and her toned legs and bright peach shoes suggested she was the kind of runner Jayna would never be—a dedicated one.

The woman—who couldn't be much older than her—flashed a smile and held up the ice cream tub. "Got it."

In her past, Jayna would have felt embarrassed for being a

clutz, but there were no judges from her modeling days scrutinizing her now. Instead, relief swept over her. "Thanks."

"Sure thing." The jogger reached down and snatched what remained of the paper bag before placing the ice cream tub in it and then rounding up the other items at Jayna's feet.

"Sorry, I should've made two trips," Jayna said.

"Hey, no worries. I've been there." Though her face and clothes were damp with sweat, there was something simply beautiful about her. She seemed completely at home in her own skin, and her green eyes sparkled in the otherwise oppressive sun.

"I'm Kaley, by the way. You live here too?"

Jayna nodded and started toward the entrance of her unit. "Yeah, just moved in."

Kaley offered a lopsided grin. "No way. Looks like we might be neighbors. I'm on the second floor."

"The third." Jayna hoped she could make it without spilling any more of her purchases.

"I can bring this up for you if you'd like."

"Oh, I don't want to trouble you."

Kaley shrugged. "No trouble at all. I just finished my run and need to cool down anyway. Besides, it looks like you could use a hand."

"You're not wrong there." Jayna's shoulders relaxed as she paused at the entrance. She really hadn't thought this shopping trip through. But then did she ever think things through? Oh, her stupid heart.

Kaley darted ahead of her to grab the door and propped it open with her foot.

"Thanks," Jayna said.

"Sure thing." Kaley followed her and then hurried ahead to press the elevator button. "So are you from around here?"

"I'm from Miami." It couldn't hurt to tell her that, right? Surely, Mario had no idea where she was anyway.

"Oh, nice. I've never been, but my boyfriend, his work partner, and I are going—not this weekend but the next. There's a boat show, and he's picking up a new addition for his water sports business. Is Miami really as gorgeous as they say?"

43

"Parts of it are." Jayna smiled. Her childhood had its shadows, but she did love her city. "It has great beaches, and if you like Cuban food, you're in luck."

"I love Cuban." The elevator opened, and Kaley blocked the door with her spare arm while Jayna hustled inside. "Can you recommend any places?"

"So many. How much time do you have?" Jayna laughed, and it felt good.

After pressing the third-floor button, Kaley turned back to her. "I'm off for the rest of the day." She hurried to add, "But I totally get if you're busy."

If she only knew how wide-open Jayna's life had just gotten.

Jayna shook her head. "No, I work remotely but have a lot of flexibility." It wasn't exactly a lie.

"Oh, what do you do?"

She should have known this question was coming, but what did it hurt to tell this virtual stranger the truth? "I'm a travel blogger and do freelance on the side."

Kaley's eyes widened. "Wow, that's like a dream job."

"Yeah." It was, until it wasn't.

Jayna hesitated. She barely knew this girl, but something about her made Jayna completely at ease—and less lonely. Should she invite her for dinner?

"I'm going to whip up some shrimp scampi and stir fry. Want to join me in an hour for dinner? Then I can tell you all about the best places for Cuban in Miami." The elevator opened, and a few more steps would take her to her room.

Kaley hesitated. "That would be so nice, but I'm actually helping at my church group's event tonight. It's our once-a-month worship and fellowship night. You should come. It's a bunch of career-age professionals like us—and there's food. Although it will probably be pizza, not shrimp scampi."

Church group. Now Kaley sounded like Beatriz.

"Thanks, but—" It was Jayna's turn to hesitate. But what? She had nothing to do but search for freelance jobs. She could save her shrimp scampi dinner for tomorrow. Besides, if there was one place Mario wouldn't be looking for her, it was in church.

"—but what time does it start?" She fumbled with her keys and then jammed them in the lock.

"It starts at six, and it's like five minutes from here. Just cross the intersection at the light and look for Crossroads Christian Church. We'll be meeting in the student center."

She pressed the door open. "Okay, maybe I'll be there."

Kaley flashed another smile. "Awesome. Well, I'll leave these here for now and hope to see you later."

"Yeah, thanks again."

Jayna used her shoe to tap the door closed and then hurried to the kitchen to rest her bags on the counter. Had she agreed to go to church?

Man, she must be desperate. But Kaley seemed so genuine, and it wasn't like tonight was a church service. It sounded like music and food, and Jayna liked both. Besides, it wouldn't be such a bad idea to meet a few people if this town was going to be her home for a while.

If Mario did catch up with her, at least there would be somebody to give the "last seen alive" report.

Chapter Nine

The frustration in the bare-bones conference room at Reynolds Investigations was tangible enough to slice with a knife. It had been only a month since Liam and the rest of Avery's team had officially occupied the space, and decorating was not high on the agenda. At least they had a table, chairs, whiteboard, and Keurig. Priorities.

Beside him sat Drew, hair still damp after today's follow-up dive. Across from them with her arms crossed like an annoyed Captain Marvel was his boss, Avery Reynolds.

In a sense, she was the captain of her small but growing team of investigators that currently numbered five. But it was just the three of them today. Tasha was currently in the field on a security job, and Blake was at his desk, buried in an intellectual property case Liam didn't envy.

He popped a K-cup in the Keurig. More caffeine might not help his headache, but it wouldn't hurt it.

"You saw nothing again today?" Reynolds directed the question to Drew and tapped on the whiteboard with a capped marker in her hand. She had used magnets to secure a faceless man's silhouette to the center and scrawled "Big Eddie" with a question mark on it. Below it, she had listed the leads on this case: Casale, Russo, Anclote Marina. The first two had strikes through them. Casale was dead, and Russo wasn't talking. The marina tip was fast drying up too.

"No, ma'am," Drew said. "The only suspicious activity is the presence of those crab traps in off season, and maybe an old fisherman simply forgot about them."

Reynolds leaned forward. "What does your gut say?"

Drew cleared his throat. "I—uh, the one brick that marina worker found must have been a fluke."

"Fluke? It's no fluke that the exact type of brick from Russo's ɔoat turns up in the Anclote Marina." She sighed and turned to ‿iam. "What about you, Bracken? What is your gut saying?"

"The only pieces that don't add up are the snorkelers in wet ;uits and the crab traps. No Floridian snorkeler is going to wear a vet suit in July. I did some digging on the pontoon boat's owner, ɔut he hasn't been in the state since winter. Rather, he's using it as ι rental to make money. We have only one name listed for each ental, and I'm running the list from the past few months through ɔur database."

Reynolds nodded, and the muscles in her face relaxed. On are moments when she did, he remembered that she was in her ₃arly thirties like himself. There was something distant and ιntouchable about her—as if she lived and breathed the case and he case only. Back when they had worked for the sheriff's lepartment, he had tried to invite her to church along with his other ;olleagues, but she always had an excuse not to come.

Since he had turned in his badge to work for her private firm, ιe hadn't invited her again. Maybe he should. She would probably ust say no. He would simply have to trust God to work in her heart, ɔecause the walls she had built around herself only He could ɔenetrate.

"Good work." She pushed back her chair and rose, her jacket loing nothing to hide the toned torso underneath. Reynolds was ethal, but she was also a natural leader and a gifted investigator. le was privileged to work with and to learn from her.

He nodded and followed Drew out the door.

"Bracken, any ETA on those results?"

Liam turned to acknowledge her question while Drew kept valking. "Should be a day or maybe Monday, because of the veekend. I'm off this weekend through Tuesday for my church rip, but I'll be checking e-mails. As soon as I get word, you'll ⷉnow."

Reynolds flashed a rare smile. "This the same church group ⁄ou went on that ski trip with?"

"That's right."

"Please tell me the girl who broke your heart won't be going."

Liam's chest tightened. He thought Reynolds would have forgotten. "You mean Kaley?"

"Yes, that sounds right. She's a nice enough girl, but I hold grudges when someone messes with my team."

Liam forced a laugh. "It's not her fault a guy can't meet her without falling for her. But yes, she'll be there. I also happen to know Reef is planning to pop the question this trip."

His boss's smile turned to a frown. "Then why on earth do you want to go?"

Reynolds didn't let down her professional front often, and that fact made him realize how much she respected him—and disapproved of those who didn't.

"Because Reef is my best friend, and I want to be there to celebrate with him. Plus, some distance from this case might be a good thing."

Reynolds nodded slowly. "Yeah, everyone needs a break."

"That goes for you too, you know."

A smirk filled out her lips, and she jabbed the marker at the silhouette on the whiteboard. "The day Big Eddie is behind bars is the day I'll take some time off. But I hope you have a fun time— just steer clear of that girl, you hear? She's not the only fish in the sea."

He grinned. "Yes, boss."

The student center door swung closed behind him, and no one was milling about the welcome area. Glancing at his watch, he started toward the stairs. Guess he was early.

Liam smiled to himself. As unsatisfying as this current case was, he welcomed the next few days off. Sure, he still had to check e-mails and answer calls, but he needed this time.

Of course, he had felt the same way last winter before leaving on the ski trip. At that time, though, he had been hopeful about Kaley.

That disappointment was behind him, and he was happy for Reef. His friend and Kaley were good together. One day, he'd find the girl who was good for him.

48

One he would also be good for.

The last thought had been milling in his mind lately. Singles his age were so focused on finding the one right for them, but maybe they needed to be thinking more about being the right one for someone else. Maybe there was a girl out there who felt less than, and he could help her see the treasure she was.

Upstairs, a few of his friends were mingling by the snack bar. Reef caught his gaze and waved him over. His friend stood a few inches higher than him but had the gift for making anyone feel at ease, noticed, and important. His suntanned features turned upward in a smile.

Reef greeted him with a firm slap on the back. "Just the man I want to see."

"Good to see you too." Liam caught his hand for a shake. "You ready for this weekend?"

His friend glanced beyond him, and his hazel eyes sparkled. "So ready."

Liam turned to see Kaley entering the hall. Happiness for his friend replaced the jealousy he'd once felt.

He lowered his voice and faced Reef again. "She doesn't have a clue, right?"

"Nope. We gotta make sure it stays that way."

Liam grinned. "My lips are sealed."

"You hear Brittany dropped out last minute? She accepted a job at a new hair salon and can't get the time off." Reef paused and jabbed him in the ribs. "Hope you're not disappointed."

He had to laugh. Brittany had hit on most of the guys during the last ski trip, but she had grown up quite a bit since then, probably due to Kaley's influence. Still, Brittany was not his type and would be one less distraction on this trip.

"Nope, I'm good, man."

Reef laughed. "I thought you might say that."

At that point, Kaley reached them. She greeted Reef with a hug and offered Liam a smile. At least they could be friends. "What's up, guys?"

"We're talking about our hiking trip." Liam covered for his friend.

49

Kaley clapped her hands. "I am so excited. Reef says he's mapped out a few waterfall hikes for the group, and the weather's going to be comfortable in the seventies. That sounds like heaven compared to our roaring nineties here."

"It will be a nice change," Liam agreed.

"So how was your day, babe?" Reef reached for her hand and squeezed it.

"Good, I met a new girl in my complex, and she said she might come tonight." Kaley glanced to a cluster of girls. "I'm going to let Olivia know so she can be watching for her too."

Kaley shifted toward her girlfriends, and Reef turned back to him. "So, tell me how your week has been. Any new leads in that case of yours?"

Liam sighed, and a weight returned to his shoulders. "No. The trail went cold. Our one lead didn't turn up any evidence or reasonable suspicion that the boaters were doing anything other than scalloping."

Although he usually kept his work to himself, Reef understood the local waters better than most, thanks to his water sports business. His friend had also proven himself to have smart instincts when Kaley had been kidnapped last winter, so Liam trusted his judgment. Still, there was no point boring his friend with the details and his own hunches, which might not turn into anything.

Reef frowned. "I'm surprised to hear that. I've been taking groups out scalloping during the day and fishing at night all week. There was one night I almost called you because we came across a pontoon boat with divers in the water."

"At night?"

"Yeah." Reef ran a hand through his sandy blonde hair. "I mean, there's nothing illegal about scalloping at night, but no one does it. The viz is a lot worse."

"But these divers were scalloping?"

"I mean, I guess so? What else would they be doing in the water?"

What else indeed. "Did you happen to notice the name of the pontoon boat?"

"Yeah, it was Yankee something. I wrote it down because I thought of you, but now I can't remember it exactly."

"*Yankee Dog* maybe?"

Reef's eyes lit up. "That's it."

Pastor TJ stepped inside the room to announce that they were starting in the worship hall, and the group shifted that direction.

"Thanks for telling me, bro." Liam followed the movement toward the hall.

"Sure thing," Reef said. "If you want, I can keep tabs on that area anytime I take a group out. If I notice anything else out of the ordinary, I'll let you know."

"I appreciate it."

Kaley darted past them toward the top of the stairway. Standing there, seemingly unsure of herself, was a woman with the posture of a model who had just stepped off the runway. Her red lips offset a warm, tropical complexion, and her dark eyes glanced around the room. She seemed to relax when she spotted Kaley.

Together, they were two of the loveliest women he'd ever seen.

"Must be Kaley's neighbor," Reef said.

Liam appreciated that his friend kept the comment casual and had, to date, refrained from playing matchmaker with him.

"Yeah, guess so."

"We'll save her a seat inside." Reef led the way toward the middle section of seats and left two on the end for Kaley and her new friend.

Soon enough, the two young women entered the hall, and Kaley guided them toward the reserved seats.

"Hey, Reef, meet Jayna. She's my neighbor I was telling you about. Jayna, this is my boyfriend Reef, and this is our friend Liam."

"Nice to meet you." Jayna waved a hand and took a seat as the band leader welcomed the group to the Thursday worship time.

Liam smiled back, hoping to make her more comfortable. She looked about ready to jump out of her skin, but there was no reason why. This group was about as friendly and chill as they came.

Maybe she hadn't grown up in church as he had. For him,

51

church was an extension of his family. If Jayna had never been to church before, he could understand her discomfort.

The worship leader started off with the song, "Reckless Love," and Liam focused on the lyrics that spoke of God's powerful, pursuing love.

He chanced a look at Jayna across from Reef and Kaley. Her lips weren't moving, but her eyes were round and—glistening? A single tear traced down her cheek.

In that moment, he prayed for this mystery girl. *Lord, if she doesn't know You, chase her down with Your love. Fight for her 'til she's found, and use Kaley—use me, if you want—but overwhelm her with Your love.*

He turned his focus back to the front as a peace settled across him. God didn't always answer his prayers the way he wanted—Kaley was proof of that—but God always knew what was best for his children.

Liam didn't have to know the answers. He just had to trust Him.

For Reef and Kaley. For the new girl. For him.

Chapter Ten

The pizza was greasy, but the company was good. Jayna munched on her pie crust in a booth with Kaley at her side. That girl made her feel as though they'd known each other since high school, not a few hours ago.

Across from them sat Kaley's boyfriend, Reef, and his friend. She couldn't remember his name and honestly didn't see a need to. He was nice enough, but she liked her men dark and handsome. Not that this friend wasn't handsome, but he was about as gringo as they came with his Irish red hair and beard. Definitely not her type. After what her modeling manager had done to her, she'd never date another vanilla boy again.

Still, she hadn't been around this many peers her age since college. This group was so diverse, not only in cultural backgrounds but also occupations. There were doctors, lawyers, therapists, entrepreneurs, and law enforcement. Yet here they all were, letting down their hair and having a good time.

She didn't understand the whole service and all the God stuff. But the group sure was sincere and friendly, and for that, she liked them.

Right then, the pastor—someone had called him TJ—strode up to their table. He wasn't anything like what she imagined a pastor would be. He wore a graphic T-shirt and jeans. His dancing eyes and grin didn't fit the stuffy persona she'd always pegged pastors as having. Plus, he couldn't be more than ten years older than she was.

"Hey, gang." He slapped Reef on the shoulder. "Hope you're all packed and ready to head out early tomorrow."

"I finished packing before coming here," Kaley said.

Reef winked at her. "Haven't even started."

Kaley rolled her eyes. "Of course, you haven't."

"We're going to have a quick meeting in a few minutes. The group is pretty small this time—you three, Matt, and Olivia. Brittany had to back out, and we never filled all ten spaces."

Kaley turned her gaze toward Jayna. "Pastor TJ, have you met Jayna yet? She and I are neighbors."

Pastor TJ extended a hand. "No, we haven't met. So glad you came tonight."

"Thanks, me too."

"Wish you could meet my wife, Jenna, but she had to leave early to put the kiddos to bed."

Jayna had already met more people than she had memory to remember. "Maybe next time."

"Hey, you wouldn't be free the next four days to join us on our hiking trip, would you?"

Was TJ still talking to her? Jayna glanced from him to Kaley and back. Sure enough, he was still looking at her.

"Who, me?" she asked.

Kaley clapped her hands. "Oh, that would be awesome. You would love it there, especially since you're a travel blogger and all. Maybe you'd even get some ideas for your blog. It's beautiful."

Really? This group that had just met her was inviting her on a trip? She didn't know whether to feel honored or worried.

Jayna cleared her throat. "Where actually is *there*?"

"Beech Mountain, North Carolina," Reef spoke up. "I've been going there since I was a kid. Usually, our class plans a ski trip each year, but there are some amazing hiking trails and waterfalls, perfect for a summer trip. So I told TJ I'd organize the itinerary if he'd put together a trip."

TJ nodded. "Like I was saying, it's a pretty small group, but we have a nice-size cabin rented."

A dozen excuses raced to the tip of her tongue. She couldn't go on a trip with virtual strangers. But then, wasn't that what she did for a living? Travel, turn strangers into friends, and blog about the experience?

It wasn't like her calendar was full. She could freelance from North Carolina as well as she could in Lutz. Being gone a few days shouldn't be a problem with Meredith either.

Jayna swallowed and glanced back to Kaley's smiling face. She sure could use a friend, and North Carolina would be the last place Mario would look for her.

"How much does it cost?" Not that money mattered. She had plenty in the bank saved up and invested from her modeling years.

TJ pulled up a chair from another table and folded onto it. "Just a hundred and fifty toward the cabin, plus some meals. We'll have regular devotional time, plus a healthy combination of quiet time and group activities. I always feel refreshed and closer to Jesus when I come back."

Jayna wasn't sure about the *closer to Jesus* bit, but she sure could use refreshment. "Sure, why not? What time are you leaving tomorrow?"

"Yay!" Kaley's eyes danced.

TJ wrinkled his eyebrows. "What time did I put on the schedule?"

The ginger-haired man across from her grinned. "Six o'clock sharp."

Sharp. Mario always used that word whenever referring to time. It had struck her odd for someone who lived in the Bahamas, but the man did follow his clock religiously.

Another reason to avoid the ginger. Though he was different from Mario in every other way, this one similarity was one too many.

"You can ride with me to church if you want," Kaley said. "I'll be heading out around five-fifty."

That would be perfect. She could return her rental car tonight and Uber back to the condo. She'd figure out a more permanent car situation when she returned since she'd left her car with her parents.

"Sounds great." Jayna nodded and then scooted to the end of the booth. "Well, if we're leaving that early, I need to get home and do laundry."

"Can you spare five minutes?" TJ asked. "We're going to have a quick meeting, and I need to get your e-mail so you can sign the waiver."

"Oh, sure." Jayna paused at the end of the seat. She would

stay for the meeting and then hustle. For the first time in the last forty-eight hours, her heart felt lighter. Travel was the answer to her broken heart.

You're running. A voice whispered in her mind.

No shame in that. Getting extra distance from Mario seemed the safest option right now. Besides, her job was traveling. What better way to forget her latest mistake than getting a fresh perspective in a new place?

Whatever Beech Mountain had to offer, she was prepared to embrace it with open arms.

Maybe she should have asked about the drive time before agreeing to this trip. Jayna uncurled herself from the back of the van and stuffed her laptop in her bag as the van reached the cabin's driveway. At least she'd gotten some writing done, but if she had to listen to one more game or karaoke competition, she might have lost her mind.

Goodness, this group played hard. Part of her admired them for it, and part of her wished they would all take up reading.

Also, it would have been nice if Kaley had warned her that from the church, she would be driving separately with Reef. That left Jayna with Pastor TJ, the ginger, and a couple who clearly liked each other but pretended not to. Great.

Nearly twelve hours later, they had arrived, and the place was stunning. The sinking sun wrapped the log cabin in a warm glow and highlighted the surrounding woods. They'd already spotted half a dozen deer, and Ginger Ale had even said he'd seen a bear on their last trip.

She had to give it to Ginger Ale. That was her new nickname for the redhead since Ginger seemed too feminine for a guy.

So yes, Ginger Ale. He was nice—even if she couldn't remember his name and at this point, felt like it was too late to ask again. He was the least loud of the whole group and the only other one who'd been working on his laptop in the van. He'd even slipped her a pair of disposable earplugs so she could concentrate.

She had seen the same yellow foam buds poking out of his ears at one point.

When he had finally taken a break from his laptop, she'd asked him what he did, thinking maybe he was a writer too. He said he was a former cop now "in the private sector of law enforcement." What did that even mean? Maybe he was a security officer, but she couldn't imagine why a security officer would need to work on his laptop on vacation.

When she jumped out of the passenger van, the cool evening air hit her hard. How could this place be so chilly when Florida was a sauna? She'd have to buy a long sleeve shirt or something. All she had was one pair of blue jeans, a yoga outfit, and a few tanks and shorts which now felt ridiculous to even have packed.

Hopefully, there would be a tourist store where she could buy a hoodie.

Even with the chill, she couldn't help but feel a little bit like she was stepping back to a simpler life. The mountain air was like a candle fragrance, and if she could bottle the rustic two-story cabin and rolling landscape, she would.

Olivia—one half of the in-denial couple—whistled as she exited the van. "This place is amazing,"

"Yeah." Jayna followed her up the porch steps lined with a double swing and rocking chairs.

Ginger Ale plugged in the access code while TJ and Matt—the other half of the awkward couple—unloaded most of the bags.

Jayna carried her own. All she had to her name right now was his duffle and her laptop. She'd left her Calvin Klein purse and suitcase in Bimini to suggest she'd return as promised. Though she was used to traveling in style, there was something freeing about his new simplicity.

A crunching noise on the gravel signaled the arrival of Reef's Subaru as Ginger Ale unlocked the door. Olivia scurried inside, but Jayna sank onto the porch swing. The evening was too nice to waste, and besides, she didn't care where she slept as long as someone left her a couch.

Kaley ran up the steps to greet her with a hug. Goodness, she'd met the girl yesterday, but the show of affection warmed her.

57

When was the last time someone had hugged her without expecting something in return?

"How was the drive?" Kaley readjusted her backpack.

"Oh, you know." Jayna didn't want to complain. "Long."

Kaley glanced over her shoulder and lowered her voice. "I'm sorry about the van, but I promise, Reef's Subaru takes getting used to. After six months of dating, I'm still not acclimated to some of his 80's big-hair favorites."

Jayna couldn't help but laugh. She liked Reef more and more. "I'd take big-hair rock over off-key karaoke any day."

As the last of the group funneled inside, Jayna begged off with an excuse to watch the sunset. Their voices faded inside but were punctuated with excited squeals from the other girls.

She sighed. If it weren't for the bugs, she'd be quite content to sleep right here. Yet watching the sunset sent a pang to her heart. The last sunset she'd enjoyed had been her engagement evening. It had promised the beginning of all her hopes and dreams—only to mock her the next morning.

On second thought, maybe she hated sunsets.

She hopped to her feet as the porch door swung open and Ginger Ale poked out his head.

"Hey, there you are. Just want you to know your room is the first door on the left upstairs."

Jayna shrugged her computer bag on and grabbed her duffle. "I have my own room?"

"Yeah, we agreed it's fair. Reef and I are sharing a room, and TJ has the couch." He paused to grin. "As you experienced, the group is great but a bit suffocating at times. We figured you might want your own space. But Kaley and Olivia are right across the hall from you if you need them."

"Thanks." She offered a smile and skirted past him inside.

"Great. I'll be in the kitchen helping Olivia, and I think the others are unpacking."

At the mention of kitchen, Jayna's stomach growled. Their burger lunch stop had been seven hours ago and too greasy to be satisfying.

She reached the stairway and hesitated. "If you need any help, et me know. I—I like to cook."

"I'll let Olivia know. She's kind of a kitchen hog, but I convinced her to let me plan one of the meals. We never say no to help."

Ginger Ale, a chef? No, chef was probably too generous. At least he could cook or cared enough to try.

She tapped open her door, and the evening's warm glow illuminated the room, thanks to a large window. Her heart swelled. This group of strangers had left her with her private room, complete with a quilt-covered queen bed, bureau, and worn lavender sitting chair.

This might be the best one-hundred and fifty bucks she'd ever spent.

But she couldn't let the group get too close. Who knew when she would have to move on? Still, for this weekend, she could pretend to have friends, to be carefree—to not be engaged to a murderer.

Chapter Eleven

In the pre-dawn twilight, Mario set his diving gear on the damp beach sand and finished zipping up his wetsuit. Though he couldn't see the powerboat, he could hear it, which meant he had mere minutes before Kevon arrived.

Since he started working with Kevon, he had yet to get a full night's sleep. The man either demanded his time at night—or Mario couldn't sleep from wondering what he would ask next.

"Remember why," he muttered and rubbed the ache from his eyes. The money was what he needed, what his family needed. Maybe he had sold his soul to the devil and would never be free of him—but no man had better reasons for doing so.

Late last night, Kevon had texted that he had a job for him and to bring his diving gear. Mario could only hope this job didn't involve a dead body.

Stowing the last one had cost him his fiancé. Somehow, he had to convince Jayna to see his side of things. He wanted to protect her—still wanted to marry her. If he couldn't—Mario swallowed bile thinking about what might happen to her.

No, he wouldn't let his mind go there. Kevon had promised to help him get her back, and Mario would hold him to his word.

The power boat's silhouette appeared off shore, and Kevon killed the engine before gliding partway onto the beach.

"You ready?" Kevon called from the boat.

Mario hefted his gear bag over a shoulder and grabbed his tank with his free hand. "Yeah."

"Throw in your gear, and then push us off."

At least Kevon couldn't see his eye roll. No one should throw a scuba tank. Stepping into the surf, Mario placed his gear inside and then grunted as he pushed off from the sand. The warm water seeped through his suit, encouraging him to relax. Being in the water had always been his escape.

Water had been his parents' gateway to freedom, and water
jobs like this would help him buy his cousins' freedom too. One
day soon.

Mario pulled himself over the boat's edge and, once inside,
nearly tripped on a long wound-up rope. Were those buoys? He
had a dozen questions to ask Kevon, but he bit his tongue. This
man could not be pushed.

Instead, he settled into the front of the boat and faced the
receding shoreline. The warm lights from his resort glowed and
cast long reflections on the face of the water. Any time of day or
night, Bimini waters were paradise.

Kevon steered the boat toward the edge of the small moon-
shaped beach and then put it in neutral. "Get ready."

Mario stood. "Care to share what I'm supposed to do?"

The impossible man nodded toward the floor of the boat.
"Grab the rope buoy. I need you to tie it off to one of the trees on
shore, and then once you're back in the boat, you can drop the rest
of it in place while I steer."

The hair on his neck bristled. "Why am I roping off part of
our snorkeling area? I already have the beach closed."

"It's because I can't take the chance some busy-body guest
of yours discovers our traps underwater. You can explain to new
guests that they are not to snorkel in this area or explore the
surrounding beach. It's too dangerous because of hurricane debris
in the water."

That was the story Mario was already telling his guests. A
new rope barrier wouldn't make a difference—except to ease
Kevon's paranoid fears.

With a sigh, Mario strapped on his mask and headlamp and
clicked it on. This job would've been a lot easier in daylight. At
least he didn't need to bother with his tank, which Kevon had told
him to bring just in case.

After pulling on his fins, he grabbed the end of the rope buoy
and swung his legs overboard. "Be right back."

"Make it quick."

Right, because swimming in the dark, making his way to a

61

rocky shoreline, was so easy. The last thing he needed was to slice himself on one of the rocks.

When he reached them, he yanked off his fins and picked his way onto the rocky ledge. Securing the end of the rope to the stump of a tree, he then retraced his steps, retrieved his fins, and began his swim back to the boat.

Once he cleared the larger boulders, he relaxed. This part of the swim was enjoyable. An array of fish and nurse sharks darted around him. He needed to snorkel more for fun—not to babysit tourists. When Jayna came back, he could show her some more of his favorite places.

A knot formed in his stomach. Would she come back? Could he make her understand? He would ask Kevon for an update before going back to shore, whether the man volunteered one or not.

Back at the boat, he removed his fins a final time and hefted his body over the edge.

Kevon grunted. "I'm going to idle around the point, and I want you to drop the rest of the buoy rope as we go."

Mario nodded. This part, at least, should be easy. With the last of the rope buoy in the water, he finally relaxed and turned to face Kevon. "Are we good?"

"One more thing." Kevon cut the engine. Then, standing, he yanked the cushion off his seat and pulled out a black duffle bag and slung it toward Mario's feet.

Mario's skin crawled. It was the same black fabric as the one he'd stuffed into his freezer. But this one was smaller—a duffle bag.

"I need you to dive here and place this bag in one of the crab traps below. That's all for tonight."

He hesitated. Why was he the one diving to the crab trap? Did Kevon want to implicate him in whatever operation he was running here?

"Is there a problem?" Kevon rasped.

He had to play cool. "No problem. Just let me ready my dive tank, and I'll get started."

Guess he would be using the tank after all. After checking his oxygen, he then forced his feet back into the fins and slid over the oat's edge. "Hand me the bag?"

Kevon chucked it into the water next to him.

Bile climbed in his throat, but he swallowed it down, etrieved the bag, and began his descent.

This part of the snorkeling area was deeper and less rocky, vith fewer fish. He flicked on his headlamp again and hoped it lidn't illuminate a bull shark. They weren't usually this close to shore. Still, encountering one was possible.

Something metallic glinted below, and he zeroed in on the :rab trap's frame. He hoped Kevon knew what he was doing. Jsing those contraptions during off season could land a hefty fine. √laybe that was another reason for the rope buoy.

His fins settled on the bottom, creating a mild silt cloud. While it settled, he felt for the zipper on the duffle. If he were isking his life, he might as well know what it was for.

He bent his headlamp down to illuminate his hand. Pulling)ack the zipper, he scanned the opening.

Sweet relief. No body parts. In their place was brick after)rick, wrapped in a colorful watertight mesh. Black, purple, and ʒreen, each brick had its own identifying number.

All along, he'd suspected Kevon was running a black-market)peration. He'd also guessed it was drug related. Somehow, seeing he proof firsthand still gave him chills. If he ever got caught ielping Kevon, he'd be looking at serious jail time.

Yanking the zipper shut, he unhooked one side of the trap so ıe could stuff the bag inside. Then, scanning the open water for ;harks and finding none, he kicked his fins and began the ascent oward the surface.

At least Kevon hadn't left him to make the long swim to ;hore. One more time, he climbed up the edge of the boat, which vas more of a chore with a mostly full tank. He tugged off his nask and headlamp.

He didn't need it anymore. The first hints of dawn warmed he horizon, giving the calm ocean surface a purplish glow.

Kevon started the engine, turned the boat around, and headed or shore. A man like him didn't enjoy the discovery of daylight.

Impatience rose within Mario. Was Kevon going to pretend

Jayna hadn't happened and that he hadn't promised to help him find her? Today was Saturday. Were they leaving to get her or not?

Mario cleared his throat, hoping Kevon would take the hint. The man scowled and focused on him. "I'm taking a yacht to Miami at ten this morning. If you want to join, I'll meet you on your yacht at nine forty-five."

"Have you found—her?" Mario hated the way his throat tightened.

"Yeah, she's in North Carolina." Kevon snorted. "With a church group. Like that cover wouldn't be easy enough for us to discover."

A church group? Mario frowned. Jayna hadn't struck him as religious. She must have been scared.

Kevon eased the boat closer to shore and motioned for him that the ride was over. Thankfully, it was still a good thirty minutes for the sunrise—before his hopeless romantic guests would be up.

"I'll be waiting on the yacht at half past nine." Yes, he would be ready early. Mario stuffed his fins back in his bag and swung it over his shoulder.

Kevon leveled a hard glare on him. "We'll try getting her back the nice way—with your sweet-talk and all. But if she doesn't come easy, don't interfere with my methods. Understood?"

"Yeah." Mario swallowed. Surely, Jayna would listen to him, listen to reason. Whatever methods Kevon referred to wouldn't be necessary.

At least, he hoped not.

Chapter Twelve

Singing. Who was singing?

Jayna squinted her eyes and rolled to her side. Golden sunlight filtered through the cracks of her paisley-patterned curtains and fell onto her sheets.

Feet padded outside her room, and the music grew louder. Oh, that wasn't just anyone's voice. That was Ed Sheeran crooning about finding his beautiful someone.

Perfect.

Like everything her love life was not.

What crazy person on this singles trip felt that playing "Perfect" was a good wakeup call?

She pegged Reef or Kaley. Those two clearly had it bad for each other, but did they have to torment the rest of the group?

Her stomach grumbled, and Jayna rolled out of bed. After tugging on black yoga pants and layering two tank tops, she spun her hair into a messy bun and crept downstairs. Maybe she could get in on the breakfast-cooking action.

She followed her nose to the bacon aroma where she found Olivia singing along to another love song which blared from her smartphone.

Jayna kinked an eyebrow as Olivia noticed her mid-note. "Darlin', Dar—Oh hey, Jayna."

"Hey." Jayna glanced at the bacon, which looked perfectly crisp. Maybe this Olivia girl really could cook. "So, what's with you and all the feels this morning? I didn't expect to be serenaded by Ed Sheeran on a single group's trip."

Olivia's curly brown hair bobbed right along with the smile playing on her face. "Just setting the mood."

"Oh." Jayna scanned the counters where Olivia had started prepping pancakes and also pulled out an egg carton. "So, are you and Matt an item?"

The curly hair bobbing came to a screeching halt, and Olivia's dark brown eyes widened. "Wha—no, we're friends. The music is for Kaley."

Jayna had her doubts about the friend status between Olivia and Matt, but today was only day two with this group. She clearly wasn't understanding why Olivia was playing music for Kaley, who wasn't even present, or what she meant by "setting the tone," but breakfast was more important.

"Can I help you with the eggs or pancakes?" She gestured to both. "I love cooking."

Olivia's eyes lit up. "Really? If you want to scramble those eggs, that would be great."

Scrambling was so basic, but she would whip up the most fluffy, moist eggs. "I'm on it."

"Oh, and there's a fresh pot of coffee over there if you want it. Coffee is one of Kaley's love languages, so even though I don't drink it, I brewed a pot."

Not drink coffee? Maybe that explained Olivia's quirks.

"Thanks." Jayna helped herself to a mug and filled it halfway. "Am I missing something with the whole mood thing though? Ed Sheeran, coffee—you're either a great friend or something's brewing."

"Besides the coffee?" Olivia chuckled at the pun. "Yeah, something's brewing all right. But I am sworn to secrecy."

Way to make the new girl feel out of the loop. Jayna popped open the creamer and added a splash to her coffee. She needed just enough to take off the bitter edge. A quick sip told her that though Olivia didn't drink the brew, she at least knew how to select some decent beans.

Even if the girl wasn't willing to spill her secret, at least she was kind enough to share the coffee and kitchen with her. Maybe this group was weird, but they were at least nice people.

"Good coffee." Jayna set down her mug on the counter and pulled a frying pan off the rack above the stove.

"Glad you like it." Olivia swiped on her phone and then clapped. "Oh, this one is perfect."

Moments later, one of Beyonce's hits started blaring, and Olivia snapped her fingers in time on her way back over to the pancake mix.

Jayna laughed out loud, and soon, was swaying her own hips in time to the beat. A church group that made breakfast with Beyoncé background music? Fine by her.

She caught Olivia's gaze and grinned as the popular song for single girls ran its course.

Olivia smiled back before singing along.

Jayna couldn't sing, but thanks to her modeling years when she dabbled in dance, she knew the whole J-Sette dance routine from the music video. Soon, Olivia was laughing and clapping while Jayna flicked her hips and wrists.

As she spun around, movement in the doorway made her freeze. There stood Ginger Ale.

Heat rushed to her face as he clapped his hands. "Bravo! But if dancing and singing are pre-requisites to kitchen help, then I'm out."

Jayna tried to hide behind her coffee mug. "Oh, I can't sing."

"But she can dance." Olivia turned to Ginger Ale. "So, you want to help with breakfast?"

"If you'll let me."

Olivia retrieved her pancake bowl. "What do you think, Jayna? Do we need more help?"

"Well, what else is there to do?" Jayna replaced her coffee on the counter and started cracking eggs to give her nervous energy somewhere to go. Her face still felt about as red as the burner.

"Cinnamon rolls."

"I'm sure Gin—he—can manage." Jayna choked on her words. Had she almost said her nickname out loud? Man, this morning was spiraling out of control.

"Oh, I'm Liam, not Jim." His eyes twinkled as if he guessed what she had been about to call him but covered for her anyway.

Jayna went searching for a whisk and found one in a nearby drawer. "Sorry, I'm bad with names."

"It's easy to forget."

She turned to face him. Did he mean his name was easy to

forget, or he was easy to forget?

But Liam had already opened the fridge and was rummaging around for the cinnamon rolls.

A twinge of sadness pricked her heart. Was she easy to forget too? Part of her hoped Mario would simply move on with his life, but part of her also wanted to know he had really cared about her as someone who was more than a pretty face. Yet all her ex-boyfriends had certainly moved on. To them, she was nothing more than a conquest.

She cleared her throat and turned toward Olivia. "I think it would be great if Liam handled the cinnamon rolls—and started a fresh pot of coffee."

There, at least the guy had a chance to help in the kitchen, which was what he said he wanted last night. Any guy should be able to follow Pillsbury directions.

Liam placed the cinnamon roll tube on the counter and searched a lower cabinet for a cookie sheet. "These won't be Pioneer Woman worthy, but I promise not to burn them."

Jayna arched an eyebrow. This guy followed Pioneer Woman recipes? Maybe he did know how to bake.

"What?" Liam met her gaze with a smile. "You don't like Pioneer Woman cinnamon rolls?"

"Oh no, I do." She turned on her burner and finished whipping together the eggs. "I'm impressed you even know who Pioneer Woman is."

"I told you I like to cook—and well, bake too." He pulled out a metal sheet that had seen better days.

"What else do you like to do?" This cop-chef was certainly not fitting the typical gringo profile.

"You mean other than work on vacations?" Olivia snorted. "I will never understand workaholics."

"Hey, I enjoy plenty of other things." Liam popped the cinnamon roll container and placed the pre-formed rolls on the cooking sheet. "For the record, I love to fish. Deep sea fish, fly fish, shore fish, you name it."

"Nice," Jayna said. "Sushi is my favorite. Have you made that before?"

"No, but I know the best place in town for it. We should all go sometime."

"Yeah." She didn't plan to stay in Lutz any longer than necessary, but he didn't need to know that.

For the next few minutes, they worked in silence, well, relative silence. Olivia didn't turn off her mood music because Liam had joined them. He even lip-synced along to a few Taylor Swift songs.

Liam was just pulling his cinnamon rolls out of the oven when the rest of the crew arrived. TJ beelined for the coffee. Matt looked as though he had tumbled out of bed, but he perked up when he spotted Olivia. Reef reached for Kaley's hand, and the girl literally glowed.

Oh.

Shoot.

Mood music.

A trip to the mountains.

With your girlfriend and her crazy friends.

Reef was going to propose.

Jayna's stomach turned sour, and her perfect eggs didn't look so appealing anymore. It wasn't that Kaley didn't deserve to be happy. She did. But Jayna couldn't be at the epicenter of a perfect proposal when her own magical moment had ended so awfully days before.

She fumbled for her empty coffee mug and got in line behind TJ. "So, what are we doing again today?"

TJ chugged his black coffee. "Ask Reef. He planned everything."

The knot in her stomach only grew. Of course, he had.

Reef hovered around the cinnamon rolls but looked up at the mention of his name. "Reef did what?"

"You planned all our hikes," TJ said.

"Oh, right." Reef's face lit up. "We're going to do Linville Falls this morning, grab lunch in Banner Elk, and then do a sunset hike at Roan Mountain."

Kaley snaked her arm around Reef's and beamed up at him. "Please tell me we're doing lunch at Banner Elk Café."

He dipped his head toward her. "Yes, I know it's your favorite place."

Jayna's eyes widened. Was he going to kiss her in front of them all?

But Kaley only batted his nose playfully and then released his arm before heading toward Jayna and the coffee line.

Kaley snagged an unclaimed coffee mug from the cabinet and stepped next to her. "Morning, Jayna. How'd you sleep?"

Jayna swallowed. She didn't want any part of this girl's day, but she couldn't spoil it for her. "Fine, and you?"

"Like a baby. Poor Olivia was all keyed up from the drive, though. Guess I was asleep by the time she finally came to the room."

Keyed up helping Reef plan your engagement was probably more like it.

Jayna refilled her mug and then reached for the creamer. "I'm not a great hiker. Do you think we'll stop by the cabin between hikes?"

Kaley poured her own coffee and nodded. "Yes, we're coming back to Banner Elk for lunch, and my guess is we won't need to leave for Roan Mountain until late afternoon. That will give us plenty of time to rest. Reef says these hikes are gorgeous, so you won't want to miss either."

Jayna forced a smile. "Creamer?"

"Oh, yes, thanks." Kaley waited to add it because TJ started praying over the food.

This group sure did pray over everything. They prayed before starting the drive yesterday. They prayed over breakfast, lunch, and dinner. And now breakfast again. With this much prayer, at least no one should get food poisoning.

Someone bumped her in the shoulder. "Hey, these eggs are the perfect combination of cheesy, moist, and fluffy."

She glanced up to find Ginger Ale—Liam—pointing at his plate, which consisted of a cinnamon roll, a few bacon slices, and lots of eggs.

This guy was so easy-going and refreshingly different than most of the guys she knew, but something still warned her to keep

70

her distance. "Glad you like them."

His eyes twinkled. "Hope you can say the same about my cinnamon rolls."

She rolled her eyes. "Send my regards to the dough boy."

Liam winced. "Ouch. But if you stick around, I'll bring those Pioneer Woman cinnamon rolls to church for breakfast one month. I promise I can bake." He passed her a plate. "Better get some before Reef eats it all."

"Hey." Reef spun ahead of them in line. He had scooped eggs onto two separate plates. "These aren't both for me, you know."

Behind them, Kaley laughed. "Babe, just remember I don't eat as much as you."

Reef looked sheepishly down at the piling heaps of eggs. Then, he halved one of the portions and scooped the rest back into the pan. "Right. I got you, babe."

Jayna felt her stomach pinch again. Could she even stand half a day with these two lovebirds? But if Reef were as romantic as he seemed, he would probably wait until sunset. She could at least see the waterfalls before bowing out of the day's activities.

As she waited in line for a cinnamon roll, she sucked a deep breath. She could deal with this day.

Liam flashed her a concerned look. "You okay?"

Goodness, did nothing escape this guy?

"Yeah, I'm fine." She snatched a cinnamon roll to go along with her coffee and then hurried from the kitchen. If skipping out on her own eggs and the healthy part of breakfast saved her from more lovers' banter, she could deal with a light breakfast.

Clear headspace and the front porch swing were calling her name.

Chapter Thirteen

Liam risked a glance in the rear-view mirror as he drove the passenger van into the parking area of Linville Falls. Jayna sat in the far back seat and had been strangely quiet since breakfast.

Had he missed something? She seemed relaxed before everyone came down for breakfast. Finding her mid-dance when he reached the kitchen had not been how he expected his day to start. He had to stop rewinding the mental tape of her hips snapping in time to the music.

Beautiful though she was, Jayna tugged at something deeper inside him. He had seen enough hurting people in his line of work to know when someone had put up walls. Jayna was hiding from something, but every once in a while, her true self surfaced from behind the carefully constructed veneer.

That true-self was worth knowing. If she would let him.

He spotted an empty space on the far end of the dirt parking area and made a beeline for it, though he was careful to avoid a group of hikers and their dogs. For mid-morning, this place was already packed. He sure hoped Reef could find a waterfall overlook that wasn't brimming with tourists for popping the big question.

His stomach churned as he shifted to park. Man, he wasn't getting engaged, and he was still nervous. He'd promised Reef he would video the proposal live on his phone and then take pictures afterward, but he had envisioned a quiet overlook where he had plenty of space to work.

Not a situation where he would have to double as crowd control.

Behind him, Matt pulled open the sliding passenger door, and the others piled out. Liam popped his own door and then pocketed the keys. The last thing he needed was losing them and everyone having to pile into Reef's Subaru for a game of telephone booth—when his best friend would definitely want alone time with his new fiancé.

Olivia was by his side. "You ready?"

"Hope so."

She lowered her voice as if a waiting mob of paparazzi might arrive at any minute to spoil Kaley's proposal. "I'll video from a different angle, so one of us is bound to get a good shot. Any idea where he's going to do it?"

He scanned the parking lot for Reef's Subaru and spotted it toward the trail entrance. He motioned to TJ, indicating where Reef was parked, and the group started hiking that direction. "I've never been here, but Reef said there are several waterfall overlooks. If they're all crowded, he'll wait for one to clear first—and maybe you can put Matt and TJ on crowd control."

"I'm on it." Before she darted away, she hesitated and tilted her head toward the others who were a few paces ahead of them. "What about Jayna? Do you think we should tell her?"

He paused. Jayna trailed behind TJ and Matt, pretending to scroll on her phone.

Pretending because there was no signal out here, even for agents like him who used only the best service.

"I'll leave that up to you. If you get a chance, it might not be a bad idea so she doesn't feel like the odd person out."

Olivia waved to Reef and Kaley who were waiting for them by the trailhead. "Right. I'll try to tell her when you-know-who isn't within ear shot."

Liam chuckled. Olivia was taking her assistant-to-the-future-groom role even more seriously than he was. She hurried forward to greet Kaley with a bear hug as if they'd been separated for days, not half an hour.

Meanwhile, Reef stepped toward him. In his left hand, he clutched his DSLR camera case. It was the perfect way to conceal the ring box and keep Kaley from guessing anything was out of the ordinary.

With his free hand, he slapped Liam on the back a little harder than usual. Guess Reef was more nervous than he let on.

Even his face seemed flushed. Reef dropped his voice. "Glad you're here, man."

Liam punched him playfully in the shoulder. "You know I got you. Today is going to be great."

Reef's face lit up with one of his hallmark smiles. "Yeah, it is." His friend hurried ahead to rejoin Kaley and reached for her hand while she chatted with Olivia.

Kaley smiled back and then continued her conversation.

Liam chuckled, content with his position as last in line down the trail. She didn't have a clue that today would become one of the most special memories of her life.

But then she did keep playing with her hair as if it were out of place or somehow less lovely than it was.

Was she picking up on Reef's nerves?

Oh, this was going to be fun to watch.

His gaze drifted to Jayna. She hung behind the other girls who were too engaged in conversation to notice. She seemed to be watching the oncoming hikers as if expecting to find someone she knew.

Odd. She hadn't mentioned having family or friends up this way, had she?

She froze. Good thing he was paying attention, or in a few strides, he would have walked right into her.

"What—" but his voice trailed off as he followed her gaze to a hiking couple and their dog who were approaching them.

The dog tugged at its leash to sniff at them and wagged its tail in greeting.

Maybe she was scared of dogs?

Liam slipped in front of her and bent down to greet the dog. It was a mid-sized dog with friendly brown eyes and a light, almost golden coat. Its twisty-tail wagged as fast as it could.

"He won't bite," the man said. He was an athletically built man about Liam's age with rich tan skin that never burned the way his did.

"May I?" Liam held out his hand to the dog.

"Of course."

The dog licked his hands and seemed to soak up all attention.

74

"It's a beautiful dog. What breed is it?"

"Thanks," the woman said. "He's a Shibu Inu."

"Good dog." Liam gave the animal one last pet before standing. "You folks have a great day."

"You do the same."

He turned to find Jayna hurrying to catch up with the others who hadn't stopped walking. Ugh, for a day where he was supposed to be Reef's wingman, he was already slipping up. Liam broke into a jog until he reached Jayna's side.

"Hey, did you know that couple?"

She narrowed her eyes and shook her head. "No."

"Not a dog person then?"

Jayna didn't look at him but picked up her pace to close the gap between her and the other girls. "Yeah, I guess not."

He fell behind, giving her space. She was lying for some reason. Something had happened back there, something he had once again missed.

Either the couple or the dog had reminded her of something that had enough hold over her to make her freeze to the spot.

Jayna wasn't just hiding from something. She was terrified of it.

The waterfalls were beautiful, but did they have to see them from every angle? Jayna paused for breath as the group resumed hiking upward to yet another vista. They had first hiked down to a scenic spot at the base of the falls and then hiked up to a stone overlook. However, above them was yet another stone overlook, and apparently, that's where everyone was headed.

Her feet ached, and she glanced down at her now dirty shoes. Next time someone invited her on a hiking trip, she would invest in a good pair of boots.

Someone slid on the gravely walkway ahead of her, and Jayna glanced up to see who it was.

Olivia stepped her direction, a nervous smile on her face. "Hey, can I talk to you real quick?"

"Uh, sure." Jayna checked her footing and resumed the climb.

A sneaky smile spread across Olivia's lips, and the girl cast one last look over her shoulder to make sure no one else was in earshot. "Okay, so Reef is going to propose. Liam and I are going to video it on our phones from behind them—different angles—and TJ and Matt are going to stay behind on the trail up ahead for crowd control. I just don't want you to be surprised."

"Oh." The word froze on her lips, and something like dread gripped her stomach. She had chosen the wrong walking trip to avoid the proposal, and now, she had to play along.

She shook her head. "I mean, of course. I'll hang back."

"Isn't this amazing?" Olivia giggled and quickened her pace. "Kaley has no idea."

Jayna fell into step behind Olivia as the trail narrowed. Ahead, it opened into the stone overlook that no doubt provided yet another beautiful waterfall view. TJ and Matt were standing right outside the entrance, half concealed behind some shrubby trees.

"I'm not too late, right?" Olivia whispered to Matt.

He shook his head. "They've been talking and asking Liam to take pictures. It should be any minute now."

Olivia turned to give her a thumbs up and then hurried to join the group on the overlook. A couple came up from behind them, heading straight for it.

TJ held up a hand and spoke in a low voice. "Hey, would you mind coming back in a few minutes? My friend is getting ready to propose right here."

The couple's eyes lit up. "No way! Yeah, sure, we'll come back."

Jayna scanned the trail behind them. Several more hikers were already heading their way. This proposal spot was photogenic, but it was far too crowded for her taste.

It wasn't anything like Mario's secluded yacht at sunset. But then maybe if they had been less secluded, she would have made wiser choices.

Her face flamed at the memory, and she turned her focus to the overlook. She couldn't help it. In the middle of someone else's happily ever after was the last place she wanted to be, but her curiosity got the better of her.

Olivia darted back toward them in the trail. "Jayna!" she whispered and motioned her to come over. "I need you."

Jayna's heart thudded. She was already too close to the epicenter of this proposal. "What for?"

Olivia pointed at her phone. "My phone is dead. I thought I charged it last night, but it won't turn back on. Do you have your phone on you? Can you help?"

There was no time to think. Reef had turned Kaley to face the falls and was whispering something to her. Any moment would be their moment.

Biting her lip, Jayna nodded and hurried behind her to the overlook, being careful not to make much noise.

Not that Reef or Kaley would have noticed an elephant. Her head fit perfectly on his shoulder, and his arm wrapped tightly around her waist.

Jayna caught Liam's gaze. He was positioned on the far side of the overlook, so she could record right at the entrance. Whipping out her phone, she tapped the camera app and swiped to video.

Taking a deep breath, she pressed record and tried to still the trembling of her hand.

Reef removed his arm from Kaley's waist and slipped his hand into hers. Then he gently spun her around and dropped to one knee.

A roaring in her ears kept her from hearing Reef's words, but she didn't need to hear them. She had a front row seat to the love written on that man's face.

Had Mario's face looked that way? She thought she had seen love written there, but perhaps it had been only lust. For that moment in time, she had felt special, wanted. Then that moment shattered.

Tears trickled down Jayna's cheeks as Reef pulled a ring box out of his camera case and opened it to Kaley. Her hands flew to her mouth, but she nodded and blurted, "Yes!"

Reef was back on his feet in a flash, wrapping her in his arms and leaning in for the most tender kiss Jayna had ever witnessed.

77

Then Kaley started happy crying, and Olivia burst through the clearing clapping and crying. TJ and Matt emerged as well, hooting and cheering.

Jayna wiped her eyes dry with the back of her hand and stopped recording. She had done what Olivia asked, but she needed air, needed space.

Just then, Liam was at her side. "Wasn't that beautiful? How did your angle turn out?"

He leaned closer and gazed down at her phone. Would she really have to relive someone else's love story again?

But as she tapped to retrieve the video, someone burst through the clearing behind them. It was the couple from earlier.

"Congratulations." Their broad smiles—were directed at her.

Jayna flinched and glanced at Liam. He was standing much too close and leaning in to see her video.

She stepped away from him, shaking her head. "Oh, no, we're not—I mean, he's not my—"

"The happy couple is over there." Liam directed them toward Reef and Kaley, who was showing Olivia her ring.

Relief washed over her at Liam's redirection. Had he sensed her discomfort? Or perhaps he couldn't imagine himself with her.

The thought shouldn't burn her. After all, she was the one who had vowed never to fall for a gringo—let alone a ginger.

The woman wagged her finger at Jayna before reclaiming her partner's hand. "Oh, well, maybe it will be your turn one day too."

Mercifully, the couple moved toward Reef and Kaley, but Jayna felt the heat rushing to her cheeks just the same. It had been her turn—it was supposed to be her turn. Tears burned the insides of her eyelids, but she blinked them away. At least with her sunglasses, Liam couldn't see them.

Beside her, he was—chuckling?

She narrowed her eyes and faced him.

He cupped a hand over his mouth. "Sorry, but that was funny. Can you believe they thought we were engaged?"

She was right. He couldn't imagine himself with a girl like her in a hundred years, which was fine. He was definitely not her type.

"Yeah, hilarious." But her tone was much too dry.

Liam's smile vanished. "Hey, I didn't mean it like that—"

Jayna flipped her long ponytail and nodded toward the trail. 'I need to use the bathroom. I'll meet you guys back at the van."

Before he could respond, she jogged away. Each step in her not-hiking-boots reminded her she didn't belong with this group of Jesus-loving hopeless romantics.

Their version of love and romance was make-believe anyway. It didn't last—wouldn't last.

Happily ever after was only in fairy tales. Real life involved waking up to the reality that she was alone and always would be.

Chapter Fourteen

Liam followed his party into the restaurant. Banner Elk Café brimmed with guests, but when Reef told the hostess he had just proposed to his girlfriend, she managed to clear a long, narrow table for them adjacent to the bar. Liam slid onto a stool across from Reef and Kaley, who had insisted Jayna sit next to her and across from Olivia.

He had to give Kaley points. For someone who had been proposed to by the man of her dreams, she was still mindfully present of other people.

Jayna had looked reluctant to sit next to her, but the only other option was the seat next to him that Olivia currently occupied. And ever since Linville Falls, Jayna had treated him like he had rabies.

Liam sipped his water and perused the menu, though he already knew what he wanted.

It wasn't Banner Elk's French dip sandwich, delicious though it always was. More than lunch, he wanted to help the wounded woman who was painfully avoiding eye contact with him.

There was no other way to describe her. From her PTSD-like reaction to the dog on the trail to her flight response after the proposal, she was a girl on the run from pain in her past. He was no therapist like Kaley, but Jayna clearly needed counseling above his pay grade.

She also needed a friend but wasn't about to let anyone get close to her—least of all him.

He could still try.

Liam tapped the menu and spun it around so Kaley could see. "Don't forget their coffee menu."

Her eyes lit up. "Right, this place is the best. Jayna, you've got to try their lattes. And Olivia, their hot chocolate is like dessert."

Jayna nodded but kept her eyes glued to the menu.

"I remember," Olivia said, "but it's a little warm for hot chocolate, don't you think?"

"Warm?" Reef wrapped an arm around Kaley's shoulder. "It's almost one-hundred-degrees in Florida, so I think seventies should be plenty cool enough for hot chocolate."

"Hot or not, I'm getting their London Fog," Liam said.

Jayna finally glanced up. "A London what?"

Ah, yes, she had a love for travel. Maybe that was a connection point.

"A London Fog," Liam said. "It's Earl grey tea with vanilla flavoring and the frothiness of a latte."

Olivia chuckled. "That sounds a little bland compared to a decadent hot chocolate, don't you think?"

But Liam hadn't broken his eye contact with Jayna. "Maybe not, but there's something soothing and comforting about it."

There, he coaxed a little smile from her.

"Maybe I'll try it," she said.

"Good. It's on me then." He folded the menu and held up a hand as Jayna opened her mouth to protest. "I insist. That way, if you don't like it, you can get something else. Their lattes are good, like Kaley said."

Across from him, Kaley nuzzled her head against Reef's shoulder. "This day could really not be more perfect. I can't believe you guys were all in on this."

"Hey, Reef needed someone for crowd control," TJ chimed in. He and Matt sat on the other side of Reef. Liam got the feeling Matt would have much preferred his spot next to Olivia, but Liam wasn't about to trade a chance to rebuild the rapport he'd lost with Jayna. And by now, Matt should know him well enough to realize he wasn't competition for Olivia.

"Did they tell you, too, Jayna?" Kaley asked.

Jayna dropped her gaze and seemed to study her water glass as if her life depended on it. "Olivia told me right before it happened."

"But that's not all," Olivia said. "My phone died as I was supposed to video, so Jayna stepped in and took over."

81

"Wow, thanks, girl!" Kaley leaned over to hug Jayna, who visibly stiffened but didn't yank away.

Jayna shrugged her shoulders. "It was nothing."

Kaley rolled her eyes. "Nothing? Nothing to you, maybe, but everything to me. Do you have your phone with you? Can I see?"

Liam held his breath. Jayna shifted in her seat. Was it the attention that bothered her or the idea of giving up her phone?

"Uh, yeah, I have it here." Jayna tugged her phone from her back pocket and placed it on the table.

As she pulled up the video, Liam detected subtle movement behind Jayna at the bar. He diverted his gaze to a lone man sitting there, his martini untouched.

His camera phone tipped up and aimed at—Jayna.

Liam sucked a breath and wished he hadn't left his phone in the van.

Who was this man? Was he admiring Jayna for the beauty she was? But taking pictures of random people was still creepy.

"It's so perfect." Kaley's voice drew him back into the conversation. "Thank you so much for capturing our moment."

Jayna's cheeks turned pink. "Glad you like the video."

Kaley looked as if she was about to replay it again but then thought better. "Can I text this to myself?"

"Sure," Jayna said.

Kaley tapped on the phone, and then her eyes widened. "Oh, you're getting a call from—Mario?"

Liam risked a glance at Jayna. The pink had fled her cheeks. What looked very much like fear filled her eyes.

At that moment, the waitress arrived. "Is everyone ready to order?"

Jayna took her phone from Kaley. "I'll text you the video later. Excuse me. And I'm not hungry."

With that, Jayna slid off her stool and rushed toward the bathrooms.

The waitress arched an eyebrow. "Well, are the rest of you folks hungry?"

"Starved," Olivia said and plunged into her order.

But Liam wasn't listening. His gaze trailed the space where

ayna had disappeared—and the now-vacant spot at the bar from where the man had vanished as well.

ayna cupped the steaming London Fog the waitress had delivered, hoping it would chase away the chill that now surrounded her heart. Why did Mario have to call her here? And what had she been thinking when she answered it?

Jayna darling, are you there? Hello? Please talk to me. It's not like you think.

She hadn't said a word, just listened to his voice, thick with a Bahamian accent from having grown up in Bimini.

I'm going to do right by you, I promise. And I will once I find you.

She had hung up then, a surge of panic sending her finger slamming into the end call button. Once he found her? Was he looking for her? Did he even know where to look?

Not even her family knew where she was.

She sipped the subtle richness of the London Fog. Liam was right. It was soothing. But her stomach growled as the waitress returned with everyone else's food. She should have ordered something.

Not that she could keep a meal down after Mario's call.

"Grilled cheese and chili?" the waitress called out.

"Oh, right there," Liam pointed. At. Her.

"But I—"

The waitress set down the plate in front of her and then called out, "French dip?"

Liam motioned to his place and then thanked her before she moved on to the others and their orders.

Jayna leaned forward, voice low. "I didn't order anything."

Liam offered a charming smile in return. "I hope you like grilled cheese. You were gone, and I didn't want you to go hungry. We put in several miles this morning, and we still have Roan Mountain to hike. The London Fog may be delicious, but it's not filling."

There was no guile in this man, just genuine concern for her. Of all the friends here, he alone had thought to order something for her, simple though the meal was.

Maybe she could eat something.

"Well, thanks."

"You're welcome." Liam glanced around the table. "I'll pray, and then we can all dig in."

Here we go again with this prayer thing.

The others nodded and bowed their heads. Jayna followed their example, though she kept her eyes open. Bea would love this group. Her sister was into prayer and stuff like that.

"Dear Father," Liam started, "thank You for this special day, these amazing friends, and this food. Bless it and our time together. Amen."

Jayna blinked. That was it? Yet Liam's words and tone were so sincere that they touched a space deep inside her. He really believed his Father was listening.

But she could think more on that later. The grilled cheese was even better than it looked, and the chili had a decent spice. Her nerves were starting to unwind when Olivia turned to her from chatting with Kaley. "So, who's Mario?"

Her last bite lodged in her throat. Really? The girl who couldn't seem to decide her own relationship status was going to get nosy with her?

Jayna reached for her water and swallowed, hoping not to choke. Then, taking a steadying breath, she leveled her voice. "He's a contact from my last job."

"And what do you do again?"

"I'm a freelancer and blogger, so I do lots of things." It was time to get the subject off herself. "What about you?"

Olivia stabbed her salad. "I do physical therapy, but I sure needed a break. This trip came at a good time for me, you know? Burn out is real."

"Yeah." Jayna scooped another bite of chili.

From the other side of Kaley, Reef cleared his throat. "So, what do you guys think about adjusting our plan this afternoon? We could go to Roan Mountain to hike after we finish here and

hen relax at the cabin this evening. I'll order Brick Oven pizza—
ny treat—for everyone to celebrate tonight. And then we can do
he group devo TJ asked me to share."

Matt nodded. "Sounds great." He glanced down the table in
)livia's direction. Maybe he would have preferred her seat across
rom Olivia, but he would have enough time on this trip to make a
nove.

Here's hoping he would take Olivia off her hands and keep
he girl too occupied to ask more nosy questions.

Kaley and Reef had a new reason to spend more time together
his trip, and Pastor TJ was on the phone a lot with the case worker
or the foster child he and his wife were trying to adopt.

That just left Liam for her to shed. He might be harder,
)ecause he always seemed to be paying attention.

"I'm ready for a nap, not another hike." Kaley ribbed Reef.

He wrapped his arm around her shoulder. "You can nap on
he drive. But trust me, you're going to love Roan Mountain."

She pecked his cheek. "I love you."

Jayna looked down at the last of her chili. She had wanted to
,kip out on Roan Mountain, but now, it looked like she didn't have
ι choice but to join the others. Still, with Mario—and probably
<evon—at large, did she really want to be left alone?

That was ridiculous. They couldn't possibly know where she
vas.

,he might not have wanted to hike more, but Roan Mountain was
vorth it.

If only her blistered feet would agree.

Jayna shut off the water to her shower and quickly dried off.
\eef's plan had been pretty perfect. They'd hiked a few miles and
,napped group pictures. That these virtual strangers included her
nto their group made her feel like family.

But then most of the pictures had been of the newly engaged
:ouple, which once again, reminded her of everything she'd lost.

Reef and Kaley seemed perfect for each other. Would they

last? Would she ever get that lucky?

Twisting her towel around her hair, she shrugged on another tank top and pulled on her one pair of jeans. The moment she stepped out of the shower, the cool cabin air prickled her skin. She did owe Olivia for insisting the group stop at a roadside tourist t-shirt place. At least she now had a "Beech Mountain" hoodie to keep warm.

Shivering, she snapped off the tag on the sleeve and then pulled the fabric over her head. It was bulky but couldn't hide all her curves.

You could wear a paper bag and still be the most beautiful girl in the room, her sister had once told her.

Well, she'd rather no one notice her, at least for a long time anyway.

If only Liam would stop being so nice. He wouldn't if he knew what kind of girl she was, what kind of things she'd done.

But she had to give him credit. When he looked at her, he looked at *her.* She often caught him searching her eyes as if trying to read her, unlike Kevon and even Mario whose gazes raked over her figure.

From outside her room, a door slammed and someone called out, "Pizza's here!"

Reef must be back. She slipped her fuzzy socks over her wounded feet and tossed aside her towel to brush through her hair.

Her stomach overrode her desire to dry it. Who knew hiking could make someone so hungry?

Yanking her door open, she stepped into the hallway.

Without looking first.

"Whoa!" Liam tried to stop but tilted toward her.

Her own fuzzy socks slid on the wood floor, and she fell right into him.

Chapter Fifteen

Liam wrapped an arm around Jayna's back to keep her from falling and stared into her wide, dark brown eyes. She wasn't wearing a trace of makeup, and she didn't need to.

Her wet hair sent prickles up his arm, and the tropical, coconut scent of her shampoo made him want to hold her a second longer than he should.

She floundered to find her footing, and he pulled her toward him so she could be more vertical.

Her face turned velvet as she nodded for him to let go. "So—sorry."

"No. I'm sorry. I wasn't paying attention." He released her, and his arms suddenly ached for her absence. Clearing his throat, he stepped backward. Being too close to her made him think impossible things. "Reef just got back with the pizza, so—"

"Great, I'm starving." She clipped her words and spun toward the kitchen.

His chest tightened at her hasty retreat. She had to know he meant her no harm. Why was she always in flight-mode?

"It's not you, man," he muttered to himself. He'd faced his share of rejection—hello, Kaley—but Jayna was different. She wasn't rejecting him. She was running. He couldn't let his own wounds from past relationships make him withdraw. His gut told him she needed a friend.

Swallowing his pride, he followed the now-empty hallway to the kitchen where a deep voice was laughing.

Reef. His friend radiated joy at claiming his fiancé. While the stab of Liam's own disappointments tempted him to retreat, he knew his place was to celebrate at his friend's side.

How many times would he have to die to himself in five minutes? Liam forced a smile he didn't feel but trusted that Jesus could help his heart follow.

Reef waved him into the kitchen and cast a wink at Kaley. "Finally, a reasonable person has arrived. Can you believe this girl, Liam? She prefers plain cheese pizza when she could have supreme."

"That's crazy talk." Liam offered a tilted grin.

"I know." Reef ran a hand through his sun-bleached brown hair. "What am I going to do with her?"

On the other side of the kitchen island, Kaley helped herself to a cheese slice and blew Reef a kiss. "Love me forever."

Reef's face broke into an even bigger smile. He strode toward Kaley, stepped behind her, and wrapped his arms around her waist. "I plan to."

Matt waved his arms in time-out from his spot next to the sink. "No PDAs on the singles' trip."

Next to Matt, Olivia elbowed him in the ribs. "Oh, give them some slack. They just got engaged."

Liam risked a glance at Jayna, who had isolated herself to the corner by the refrigerator. She watched Reef and Kaley with— jealousy?

Not that he could blame her. He wanted what they had too.

Maybe the tightness between her eyes wasn't jealousy. Maybe it was closer to doubt. Surely, she had to see that what this couple shared was the real deal?

Liam shook his head and helped himself to a paper plate. But then, what did he know about love? Still, he knew Reef, and there was no truer friend. Reef would be true to Kaley, even when life got hard.

The sliding door behind the dining table squeaked open, and Pastor TJ appeared, phone in his hand. "Sorry, that call took longer than planned. You guys didn't have to wait for me."

Reef released Kaley and filled his empty hands with a plate. "You're just in time to say grace."

"Well, great. Circle up." Pastor TJ stepped toward the island and bowed his head. "Dear Lord, thank You so much for this special day for Reef and Kaley, for safety hiking, and for this time of celebration. Bless this food and our fellowship. Thank You for knowing what we need right when we need it. Amen."

"Amen," Liam whispered. TJ was right. God knew what each of them needed and when they needed it. He had to remember that.

Jayna couldn't eat another bite, but that Brick Oven pizza was rave-worthy. When was the last time she'd allowed herself to eat three slices? She eyed the remnants of her crust and willed herself to stop. Though it had been a decade since her sister had caught her purging a meal, she didn't want to feel the guilt of wanting to do the same later tonight.

"Okay, before everyone goes into a food coma, Reef has something to share with us." Pastor TJ collected empty plates on the table, and Jayna added hers to the pile. "Let's meet in the living room in five."

Her stomach churned. Something to share with them? Hadn't Reef shared enough today? C'mon, they all had to witness his proposal.

Maybe she could excuse herself, say she was tired. But part of her wanted to know what made a guy tick who seemed as genuine as Reef.

Matt yawned across from her. "How are we supposed to pay attention with all this food on our stomachs?"

Olivia swatted him with an extra plate. "I've got the fixings for ice cream sundaes for those who stay awake after Reef's devotional. Is that motivation enough?"

Ice cream too? Jayna rubbed her bloated belly. She should pass on that.

Reef and TJ were the first to head for the living room, and Kaley and Liam followed close behind. Matt had offered to take out the empty pizza boxes and full trash bag to the garbage bin, leaving her and Olivia behind to finish cleaning up.

"Could you help me set out the ice cream and fixings afterward?" Olivia replaced the trashcan with a new liner while Jayna wiped down the table.

"Uh, sure." She hesitated. "Just don't let me eat any, okay?"

Olivia arched an eyebrow. "Girl, you're basically a model. How can you say no to ice cream?"

Jayna's mouth went dry. Olivia had no idea that her old demons still found ways to torment her. "I—um—am sensitive to dairy. I already had too much pizza." It was a lie, but it seemed safer than the truth.

"Oh, sorry. Do you need a lactose pill? I packed some because Matt's stomach gets upset sometimes with dairy too."

A smile tugged at Jayna's mouth. Why couldn't this girl see she cared about Matt? People who weren't lactose intolerant didn't pack lactose pills for just anyone.

Jayna wrung out the dishcloth and draped it over the sink to dry. "Thanks, I may take you up on that offer."

Olivia nodded and started for the door. "I'll grab them and meet you in the living room."

"Okay." Jayna swallowed as she disappeared. Goodness, this crew was kind. They made her feel less like the outsider she was.

Still, she couldn't let anyone get too close. If she did, she would cause hurt feelings when the day came that she had to disappear.

Maybe she wouldn't have to. Maybe she could start new in the Tampa area with this quirky group of friends. As long as her past didn't catch up with her.

After helping herself to a glass of water, she traced Olivia's path to the large living space, complete with a wraparound couch, recliner chair, fireplace, and pool table in the corner. Reef had pulled a few kitchen chairs and sat on one next to TJ. Kaley motioned for Jayna to join her on the couch, but she pointed to the recliner chair. It was its own little island away from the others, and she preferred it that way.

Funny how she was avoiding the very girl who invited her on the trip. But Kaley couldn't have warned her she was about to get engaged. The girl was living a dream-come-true, and well, Jayna couldn't relate to someone with a picture-perfect life.

Matt emerged from the kitchen, and Olivia bounded down the staircase with a pill bottle and two fuzzy blankets in tow. She tossed a blanket at Kaley and then tracked toward Jayna.

"Thought you might want a blanket." Olivia held one out to her and then shook the small bottle in her other hand. "I've got these for Matt, so if you want one, let me know."

Jayna accepted the blanket, a black and green checkered fleece that felt like a warm hug. "Thanks. I'm good for now."

"Sure thing." Olivia turned to squeeze next to Kaley on the couch and tug half the other fleece over her legs. Matt claimed a space on the other side of her, leaving only one person missing.

Liam.

Footfalls sounded on the staircase, and moments later, he emerged, gripping his cell phone in one hand. There was a new thinness to his lips as if he'd received news. Bad news?

She felt her face warm and buried her nose in her water glass. She shouldn't stare. Goodness, she had already fallen into his arms once tonight. The last thing she needed was for anyone in the group to think she had a thing for Ginger Ale.

Which, of course, she didn't. He was the gringo stereotype with ginger hair—like the modeling manager that had taken advantage of her innocence.

It had been a few months into their working relationship. She had been finishing the end of a swimsuit shoot for a junior's brand, and Travis caught her in her bikini on the way to the changing room.

"Got a second, Jay?" He'd placed a hand on her shoulder.

"Yeah, sure."

"I've got someone for you to meet."

Travis led her to the back of the shooting studio into a small, windowless room. But an older man was working behind a camera, adjusting the lighting for a green screen. He didn't say anything to her but nodded toward a privacy panel.

"Another job?" she asked as he handed her a sparse black bikini. "I thought we finished the swimsuit shoot."

"We did. This is extra." To her surprise, though, he followed her behind the changing screen.

"What—"

Travis had gripped her shoulder. "Listen, you want to succeed as a model, right? This guy has connections. Big ones. You do this

91

job, and your modeling calendar will be set."

Her eyes had traced to the swimsuit fabric—more like a bunch of strings. Her mom already wasn't happy she was modeling two pieces, but this could hardly be called any kind of piece.

"But—"

"You have to do everything I say, no questions asked. You blow this, and you might as well kiss your future good-bye."

"Okay, but—"

"No 'buts,' just do." His fiery green eyes had sparked with something she'd never seen there before. It wasn't professional, that was for sure.

She gulped. She was only sixteen. Surely, he knew the laws better than she did for underage models. She didn't have anything to worry about.

"Okay."

"Now be quick about changing. See you out front in a minute."

She removed her cute bikini and tried to figure out the stringy business. When she finished, she didn't need a mirror to tell her it left little to the imagination.

You do this one job, and your modeling career will be set.

Her mom would be furious. Her sister, too. But it was just a job. And she could trust her manager.

Trembling, she squared her shoulders, raised her head, and then stepped out from the screen. The photographer and Travis looked up the minute she did.

Travis had never looked at her like she was raw meat before, but that look—he wanted to devour her. This was a bad idea. She should leave—

"Right in front of the green screen," the photographer said. Travis was instantly by her side, hand on her backside, propelling her forward. He'd never touched her this way before.

"Relax," he whispered. "You look like a million dollars."

She willed her lip not to tremble as he continued to touch her, guide her into a dozen angles for the shoot. She had never done such provocative positions before.

Blinking back tears of shame, she glared down the

photographer as he devoured her with the camera lens, and Travis devoured her with his eyes. It had been only the beginning of his devouring.

She had been such a fool for believing her career justified obs like that one, which only led to more and more shameful ones. If Bea hadn't discovered her secret and forced her to quit, where would she be now?

Maybe in the same boat as Mario, with such a deadened conscience that he could justify a decapitated body as a means to an end.

Someone pulled up a chair beside her, shaking her from the nightmarish memory. "Sorry I'm late," Liam said. "My partner left a voicemail, and I needed to respond."

"No worries, man." Reef tugged his Bible off an adjacent end table. "Would you open us in prayer?"

"Glad to." Liam bowed his head and started praying, thanking God for His goodness, praying for His blessing on Reef and Kaley—

She stopped listening and pulled the checkered fleece more tightly around her shoulders to fight a shiver. She would never be free from her past. There was too much of it. And she could never trust a ginger again, no matter how nice his prayers might sound.

Chapter Sixteen

The moment Liam finished praying, Jayna's gaze darted to Olivia and the lactose bottle she'd placed on the coffee table. That was her ticket to escaping the group and getting alone to wrestle with her bitter memories.

But her conscience pricked her. Being alone never made her anxiety go away.

"If you have your Bible—or your phone—take a look at Genesis 16," Reef said.

Jayna wished she could disappear. The Bible Beatriz had given her years ago was collecting dust on a bookshelf somewhere, and Jayna had left her phone in her room.

Something brushed her arm, and she jerked to see what it was.

"Sorry. I didn't mean to scare you," Liam said. "I thought you might like to use my Bible. I have the app on my phone."

Jayna glanced to the armrest, where he'd opened his leather Bible to Genesis for her. At least it would give her a point of reference.

"Thanks," she murmured and slid it onto her lap.

Reef was talking again, and she turned her attention back to him. "Just a little backstory before we dive into the text. Remember that God promised Abram that He would bless him and his wife with a son and that his descendants would be as numerous as the stars. He was seventy-five years old when God made this promise, and a decade later, he and Sarai were still childless. At this point, his wife wanted him to force God's hand by having Abram sleep with her servant. I know, it's pretty R-rated stuff, but there's a lesson for us here. Would someone read verses one through four?"

"I got it," Olivia said. "'Now Sarai, Abram's wife, had borne him no children. And she had an Egyptian maidservant whose name was Hagar. So Sarai said to Abram, "See now, the Lord has estrained me from bearing children. Please, go in to my maid; perhaps I shall obtain children by her." And Abram heeded the voice of Sarai. Then Sarai, Abram's wife, took Hagar her maid, the Egyptian, and gave her to her husband Abram to be his wife, after Abram had dwelt ten years in the land of Canaan. So he went in to Hagar, and she conceived. And when she saw that she had conceived, her mistress became despised in her eyes.'"

"Thanks, Olivia." Reef nodded at her. "At first, it looks like Abram and Sarai helped God along. I mean, their plan worked, didn't it? Hagar got pregnant and gave them a son. But Ishmael wasn't the son of promise, and because Abram and Sarai rushed ahead of God, Israel and Ishmael—aka, the Arab nations today—are locked in constant warfare."

Jayna sucked a breath. Wow, she had no idea that the ongoing conflict in the Middle East stemmed from one couple jumping the gun on God.

Reef scanned the room as if to intentionally make eye contact with each of them, even her. "Some of you know me better than others, so I'll tell you a little of my story. I come from a pretty messed-up home. My mom was an alcoholic, and my dad raised me on his own."

"He did a good job, too," Kaley said softly from the couch.

Reef smiled her way before continuing. "He did do a good job, but I underestimated the hurt I internalized. All through my twenties, I dated around, sure I'd find the right girl, settle down, and have the home I always wanted."

Jayna squinted at Reef. She'd never thought about how old he was. He was in great shape and certainly not lacking in the looks department, but he wasn't twenty-something any more.

"I watched many of my best friends—including TJ here— marry young, have one kid, and then another." Reef chuckled. "It was like I was always the groomsman and never the groom."

Goodness, she could relate to that, and she was still in her twenties. How long had Reef waited for Kaley?

"Due to the nature of my business, I met lots of pretty girls, but none of them loved Jesus the way I hoped my future wife would. Again and again, God told me no, and I started to doubt if

He'd ever give me a yes."

"And just to clarify," TJ piped in, "you didn't have a direct word from God that you'd even get married."

Reef laughed. "Exactly. God doesn't tend to speak audibly today, but He does speak clearly in his Word. Although there were no promises that said 'Reef would get a wife,' there were plenty of instructions to live godly, to avoid immorality, and to wait on God."

Jayna dropped her gaze to the text in front of her. She had certainly failed on those counts ever since her modeling days desensitized her sense of modesty. Although it had been terribly wrong of her manager to take her to the shoots he did, she always had a nagging thought that she could say no. But she hadn't been brave enough. If this God promised good things for His people, why hadn't He promised something good for her?

She tried to swallow the resentment, but it left a bitter taste.

Reef's expression turned serious. "I'm not here to hold myself up as a model. I made my share of mistakes along the way and didn't always handle relationships well."

He paused. "I suppose you could say that it's easy for me to tell this story now, because the most wonderful girl in the world just agreed to marry me. But my reason for telling it is to encourage you that God is writing each one of your stories. It may be messy, but if we wait on Him and submit to His plan for our lives, He will write a better ending than we ever could."

Jayna sneaked a glance at Kaley. Her face was radiant. She was a lucky girl.

But her smile tightened. "Could I add something, Reef?"

"Of course."

Kaley bit her lip. "Sometimes, God allows tough things to happen to us while we're waiting on Him. Still, those hard situations are better than rushing ahead of God like Abram and Sarai and living with the consequences."

Tough things? Jayna scrunched her face. Kaley's life seemed picture perfect.

Kaley tugged at the fleece she and Olivia were sharing. It was a protective move Jayna understood too well.

"Most of you know what happened last winter here at Beech—with me being kidnapped and almost trafficked on account of a client I represented."

Jayna's jaw dropped. "What?"

Liam leaned toward her. "It's a crazy story. I'll fill you in later."

Kaley flashed a sad smile her way and continued, "There were moments I almost wrote off God. Why wasn't He listening? Didn't He care? Then I realized that although we can't always control what happens to us, we do get to choose our response to it. In our most painful moments, He is most present. We simply need to call out to Him."

Jayna's thoughts swirled. She hadn't been able to control many of the things that happened to her in the past and the things that were happening to her now. But she'd never thought about still having a choice in how she could respond. That idea was—empowering.

"Thanks for sharing that, Kaley." Reef offered her another tender smile. "She's right. Waiting on God is hard enough when life is good, but when times are tough, it can be excruciating. The shame of barrenness burned this couple, but instead of taking their pain to God, they tried to fix it themselves. And when we rush ahead of God's timing, we're going to hurt others and ourselves."

Reef glanced at TJ and offered a lopsided grin. "I promised I wouldn't give a sermon, so I'm going to stop there tonight. If we read on further, we'd see how God still did keep His promise to this couple despite their disobedience. He even went so far as to change their names from Abram and Sarai to Abraham and Sarah to underscore that they would be parents of many nations—and blessed them with a baby boy named Isaac when Abraham was one-hundred years old."

He turned to gaze at Kaley. "I also hope you can see how Kaley's yes today was God's blessing from a whole lot of waiting. As singles, you know all about waiting too. I want to encourage you not to give up when the going gets hard. God might not answer your prayers the way you want Him to, but His answer will always be better."

97

Better. Jayna mentally chewed on the word. Could God really have something better for her than a life running from her past?

"Thanks, Reef," TJ said. "I'd like to add that you can't experience that *something better* if you don't know God in the first place. And knowing Him starts by believing He sent His Son Jesus to die in your place and pay the price for all your sins—past, present, and future. All He asks of us is to believe in Him as our Savior. From there, we begin a daily walk with Him to know Him more and to live for Him."

His words sounded familiar, probably something Bea had told her at one point. But Jayna had never really listened—like she wasn't right now since TJ was still talking.

"… I'd like to think everyone here has a relationship with God, but if you don't—or you feel stuck in a rut—please come talk with me or someone else after. Let's pray."

Her life was in more than a rut. Since her parents had taken her to church only on Christmas and Easter, she'd never found religion anything more than sitting in a pew a few Sundays in a year. Beatriz had "found God" sometime in college, and though she was a nicer person for it, Jayna opted not to drink that Kool-Aid. How did a person even have a relationship with an intangible being? All she had to do was believe in Him?

It seemed too good to be true. In her experience with relationships, when they seemed too good to be true, they always were.

The moment TJ's prayer ended, Olivia popped up from her seat. "Give Jayna and me a few minutes to set up and then come on back to the kitchen. I have all the fixings for ice cream sundaes to celebrate the happy couple."

Jayna uncurled herself and closed the worn Bible on her lap. "Thanks for letting me borrow it." She slid it on the armrest toward Liam.

"No problem." He reached for it and met her gaze. "Good stuff, right?"

Good stuff? Jayna bit her lip as her thoughts spiraled. Abram having sex with his wife's servant wasn't good. Rushing ahead of God wasn't good. But God staying true to His word was. Baby

saac being born to Abraham at one-hundred was certainly good
ind nothing short of a miracle. Or just a pretty story.

"Guess it depends what you mean." Jayna rose and folded the
leece. "I told Olivia I'd help her in the kitchen." She jerked her
humb that direction and hurried down the hallway. Reef's and
[J's words had given her something to think about, but if there was
ι *better* for her, God was going to have to show up and prove He
;ven wanted a relationship with her.

Iis cell phone vibrated in his pocket, and Liam stood and strode
'or the front door. He didn't need to check the caller ID to know
)rew was calling again, and he didn't want to bother the group
nside with his work call.

"Liam here." He tapped the front door closed with his boot
ιnd then settled into the swing. It offered a front row seat to the
varm colors of the evening sky. Would he ever be able to fully
·elax and simply enjoy the view?

"It's Drew," came the breathless reply. "Listen, I know
/ou're on vacation, but man, this is too good to wait until you get
)ack."

Liam pressed a smile to his lips and added a lightness to his
/oice he didn't feel. Drew was a great partner, even if he was easily
:xcited. "It's okay. What's up?"

"You remember those crab traps?"

"Of course." Liam's gaze wandered toward two deer that
;auntered across the road leading to their cabin. An approaching
;edan spooked them, and they disappeared into some trees.

"Yeah, the ones I found when I was diving near *Yankee Dog*,"
)rew said. "I went back out the other day for a closer look since I
lropped a pin of the location. You know that traps, even
·ecreational ones, must have the owner's name and address fixed
o them."

"Right, but the *Yankee Dog* was out scalloping. You don't
hink it was a coincidence they were diving by those traps?" The
;edan that scared the deer continued a slow, winding drive down

the road. They must be lost or not sure which cabin they rented.

"That was my hunch. Anyway, the traps are owned by one Enzo Martinez."

"Should that name mean something to me?"

"No, but he died six months ago."

The sedan slowed to a stop in the lawn in front of him. Great, he was probably about to get asked directions.

Liam kept the sedan in the corner of his vision while trying to focus on Drew's words. "You think someone else is using his old traps?"

"Exactly. When I dove down for closer inspection, I also noticed someone had snapped the wire around the escape rings to make bigger openings. In other words, whoever is using the traps isn't interested in catching crabs."

The sedan's passenger door opened, and a man dressed in black pants and a silver-collared shirt stepped out. With one hand, he smoothed back his dark hair, and in the other, he grasped a dozen roses.

A dozen red roses.

Liam tensed on the swing as the man walked toward him across the lawn. "Hey, Drew, I'm going to have to let you go. I think someone is lost and needs directions, but he's heading my way. I'll call back in a few."

He ended the call and stood as the man mounted the porch steps. "Can I help you?"

The stranger shifted the bouquet to his left hand and extended his right. "The name's Mario. I'm here to surprise Jayna."

Jayna.

Liam stared at the extended hand as if it had bitten him. "Excuse me, who?"

Mario flashed a toothy smile and retracted his hand. "I'm Mario. Do I have the wrong cabin? I understood this is where Jayna Scott was staying."

Everything in him wanted to lie and say that this man—Mario—had the wrong address, but he knew both Jayna's first and last name. Maybe he lived in the area, and Jayna had invited him to stop by? As far as he could remember, Jayna hadn't mentioned having any friends in the area. Something felt off.

"There is a group of us staying here." Liam stepped toward the door. "Wait here, and I'll check."

Mario's smile wavered for a moment, but he nodded. Did he grip the bouquet more tightly, and was that sweat on his collar? Why did the man look nervous?

Liam slipped inside and made sure the door latched behind him. The living room was empty, but laughter echoed from the kitchen. That's right. They were fixing up ice cream sundaes.

His heartrate quickened as he strode toward the voices. When he reached the kitchen door, Jayna's beautiful face came into view. She held a cup of ice cream and was chatting with Kaley as if she didn't have a care in the world.

His gut warned him he was about to shatter that illusion.

He skirted TJ and gently touched her arm. "Hey, Jayna. There's someone at the front door who's asking for you."

The color drained from her face. "What?"

Liam suppressed the sudden urge to wrap an arm around her shoulder and assure her she was safe. "I thought he might have the wrong cabin, but he said your full name. He called himself Mario."

Chapter Seventeen

Mario.

Jayna's whole body jerked at the name, and the ice cream cup she'd been holding slipped through her fingers.

A cocktail of emotions raged inside her as her new friends stared at her. They were clueless about the man from her past who was about to sweep into this perfect day and drag her garbage up for them to see.

The room was suddenly far too hot.

Jayna sank to the floor to collect the remnants of her dessert, but Kaley beat her to the sticky cup and melting pool that was her sundae.

"Is everything okay?" Kaley whispered. "If you don't want to see this Mario guy, have Liam tell him to get lost."

She swallowed down the words forming on her tongue. Would Mario simply get lost? If he had tracked her to a sleepy mountain community in North Carolina, he would find her anywhere. Maybe it was the ring he wanted back. Maybe returning it would put an end to all this.

"Thanks." Jayna steadied her breath and rose. "I'll talk to him." Her gaze settled on Liam's worried face. For some reason, he was the last person she wanted overhearing this conversation, but she would feel better with backup.

"Maybe Reef and Liam could come with me to make sure he leaves." No, that wouldn't do. Mario would get jealous.

"Or actually, Reef and Kaley would be better," she hurried on. "Mario and I have a complicated relationship, and it might be better that he doesn't see a guy with me and make assumptions."

A frown flashed across Liam's face, but he nodded toward Reef. "I'll be right behind you in the hallway in case you need me."

Kaley's small hand squeezed Jayna's shoulder. "Remember

you're not alone," Kaley said. "We're here for you."

Jayna bit her lip. Would they stick around if they knew the grimy details of her situation?

"Thanks," was all she could say. "I need to grab something from my room, but I'll meet you at the front door in a minute."

Without waiting for an answer, Jayna darted down the hallway to her room. Tossing her duffle bag onto her bed, she flipped open the center compartment and reached for the small inside zipper pouch.

Her fingers wrapped around the ring, and she pulled it out. Even in the fading daylight that filtered through her window, the oval diamond shimmered. She had never fantasized about an engagement ring. She had just desperately wanted one and the promise that came with it.

What a fool she had been. Now, she wanted to get rid of this one and everything it represented.

She tucked it inside her hoodie pocket and started for the door, but dread slowed her steps. Would he be furious? Men had cursed at her before.

Sucking a deep breath, she whispered a silent prayer. Did God hear her the way He heard these friends? If Reef were right and God wanted something better for her, maybe He would let this encounter end well.

As she reentered the hallway, voices were already coming from the front entryway. Liam waited like a sentinel at the end of the hallway, out of sight from the front door. For the first time, she saw him as a cop, not as Ginger Ale.

A cop who cared enough to make sure she and his friends stayed safe.

Gratitude swelled inside her. Maybe she could thank him later. Right now, she had to face her past and hopefully not give her new friends too much to gossip about.

Her stomach dropped when she caught sight of Mario's charming smile and the roses in his hand.

Shoot. So much for minimizing the gossip-worthy material.

His eyes lit up the moment he spotted her. "Darling!" Mario brushed past Reef and reached for her, but she shrank back.

"What are you doing here?" She crossed her arms.

His smile tightened, but he didn't back down. "I know there's been a misunderstanding, and I want to explain."

Jayna arched an eyebrow. So that's all a dead body was to Mario? A misunderstanding?

"I left—"

"You ran away without giving me time to explain," Mario cut her off. "Please, I'm staying in a hotel a few miles down the road. Come with me, and we'll sort things out."

His smile seemed so genuine, but he was like so many other men she'd known–a liar.

She fought against the squeezing sensation in her throat. "There's nothing to sort out, except that we were both fools."

"Give me a chance." His handsome dark eyes pleaded with her.

Her gaze drifted behind him to the black car parked out front. A shadow shifted in the front seat.

A shiver raced down her spine. "Who's that? And how did you find me?"

Mario dropped his gaze and stalled by placing the bouquet on the entryway table. "I had to find you, darling."

"Kevon?" She hissed. "That man—"

"Is resourceful." Mario's tone was pinched. Once more, he reached to touch her, but she twisted to avoid him.

Beside her, Reef and Kaley shifted closer, as if not sure what to do.

Jayna had to wrap this up fast. She plunged her hand into her hoodie pocket and then reached to grab Mario's hand that still stretched toward her.

She pressed the ring into his palm. "I'm sorry, Mario, but we made a mistake. Take your ring back, and please leave me alone."

But his touch did something to her. It broke past the shallow defenses she'd built around her heart. It reminded her of everything she'd almost had. Tears pricked her eyes, and she backed away. "Good-bye."

She choked down a sob and ran down the hall and past Liam's confused stare. Mario was calling after her, but she slammed her bedroom door shut and pressed the lock in place.

Then she fell against the door, slid to the floor, and covered her face with her hands. She didn't hold back the sobs now. She was broken beyond repair. If her past could find her here, it could find her anywhere.

Reef was wrong. Girls like her didn't have a chance for anything better than heartbreak and disappointment.

"It's not what you think." Mario's final words echoed in Liam's mind, even after Reef had kindly but firmly herded the man from the entryway and bolted the door behind him.

Liam rushed to the adjacent window and tugged back the blinds as the sedan started down the road. He snapped several pictures on his camera phone and hoped the license would be clear enough.

"What are we supposed to do with these?" Kaley fingered the bouquet Mario had planted on the entryway stand. "I don't think she wants them."

Liam gazed down the hallway where Jayna had disappeared and slammed her door. No, she didn't seem to want them. The roses were an apology that Jayna hadn't accepted.

But at one point, she had accepted Mario's ring. The ramifications ran through his mind. Jayna had been engaged to that chump.

Who was Kevon, though? He must be more than a taxi driver. Mario had indicated he needed the man to find her, and Jayna hadn't been happy about that arrangement at all.

He sighed. "I'd leave them there for now."

If only he could take that same advice about Jayna. His gut warned him he should walk away from the web surrounding her, but his professional instinct screamed that she needed help. He was a private investigator and former cop, after all. Helping others was his business.

A hand on his shoulder pulled him out of his thoughts. "Hey, man. I'm sorry."

"Sorry about what, Reef?" Liam slid his phone into his pocket and faced his friend.

"You know, about Jayna."

He stared at Reef, and his mouth felt like cotton. Surely, his friend knew he was here to support him, not chase after a new girl.

Kaley motioned toward the kitchen. "I—uh—I'll let everyone else know we're okay." With that, she hurried down the hall.

Liam shook his head. "It's not like you think, Reef. I'm professionally concerned about her. That's all."

"Dude, it's okay if you're attracted to her, but there's something really off with this situation. I don't want to see you—"

"Get disappointed again?" Liam couldn't keep the tightness out of his tone. "I appreciate your concern, but I can handle it."

Reef held up his hands. "I get it. If you need anything, let me know." He slipped past him down the hallway toward the kitchen.

Liam sighed. He didn't mean to come across as short. The whole situation had him on edge. Sure, he was drawn to Jayna, but she had a whole lot of baggage to sort through before considering another relationship.

Right now, he needed to make sure she wasn't in some sort of real trouble.

The others could enjoy their sundaes in the kitchen. He needed to phone Drew again—and not just to hear more about those crab traps.

Spinning on his toes, Liam headed for the stairs and the room he shared with Reef. The evening was still young, and no doubt, his friend would spend every waking minute of it with Kaley.

Fine by him. He needed space to think and work.

Chapter Eighteen

A buzzing noise pulled Jayna from another nightmare. Her eyes cracked open but felt like someone had glued them shut. Rather, tears had hardened on her lashes, caking them to each other and her skin.

She'd fallen asleep on her comforter and tossed her phone aside.

It continued to buzz—vibrate—from somewhere on the bed. She patted the comforter around her until her fingers grazed her plastic case. It was probably Mario calling for the hundredth time.

But when she stuffed the phone in front of her blurry eyes, a missed-call notification flashed for Beatrice.

A pang of guilt shot through her. When was the last time she'd answered her call? Part of her wanted to tell her sister everything, but Mario and Kevon had found her. Clearly, she was safe nowhere. The less her sister knew about the mess she was in, the better.

Forcing her eyes to focus, she shot off a quick text. "Not dead. Traveling right now. Not much signal. Call later."

Not dead. It had become her sister's running joke, because Jayna so seldom answered her calls. *All I want to know is that you're not dead or lying in a ditch*, Bea had said.

Well, she wasn't dead yet, but her phone almost was since she'd forgotten to charge it. There was still the possibility Mario and Kevon wouldn't relent, and she'd end up in a body bag like the poor soul she discovered.

With a groan, she rolled onto her side to reach the charger she'd plugged in by her night stand. Once inserted, she tapped her missed calls. Nine were from Mario.

She turned the phone on its face and rolled back to her pillow.

He had to give up eventually. She hadn't spilled their secret to anyone and didn't plan to.

They must know she'd found the body. Otherwise, why would they go to the trouble of finding her? Would he and Kevon not back down until they had sworn her to secrecy—or silenced her?

Her eyes burned, and she wanted nothing more than to go back to sleep for a few more hours. It was six thirty in the morning, and most of the group wouldn't be up for a while.

Maybe a shower and coffee would help her feel like a human again and kickstart her brain. She had to come up with a story to satisfy her group and hope that Mario wouldn't spring any more surprises.

Surely, there was safety in numbers, though. He had backed down last night easily enough, though Reef's tall build could intimidate anyone.

Reef, Kaley, Liam—they'd all stood up for her yesterday. She at least owed them an explanation and an apology for spoiling their night.

Rolling off the comforter, her socked feet padded to the small bathroom adjacent to her room. She turned the water as hot as she could tolerate to prick her skin and revive her foggy brain. Then she redressed, brushed through her wet hair, and slipped down the hallway in search of coffee.

To her surprise, someone had already brewed a fresh pot. A quick glance around the kitchen and dining room revealed she was alone, and for that, she was grateful. She retrieved a mug and poured herself a generous amount.

That's when she heard voices.

Jayna gently set the pot on the warmer and tilted her head to peek through the small window above the kitchen sink. There, reclining in two Adirondack chairs facing away from her, sat Reef and Kaley.

Reef's sun-bleached head was impossible to miss, and he was holding hands with the only girl wearing a newly minted engagement ring.

"... don't like him," Kaley was saying. "Did he expect her to so spend the night with him in a hotel? Ugh, what a jerk."

Jayna's face flushed. They were talking about Mario, about her. She should go before she overheard anything else, but her feet remained rooted in place.

"Most of the world doesn't see anything wrong with shacking up, Kaley. They don't know or don't care about what God says about saving themselves for marriage. We shouldn't be judging their situation but praying for them."

She bit her lip. Yeah, she'd messed up big time on that count, but Reef wasn't slamming the Ten Commandments over her head. He wanted to pray for her?

"You're right. I'm just worried for Jayna. Whatever happened between them, she has to be hurting."

Jayna bristled and pulled away from the window. She didn't need sympathy from a girl whose life was perfect. Time to take her coffee and go.

"… I'm worried about Liam."

Reef's words stopped her in her tracks. Liam? What did this conversation have to do with Ginger Ale? She tiptoed closer to the open window again.

"He wouldn't talk to me last night. I know he had a hard time getting over you, but he's been a good sport. I know he's genuinely happy for us, but man, I want him to be happy too. And I think he was getting hopeful about Jayna. It's plain as day there's chemistry between them."

"And now this," Kaley said.

Jayna clamped a hand over her mouth to hide the gasp. Plain as day? Chemistry between her and Ginger Ale?

She moved her hand to feel her forehead. No, she wasn't feverish.

Reef was wrong. He had to be. Liam was a nice guy, but he wasn't her type. Her type apparently involved dark and handsome resort owners who dabbled in murder.

Jayna took a swig of coffee. It burned down the back of her throat, leaving a bitter aftertaste. Much like her eavesdropping was doing. She'd listen just a little longer.

"Oh, did I tell you Sam called me back about the boat show?"

Reef stretched so that his long arms shot toward the sky. Then just as quickly, he searched for Kaley's hand again.

"No, is it a go then?"

"Yeah, next Friday. You know we've been looking to add another boat because business is booming. Sam found the one, and we can pick it up at the show next week."

Kaley clapped her hands. "That's wonderful."

"Sam said he's good with you coming along if you want. We can all stay at his aunt's house, and you'd get your own room."

Enough. She'd heard more than enough to remind her Kaley had everything she never would. Kaley's fiancé cared so much about her reputation that he'd put her up at some aunt's house where she'd have her own room. Mario had come knocking on the door last night to invite her to get cozy in his arms at a local hotel.

Why did seeing what she'd never have hurt so much? Why couldn't she simply be happy for Kaley?

Jayna gripped her coffee mug and retreated to her room. The answer was plain as the bags under her sleepless eyes.

She'd made too many mistakes to ever qualify for happily ever after. And now, she had to live with them.

Once back in her room, she softly clicked the door in place behind her and set her coffee on the night stand. Dare she look at her phone?

Chugging another bitter mouthful, she flipped it over to see the screen. No missed calls.

But she had one text. It was from Mario.

You may not want to see me, but we need to talk. If your friends knew why, they wouldn't be helping you.

The coffee boiled up her throat, and she ran to the bathroom in time to gag in the sink.

After rinsing out her mouth and brushing her teeth twice, she staggered back to her bed and reread the text. Once. Ten times.

Mario didn't need to veil his threat. He'd stabbed her in the one place she remained vulnerable.

She cared too much what people thought of her. She wanted too much to find safety, find acceptance somewhere.

But exposing her knowledge meant exposing his own. He

wouldn't dare. Would he?

If your friends knew ...

Jayna stood and reached to shove her few belongings into her duffle. She couldn't risk ruining anyone else's life. These friends were already starting to care about her. Hadn't she always known a new life for her was too good to be true?

Her only hope was to talk with Mario one on one and convince him they were done and she wasn't going to talk.

She wound her phone charger around her palm but hesitated to stuff it in her bag. Maybe she didn't need to pack up. Maybe she could come back afterward. After all, Pastor TJ had been nice enough to let her join last minute. She'd signed some form that she would abide by the trip rules.

But she hadn't bothered to read what they were. Hopefully, meeting up with an ex-fiancé for coffee wasn't one of them.

Would Pastor TJ even give her the okay to leave? Everyone here was an adult, but he was in charge of the group. She didn't want to be disrespectful.

Better to ask forgiveness than permission. She would leave a note and promise to text Kaley later. They should go on with their day's plans without her, and hopefully, she'd be back in time to help make dinner.

Telling herself that line tasted like hope, but she added her phone charger to her duffle anyway. Her gut told her she'd never be able to come back.

Fingers trembling, she typed her reply to Mario's text. *Okay, we can talk over coffee. Can you pick me up?*

Seconds later, her phone buzzed. *Be there in five.*

That sure didn't give her much time.

Jayna slid her sore feet into her shoes, slung the duffle over her shoulder, and tiptoed out her room and down the hall. There was a faded notepad on the living room coffee table where the owner had left directions for their stay. She tugged a blank sheet from below the top one and wrote her excuse.

Hi, Pastor TJ and friends,

Sorry for the drama last night. I handled it poorly and am meeting Mario for coffee. Don't worry or wait up for me. Have a

111

great day hiking, and I'll be back for dinner. If anything changes,
I'll text Kaley.
    J

Surely, they would see it on the coffee table. She couldn't risk going back to the kitchen and running into someone who would ask questions.

✓ With one last glance, she readjusted her duffle and unlocked the front door. Once on the porch, she closed it with a soft click and stepped down the porch stairs. She might as well start walking. Only one road led to the group of cabins, and the exercise helped distract her from facing what lay before her.

The crisp morning air tempted her lungs to breathe more deeply and savor this moment. It might be the last peaceful moment she enjoyed for a while. She paused and glanced back at the cabin. Her heart tugged her back in its direction.

But she could never enjoy true freedom until she faced her mistakes.

A car's engine snapped her to the present, and she jerked her gaze forward. The same black sedan from yesterday was cruising her direction.

She swallowed hard. Only moments separated her from her ex-fiancé and the dangerous web he was pulling her into. She was still on the fence about God, but if He were real, now was a good time to pray.

The black sedan slowed to stop a few feet away from her, and the passenger door popped open. Mario stepped out but didn't bridge the distance between them.

Gone was the desperately romantic façade he'd played last night. In its place was a cool aloofness, a distrust she'd never seen before.

If he was waiting by the passenger door, that could only mean Kevon was driving.

That there would be no coffee date between just Mario and her.

That whatever she told Mario, Kevon would hear.

Still standing his ground, Mario held out a hand to her. She picked her way toward him and steadied her chin. They had to now she was terrified, but she didn't have to show it.

She paused next to the back passenger door but did not accept his hand. "Mario."

He dropped his arm and reached to open her door. "Jayna." His gaze swept over her yoga pants and hoodie, and something like a frown tugged at his lips.

Her heart pinched. Liam hadn't frowned at her for looking comfortable last night. He'd looked at her in a way that made her feel seen.

Had Mario ever seen her? Or had he simply seen her pretty dresses and sensuous curves?

He motioned for her to get inside. "We have a lot to talk about."

She lowered her duffle onto the seat. "I suppose we do. How does coffee at Banner Elk Café sound?"

Mario blinked. He hadn't expected her to have a plan.

He didn't need to know she was making this up second by second. She cleared her throat. "They have a really great London fog, and I could use breakfast."

The first hint of a smile flickered across his face. "Banner Elk Café, it is."

But the moment she slid into the backseat and Mario closed the door, Kevon cast a steely glare in the rearview mirror to remind her who was calling the shots.

Her gut twisted. Something told her she wouldn't be back in time for dinner.

Chapter Nineteen

Rap. Rap—Rap—Rap.

Liam squinted and rolled to his side. The comforter he had meant to crawl under last night lay crumpled beneath him. His laptop rested next to his pillow.

So much for his resolve not to work in bed.

The knocking on the door came harder. Reef's bed was empty, and his roommate didn't need an invitation to enter.

"Who is it?" Liam's voice came out more like a croak.

"It's TJ. Can I come in?"

"Yeah." Liam swung his legs over the bed's edge as TJ cracked open the door.

"Hey, sorry to wake you, but you need to see this." TJ strode toward him. He held out a folded piece of paper in one hand.

Adrenaline pushed him to his feet, and he reached for the paper. "What's wrong?"

Worry creased TJ's eyebrows. "Jayna's gone."

His gut twisted, but somehow, he wasn't surprised. Running was what that girl seemed to do best. "Gone?"

TJ nodded toward the sheet. "Read it."

He did, but his confusion only grew. Why would she agree to meet with the man she couldn't stomach last night? What had changed in a few hours?

A dozen scenarios ran through his mind, and all of them involved some control Mario had over Jayna. Did he know some secret about her? Was he threatening her or someone she cared about? Maybe blackmail was involved? His cop instincts went to worst-case scenario, but maybe the truth was simpler. Perhaps she was so afraid of being alone that she returned to a man who had broken her heart.

Hadn't the last few days shown her that she had new friends?

Liam shook his head. If Jayna were running from something, why did she run to a man who had caught up with her in the most unlikely of places?

"Thanks for showing me this, TJ. May I hold on to it?"

TJ shrugged. "That's fine with me. Do you think she'll be back for dinner like she said?"

Liam hesitated. He was still waiting to hear from Drew on the license plate from last night. Maybe there was an e-mail in his inbox that would provide some answers.

"I hope so." Liam reached for his phone on the windowsill edge. He had half a dozen new e-mails and a text from Drew.

TJ turned for the door. "I'm going to get some breakfast and tell the others. I guess we'll still plan to leave after devos for Grandfather Mountain. At least Jayna can text Kaley if she needs anything."

"Yeah." Liam responded absently as he flipped open his laptop on the bed. "I'll be down for breakfast in a few."

TJ arched an eyebrow. "I thought this trip was a vacation for you?"

Liam offered an apologetic smile. "You know the saying, 'crime never sleeps.' I might have to do some work today. If I need to stay behind, at least I'll be here if Jayna comes back."

"*If.* You don't think she will?"

Liam needed to be more careful with his words. "Guess the cop in me always anticipates the worst."

TJ nodded and slipped into the hall. "See you downstairs."

Liam was already skimming Drew's text. *License plate is a rental. Do you want me to contact the agency?*

If Jayna hadn't disappeared this morning, he would say no. But he'd rather raise a few red flags and play it safe than find out later she had left early in the morning to meet up with some kind of offender.

"Yes, just be discreet."

Drew might be young, but diplomacy was his strong point. He would get the information without causing alarm.

Hopefully, there would be no reason for any alarm. Maybe the guy was nothing more than your friendly neighborhood dentist

115

or a local middle school teacher she'd met through a dating service.

His phone pinged moments later. *On it. Check your e-mail when you have a chance.*

Drew was taking advantage of his workaholic tendencies, but right now, he was glad for the distraction. Better not to dwell on Jayna's potential problems until he had proof something was wrong.

One e-mail was from Drew. It recapped the news about the deceased crab trapper, Enzo Martinez. The man seemed harmless enough with a history of family roots in the greater Tampa Bay area. Then Liam scanned his personal file.

Born in 1988. The man had died in his prime. Why?

Cause of death. Car accident.

Accidents could mean one of two things—being in the wrong place at the wrong time or being set up.

Was this man Enzo the victim of an unfortunate accident, or had his second life caught up with him?

There didn't seem to be enough evidence to say. Liam scanned his professional history and public records, but nothing stood out as a red flag. Enzo had been part of a few fishing organizations, purchased his vessel legitimately, stayed current on his taxes and registrations.

Liam sighed. The man looked like a dead end. Literally.

Another e-mail was from Avery and time-stamped two in the morning. Did his boss never sleep?

She'd attached a few images, and the previews alone showed she'd found more cocaine bricks with the same labels.

The Coast Guard intercepted these in the port of Miami on a fishing craft bound for the Bahamas. Lucky break. The vessel's registration had lapsed the previous day. The Coast Guard craft that intercepted them happened to have a dog that alerted them to the presence of narcotics. The fishermen were taken into custody but aren't talking. Hoping to change that. I'm heading to Miami today and will keep you in the loop.

Liam grinned. Avery was like a hound dog fresh on a new scent. He hoped this lead wouldn't disappoint her.

His stomach grumbled, reminding him he needed breakfast

nd a shower. But right then, his phone vibrated.

It was Drew. Breakfast was back on hold.

"Hey, man." Liam pressed speaker so he could keep his hands ree to type a note to acknowledge Avery's e-mail.

"Dude, so guess what your man Mario does for a living." The nspoken whistle in Drew's tone sent off warning signals.

"I was hoping for dentist."

Drew clucked his tongue. "Try again."

"Local florist? He brought one of the girls here quite the ouquet."

"Not even close. Mario Delgado owns a small resort in 3imini. He's visiting on a passport and travel visa, both valid."

Bahamas? Liam sucked a deep breath. What in the world was ayna doing engaged to a Bahamian resort owner?

The words *travel blogger* popped in his mind and offered a limmer of hope. Maybe she'd fallen in love on assignment, and it ad been a fast, foolish romance. That story still didn't explain why Mario had followed her—tracked her down—in the States.

Drew kept talking. "But it's his companion that's more nteresting to me."

"Companion?" Liam's thoughts turned to the driver. What ad Jayna called him?

"Kevon Rolles," Drew supplied the name. "The rental was nder his name, though Mario was listed as a secondary driver, vhich made my research easier. But back to Rolles. He's a 3ahamian native and fisherman who makes a surprising number f visits to Florida. But here's the real kicker—he's a member of he same fishing organization as our man Enzo."

Liam's fingers froze above his keyboard. "Wait, the dead nan with the crab traps?"

"Yep, they are—or were—members of Gulf Stream Riggers, LC."

"What do we know about this organization?"

There was a pause while Drew's fingers clicked on his own eyboard. "The website is super minimal, says something about eing under construction. I'm going to have to do more digging nd get back to you."

"Roger that," Liam said.

Drew hesitated. "If this LLC turns out to be some kind of front, I'm going to have to switch your request from favor to work."

Liam's gut clenched. "Right, and you're going to need everything I know about Jayna."

"Is that the girl who disappeared with him?"

"Yes."

"What's her full name?"

Why did his throat suddenly feel like cotton? He swallowed hard. "It's Jayna Scott."

"Thanks. I'll let you know when I have anything else." With that, Drew disconnected the call.

Liam finished his e-mail to Avery and then snapped his laptop shut. He hoped Jayna wasn't going to disappear. But if Drew had scraped the top of this iceberg, she might be in the middle of something much bigger than a failed destination romance.

If that was the case, was she an innocent victim or a knowing accomplice?

Chapter Twenty

Was it only yesterday she was sipping a London Fog across from Liam at Banner Elk Café? A much different man studied her now. In the short time she had known Mario, he had changed.

Gray circles ringed his otherwise handsome eyes, evidence of sleepless nights. He'd gone from a romantic philanthropist to a man afraid of his shadow, a shadow that now took the form of Kevon.

The brooding Bahamian sat adjacent to their booth in some casual seating by the café's fireplace. He seemed to be absorbed with his smartphone, but perhaps he was straining to overhear their conversation.

Mario agreeing to her preferred coffee location was a meager attempt to make her believe she controlled anything about their relationship.

Jayna raised her steaming mug to her lips, hoping Mario would go first. She didn't know how to start this conversation. *Hi, Mario. Yes, I saw your dead body. That would have been nice to warn me about before I agreed to marry you.*

Cupping his own coffee mug, Mario leaned forward and stared into her eyes. "Jayna, you've got to know I still love you."

She choked on the hot tea and set down the mug with trembling hands, grasping for a napkin to cover her mouth.

Of anything he could have said, professing love for her was not what she expected.

"Love me?" She crossed her arms. "Love doesn't come with strings attached—or body bags."

There, she'd said it. Mario flinched as if she's struck him in the face. "I had nothing to do with that. You've got to believe me."

From the corner of her eye, she caught Kevon shifting in his seat. She had to keep her voice down.

She leaned forward and whispered, "It was in your boat."

Mario reached for her hands and held her wrists so she couldn't pull back. "You've got to listen, Jayna. Very carefully. Your life depends on it."

She bit down a retort and ignored the reflex to pull away. The intensity in Mario's eyes stilled her.

"I told you about Camilo and Gabriel. After the storm wiped out my savings, I met Kevon. His offer seemed reasonable, and my cooperation would refill my bank account to help my cousins. I didn't know then what I know now, but it doesn't matter. This job will help me buy a new life for them. Their freedom will be worth any—challenges—I take to get it."

Bile climbed her throat. "Mario, someone is dead."

"People die every day, Jayna. You and me, we have a chance to make an impact on the world, to make life better for others." He released one of her hands to reach inside his jacket pocket. When he retracted it, his fingers pinched her engagement ring. "This situation is a stepping stone. When the job's over, we'll go on to live and have all the adventures we dreamed about together."

Jayna tried to twist out of his grasp, but he only tightened his grip. "Kevon said he'll call off his hound dogs if you come back with me."

Go back to Bimini? Where Kevon could watch her every move? Pretend she still adored Mario, the man who had lied to her? No, she couldn't.

Mario either didn't notice her repulsion to the idea or pretended he didn't. "Here's the story you're going to tell anyone who asks. You came to the states to tell your family and friends our good news. You came to say good-bye because you're getting married and relocating to the Bahamas."

Finally, she succeeded in sliding her hands free of his. "Mario, that would all be well and good, but I can't marry a man I don't trust."

His face hardened, but a determined glint flickered in his eyes. "You can trust me. In fact, Jayna, you don't have a choice."

The hair on her neck bristled. How dare he—

"Kevon has contacts everywhere. I am the only man who can keep you safe, and you cooperating is the only way to keep your sister and family safe."

Jayna gasped. He was threatening Bea and her parents? Her sister had her own little family too.

Could she marry a liar? Could she live with herself if anything happened to her family because of her?

She tilted her chin up. "I can go back with you, Mario, but I can't marry you."

He tapped the table with her ring and shook his head. "The only way you can come back with me is as my fiancé."

"Fine." She bit her lip to hide the tremor she felt. "I'll be your fiancé by name, but I'm not marrying you."

His eyes flashed, but he maintained a dignified determination. "Jayna, I want a woman to spend my life with. That woman is you. Take back my ring. Return home with me, and I'll spend as long as it takes to convince you I'm the man for the job."

She wanted to spring to her feet and run. Marriage wasn't a job. It was a lifelong commitment between two people who loved and respected each other. At least, that's what her parents and sister told her.

But what choice did she have? Returning to Bimini as Mario's fiancé would help him save face, temporarily keep her alive, and hopefully, keep her family out of the equation. She could come up with an escape plan later.

If she didn't, she'd either end up married to a man she didn't love or in her own body bag.

Jayna dropped her gaze to her naked fingers. How ironic that the ring she'd always wanted now represented her worst nightmare.

Swallowing hard, she raised her left hand and pressed it onto the tabletop. "Okay, I accept. I'll give you time to convince me that we can still work. If not, I'll leave for good."

Mario squeezed the ring between his fingers. "I won't be able to save you if you do." He flashed a toothy smile. "No need to worry about that though. Back in my arms, you won't ever want to leave again."

A shudder traced down her spine. Back in his arms was the last place she wanted to be, but how could she escape?

Mario reached for her hand again and slid on the ring. "See? Perfect fit. I'm so glad you'll be coming home with me, darling."

He lifted her hand to his lips, and as if on signal, Kevon stood and stalked over to them. The man sneered her direction and then spoke to Mario. "Tickets are all set. We'll drop off the rental at the airport and catch our flights to Miami. My men will have a boat there waiting for us."

Tickets? To buy airplane tickets, they had to know her name and birthdate, but she'd never told Mario her birthday.

Whoever Kevon was, he must have friends in resourceful places.

"Ready, darling?" Mario took one last sip of his coffee and rose.

"Yes." She adjusted the diamond on her finger. It felt heavy, like her heart. "I just need to use the girl's room, and then I'll be ready."

She slipped past both men and rushed to the restroom. Only when she latched the stall door did she release the breath she'd been holding.

Tears threatened to tumble from her eyes, but she held them back. She didn't have much time, and she had to send off a text to Kaley so the group didn't worry about her.

Hey, Kaley, sorry I won't be back. Mario and I are working through things, and he's taking me home. Thanks for everything, and don't worry about me.

A tear slid down her nose. Bimini wasn't her home. Mario and she would never be able to work through things.

She was as much of a liar as Mario. Maybe they did belong together.

After wiping her eyes with the back of her hand, she unlatched the stall door and turned on the faucet. Feeling sorry for herself would accomplish nothing. She had to keep her wits with her if she wanted to survive.

They seemed sorely insufficient for the problems facing her. What she really needed was a friend.

Was God her friend? The thought offered hope that quickly died. No, she was more like Abraham and Sarah dealing with the consequences of their bad choice to rush ahead of God.

Only, her story held no hope of a promised child or redemption. Squaring her shoulders, she pushed through the bathroom door.

Mario offered a tight smile before placing a hand on the small of her back. He guided her to the rental car where Kevon waited and to whatever uncertain future lay ahead.

Liam twisted the stovetop's heat off and shifted the large frying pan to the warmer. The taco meat would be ready when his friends returned from Grandfather Mountain.

He'd already diced and chopped the avocado, tomato, and onion, which waited in covered bowls in the refrigerator. Shredded lettuce, two large cans of salsa, and far too much sour cream for their small party to consume were lined up on the shelves and ready to go.

Maybe staying behind had been a bad idea. Sure, he'd worked several hours reviewing every file and chasing down every lead he could find about Mario Delgado and Kevon Rolles. But neither one had a record, and though Rolles' frequent trips between the Bahamas and Miami raised some eyebrows, he was a fisherman. All his licenses were up-to-date. As for being part of the same LLC as the deceased crabber, the jury was still out if that fact was an odd coincidence or the tip of the iceberg for something more sinister.

As for Delgado, he was a curious one. The Cuban-born immigrant had obtained his Bahamian citizenship. Ever since he was old enough to collect an income, he'd been working for his parents on their resort. A few years back, he officially bought it from them, apparently so that they could retire. The man seemed squeaky clean.

Liam pulled open the fridge and helped himself to a bottle of Cheerwine. It was North Carolina's version of cherry cola, and one of the guys had snagged a case of it during their last trip to Fred's Mercantile.

The fizz seemed to catch in his throat, and he had to swallow hard to keep from gagging.

No use. The truth was that he'd stayed behind all day hoping Jayna would come back. A dozen scenarios had played through his mind, and none of them had happened.

The doorbell hadn't rung, and his cell phone remained eerily quiet.

He stepped to the sink and took another cautious sip. This time, the cherry fizz didn't choke him. Placing the bottle on the counter, he stared through the kitchen window to the patio where half a dozen Adirondack chairs surrounded the fire pit. After setting aside his laptop last night, he had joined the group around the fire, hoping maybe Jayna would reappear, but she had remained absent.

His gut told him she wasn't coming back now.

Noise at the front door snapped him to the present. Could it be?

Then a series of voices and banter echoed down the hallway, and his hopes fell. Jayna wasn't back, but his friends were. Maybe Kaley, at least, had news from her.

Leaving his Cheerwine behind, he strode down the hallway to greet his friends.

"... that black bear. I still can't believe his caretaker let him eat all those marshmallows," Kaley was saying.

"He sure looked like a marshmallow." Olivia set down her water canteen on the pool table in the living room and glanced up at him. "Oh, hey, Liam. How was your day?"

He stopped on the other side of the pool table and glanced at the game someone had left unfinished. "Fine. Just working."

Olivia rolled her eyes. "I thought the whole point of us taking this trip was to escape our jobs for a few days."

He smiled. The investigator in him never slept. It didn't matter if he was in the office or on vacation. "Did you hear anything from Jayna? She hasn't come back."

Olivia's expression fell, and she looked at Kaley who was fixing her ponytail. As if she could somehow look less beautiful with messy hair.

Kaley sighed. "Yes, I did, but I didn't like what she had to say."

He picked up a pool stick, chose a shot, and then aimed at the white ball. "And what was that?"

"She said that she and Mario are working through things and that he's going to take her home."

He missed the white ball by a good inch and jerked his head up to study Kaley. "Whose home?"

Kaley's forehead pinched. "I—I assumed hers. But she didn't say."

His hand went for his pocket before he remembered that he'd left his cell phone in the room to charge. He needed to get a bead on Delgado to find out.

No, he needed to wait 'til Drew got back to him on the LLC. Right now, he had no evidence Delgado or Rolles were bad news. All he had was a sinking feeling about a girl who had somehow wormed into his heart in two short days.

He returned the pool stick to the wall and cleared his throat. "Dinner's ready whenever you guys are."

At the word *dinner*, the guys snapped out of whatever story they were telling and turned his way.

"No way, you already made dinner?" Pastor TJ dropped his keys on the entry table, right next to the bright red rose bouquet Mario had delivered the night before.

"Yeah, the taco fixings are ready. Give me five minutes to warm the tortillas, and we'll be good to go." With that, he retraced his steps to the kitchen.

Reef linked arms with Kaley and trailed close behind him. "You're the best, man."

Kaley glanced at her fiancé. "Oh, c'mon. You've got to do a better job at asking him than that. You're supposed to make it special."

"Asking me what?" Liam paused midway down the hall.

Reef's face flushed. Either that, or he'd gotten too much sun on the mountain. "Er—well, I'd like for you to be my best man. That's not what I meant a moment ago, but I guess now is as good a time as any to ask?"

"Oh, babe," Kaley chuckled. "That's one way to do it."

Reef looked at Liam, clueless as to what etiquette he had messed up on.

"It would be my honor, Reef. Why don't you come get a Cheerwine and help me with these shells?"

Reef kissed Kaley's cheek and then hurried after him. "Dude, I have no idea about this wedding stuff."

"You don't have to. That's why you've got Kaley."

"You're right. Thanks."

Liam nodded but didn't reply. He was a good wingman, and

he'd be glad to stand by Reef's side. Hopefully, one day, Reef could return the favor.

But that day was looking farther out of reach, thanks to one more girl who'd managed to suck the air from his lungs and then disappear from his life like a vapor.

Liam was running hot water over the frying pan to let it soak when he felt a soft thud on his arm.

"What?" He spun to find Olivia standing there with the dish towel she'd used to flick him.

"Chef doesn't do the dishes." She pointed to the dining room where the others were still talking and laughing over seconds. "Go relax. I've got cleanup."

He turned off the water and motioned toward the hallway. "Thanks, but I need to check on something back in my room."

Olivia shook her head. "You know you're a workaholic, right? You stayed back all day to work, and now you're going to spend your evening working too? I mean, it's none of my business how you live your life, but—"

"Thanks, I'll be back down for smores later." He retreated down the hallway before Olivia could finish her lecture. She meant well, but she didn't understand the half of why he'd stayed behind.

And he didn't feel like confessing to anyone that Jayna was the real reason.

Taking the stairs by two, he soon reached the room he shared with Reef and beelined for his phone which he'd left to charge.

There were two missed calls, one from Drew and one from Avery. Might as well start with his partner.

He pressed the notification to return the call. "Drew, talk to me."

"First, Avery needs to talk to you ASAP."

"Yeah, I'm going to call her after this."

There was shuffling on the other side of the phone. "Sorry, I'm trying to eat and work," Drew said. "The big news is that this LLC— Gulf Stream Riggers—is a sham or a cover for something. I tried calling the number on the website. It's disconnected. The website tself is barely functional, yet Rolles renewed his membership two months ago. Oh, and the crew the Coast Guard just took into custody n Miami? Yeah, they're registered LLC members, too."

"So, you think the LLC might be the connection among all these >ricks that are turning up and changing hands?"

"Definitely. Avery thinks it's the link she's been hoping to find. f we can somehow get our hands on a roster, we can identify the vhole web."

His phone pinged, alerting Liam to an incoming call. "Hey,)rew, Avery's on the other line. Can I call you back?"

"Sure thing."

Liam disconnected and accepted Avery's call.

"I need you at Columbia airport in four hours," was her clipped greeting.

"I don't have a personal car. Can you arrange an Uber?"

"Done."

So much for smores with the group tonight. "Okay, so can you ell me what this is all about?"

"Rolles returned his rental car to Columbia airport an hour ago. He's boarding a flight for Miami within the next hour—and Delgado ind your friend Jayna Scott are on the same flight."

Liam closed his eyes and massaged his forehead. "Go on."

"Rolles has a yacht waiting in Miami. I'll have eyes on the ground, but my gut says they're going back to Delgado's Bimini esort. We're going after them."

He blinked. "What?"

"Someone's running drugs packaged in Big Eddie's signature vrappers between the Bahamas and Miami—and who knows where :lse. Kevon Rolles is the only known member of this so-called LLC vho isn't dead or in custody. He is the first lead I've got on Big Eddie, ind I'm not going to lose the trail this time."

"What about the guys you intercepted in Miami? Can't we learn something from them?"

"They're not talking."

"Do you think Rolles will? Because the one look I got of him, ie's a watertight box."

"Your girl Scott isn't."

Liam sucked a deep breath. What did Jayna have to do with any of this? If she were mixed up with the wrong crowd, was she as innocent as she acted? Or was her act a cover?

He shook his head. "What if she doesn't know anything?"

"She knows more than we do. Don't you wonder what made her run the way she did, or what they're holding over her that would make her go back?"

Yes, he'd wondered both those things. The answers led to places he'd rather not consider.

Still, he was a professional. Undercover work was part of his job. He would simply have to cram his raw, confused feelings about this woman into the lockbox of his heart and hope that she was smart enough to stay alive.

"I'm e-mailing you your boarding passes," Avery continued. "Drew will pick you up in Tampa tonight. Your flight for Miami leaves tomorrow at noon. Before then, make sure to lose your red hair. I'm already in Miami on this case and will meet you at the airport there—undercover as your girlfriend. From there, we'll leave for Bimini."

He knew the undercover drill, but man, she wasn't giving him much time. The idea of posing as anyone's boyfriend left a bad taste in his mouth, but questioning his boss was pointless. Besides, Avery had vowed not to let the next trail go cold. Big Eddie's dropping off the map the last few months had eaten her alive. Liam had just never imagined he'd be the one chasing down the mafia underworld's connections with her.

Still, he couldn't ignore the obvious red flag. "What if Jayna recognizes me, disguise and all?"

"It's a risk we'll take, because if she does, maybe she'll trust you. Trust is a hard commodity to come by."

"If she doesn't?"

"Undercover work is safe said no detective ever," Avery quipped.

He cleared his throat. He wasn't afraid of danger. He was afraid of his heart and one more girl breaking it.

"I'll pack my bags."

"The Uber is on its way. ETA is an hour. You guys really are in he mountains, huh?"

"Yeah."

"See you tomorrow." With that, Avery disconnected.

He called Drew back and put him on speaker so he could jam everything he'd unpacked into his duffle. "Hey, so I hear you're picking me up at the airport."

Drew cleared his throat. "Sorry about your vacation, but you know how Avery is with anything on Big Eddie."

"No worries. The group is heading back tomorrow anyway. Besides, it sounds like the agency is putting me up in Bimini."

His partner snorted. "Working undercover with Avery won't be a vacation, bro."

Oh, he could imagine. Their boss personified Type-A personality. No one pulled all-nighters the way Avery did when she was on a case.

"Well, I gotta pack. If you send me your data, I'll read it on the plane."

"On it."

Once done with the worst packing job of his life, Liam headed downstairs to break the news. Olivia would roll her eyes but probably pack him a snack. Reef would protest, but he'd have Kaley to enjoy the rest of the evening. They would understand.

One person definitely would not. If Jayna saw through his disguise when he landed in Bimini, he could only imagine what she would think of his firecracker boss hanging on his arm.

Chapter Twenty-One

Everything in her room was the way she had left it. Her flirty dress from their engagement dinner still hung lopsided on the hanger on her closet door. Her other clothes she'd left behind lay folded in the dresser.

The roses Mario had given her that night remained in the tortoise-shell vase on her night stand—but now they were dead. Their brown petals, shriveled against the stems, were supported only by the vase's brim. Many of them had already fallen onto the floor.

Apparently, the maid hadn't checked the room for a few days, and Mario hadn't given her enough notice before they arrived in the early hours of the morning.

Mario had placed an icy kiss on her cheek and told her they'd talk again in the morning. Now, morning was here, and she wasn't ready for it.

Jayna rolled on her side away from the dead roses and the window beyond that overlooked Mario's pristine beach.

For her, Bimini had lost its luster. What had once been a paradise was now her prison.

She pressed her eyes shut and imagined her simple room in the Beech Mountain cabin. If she hadn't texted Mario, she'd be waking up there today, maybe even helping make breakfast before the group started the long road trip home.

Tears slipped past her closed eyelids and wet her pillow. Maybe she could have held out a little longer, but Mario had threatened her family. She could never live with herself if something happened to her parents or Bea.

A soft rap on the door made her brush away the tear traces. "Yes?"

"Room service."

"Just leave it outside. I'll get it."

"Very well."

She felt for her phone on the night stand and pulled her cell phone toward her to check the time. Nearly nine thirty in the morning. Mario hadn't specified a time to meet, and if he'd ordered her room service, maybe he was smart enough to realize she needed space.

Or he was busy doing something for Kevon.

Slipping out from beneath the sheets, Jayna padded toward the door and cracked it open. The breakfast tray, complete with hibiscus flower, rested on the floor by her door. She retrieved it and re-locked the door before dropping the flower into the trash and setting her breakfast onto the bed.

In classic Mario style, there was a note.

My darling Jayna, I hope you slept well. I know yesterday was a long day for you, so I didn't wake you before taking out today's excursion. We'll talk over dinner. How's my yacht sound?

Jayna balled the note in her fist and threw it on the floor. If he was envisioning another romantic tryst on his yacht, he could forget it. She never wanted to set foot on that yacht again. Ever.

She hugged herself. She never wanted him to touch her again either. Love without trust was an impossibility.

She scanned the tray, complete with a steaming coffee mug, creamer in a white ceramic server, sugar packets, fresh yogurt, fruit slices, and sausage. She poured cream in the dark coffee and swirled it with a spoon. If this were her last meal, she might as well die caffeinated.

She'd taken her first sip when her cell vibrated.

Are you ever going to return my calls and texts with more than a not-dead comment?

Bea. What could she say that wouldn't set off alarm bells in her sister's head? Her gaze drifted to her breakfast tray. That looked innocent enough. She snapped a picture and sent it.

Hey, sis, I'm having breakfast in my room. The Bimini job is lasting longer than expected. I'll call when I'm heading home.

She pressed her lips into a thin line and hit send. Would she ever be able to head home?

Her phone pinged again almost immediately. *ETA, please?*

Jayna sighed and sipped her coffee before typing the only truth she could offer. *Don't have one. But you'll be the first to know. Love you.*

After eating half the yogurt, picking through the fruit, and returning the tray outside her door, Jayna tugged her laptop from her duffle and set it on the bed. She should work, write more content for Mario's resort so Bea wouldn't be more suspicious than she already was—and Mario could at least see she was earning her keep the honest way.

The post about "paradise in the details" highlighted her breakfast photo and the luxurious touches of her room. It turned out about as well as a post could for having been inspired by anything within sight of her bed.

It was well past lunch by the time she'd perfected and promoted it. After closing her laptop and plugging it in to charge, she glanced in the mirror. She needed a shower and to prepare for her meeting with Mario.

And sooner or later, she had to leave her room. She'd already milked it for all the post-worthy inspiration she could dream up, and if she could convince Mario to view her purely as a professional, she would need to serve up more post content ASAP.

Her writing was all she was willing to offer him. She was no longer on the menu.

A nagging draft flipped up Mario's collar and threatened to steal the fabric napkins from the two placemats. Dinner on the private balcony had seemed romantic before the weather decided to turn as unpredictable as the woman who should have joined him fifteen minutes ago.

What did she not understand about dinner at six o'clock sharp? He'd already had to give up his notions of a relaxing evening on the yacht when his guest relations manager quit without notice. And he had half a dozen new guests arriving by eight. William had already checked on him once and would probably reappear any minute to see if they were ready for the appetizer. Being late was downright inconsiderate.

The stair railing squeaked, a signal that his fiancé had arrived. He stiffened in his seat. Jayna had accepted his ring back, but she certainly wasn't acting like his fiancé.

Maybe he deserved that. Discovering a dead body on his yacht had to have been quite horrible for her.

But she didn't seem to understand what he had risked taking her back. Without his protection, she'd be in a body bag herself.

Jayna emerged from the stairwell. She wore a high-collared tank top and skinny jeans. It was the most librarian he'd seen her appear.

Out of courtesy, he rose and pulled out her chair for her. "How are you, my dear?"

"Good." Her tone was short but polite. "I finished a new post for promoting the resort, and it went live an hour ago."

He frowned at his water glass and flipped the wine one over so William could fill it on his next check. "Nice job, but darling, you could have taken the day off."

Her fingers snatched her napkin and fidgeted with it longer than necessary before placing it on her lap. "Just trying to earn my keep."

Warmth ran up his neck and into his cheeks, but he forced a steadying tone into his voice. "You're my fiancé. You don't have to earn anything anymore."

Her hands stilled on her lap, and she lifted her chin, which quivered so slightly he almost missed it. "I don't feel like your fiancé."

Behind them, the stairway creaked again, and William appeared, tray in hand. "Good evening, Miss Jayna. Mr. Mario, I brought that merlot you asked for. The soup of the day is peas and dumpling, and the sweet bread is fresh from the oven."

He set down steaming soup bowls and the bread basket before filling each of their wine glasses. "Anything else I can get you?"

Mario grasped his wine glass and took a much-needed swig. "That's all for now. Thank you, William."

"Yes, thanks," Jayna murmured and reached for a slice of

sweet bread. She placed it on the edge of her bowl and hesitated. "Should we—do you want me—to pray?"

The wine went down his windpipe, and he choked into his napkin. "Excuse me?"

A blush rose to her cheeks. "Never mind. It's something my friends did. I guess it was silly."

Mario scooped a spoonful of his soup. "What's silly is letting the food go cold—and your comment about not feeling like my fiancé."

Jayna picked at the bread. "I—I'm sorry. But Mario, I can't marry someone I don't trust."

He dropped the spoon back in the bowl, and it splattered all over his shirt. Perfect, now he would have to change before the guests arrived. Snatching the napkin off his lap, he tried to wipe away the mess, but damp stains remained.

Gritting his teeth, he returned the napkin to his lap and leaned forward to face this woman he was liking less and less. "Listen, Jayna, I know you're scared, but I've got to square with you. I like you—like you enough to plant that nugget on your finger and make an honest woman of you."

Her lips parted as if she was about to hiss at him, but he had to get this out before she interrupted him. "You have got to understand that I had nothing to do with that body. I didn't even know it was a body when Kevon asked me to store it. Truth be told, it wouldn't have made a difference. You already know why I'm working with him. I told you about my cousins and that I will do anything it takes to free them and give them a new life. Anything. That's why you can trust me. Because once you are mine, I will never give up on you."

Her eyes sparked like the lightning in the distance. "That sounds wonderful in theory until you consider that someone else is suffering because of you. I mean, who was that poor soul in the bag?"

"I don't know, and frankly, I don't care. I can't be responsible for everybody. But I can be responsible for somebody, and that somebody is you. Trust me, okay?"

Trust him? How?

Jayna shivered as a gust of wind swirled through her clothes and hair. The same story that had made Mario rise to sainthood in her eyes now dragged him through the mud. Wanting to help his cousins was wonderful, but at what price? She knew too well that wrong means never justified a good end, but she wasn't about to bare her soul to Mario about her modeling days.

Liam's face flashed in her mind. He was a cop. His whole life was protecting people he didn't know or might never meet again. Not because it was convenient, but because it was the right thing to do.

She shook her head and tugged the ring off her finger. She slid it across the table toward him. "No, Mario. I can't trust somebody who doesn't care about the nobody in the body bag. I will stay and help promote your hotel for as long as you need me to help save your face, but I can't marry you."

Mario's handsome features hardened, and he did not reach for the ring. "Be very careful, Jayna. If you are not my fiancé, I can't protect you."

Her hand froze a few inches from where she'd dropped the ring on the tablecloth. "Are you threatening me? I've done nothing wrong, Mario."

His jaw relaxed enough to let a smile flicker across his lower lip. "No. I would never threaten you. But Kevon knows what you saw. I promised him that as my fiancé, you and I were a unified front and would never speak of it. He doesn't trust you, but he agreed to my plan."

"Plan?" She took a bite of her bread. Its sweetness was a sharp contrast to this conversation.

Mario sipped more of his wine. "In a week's time, I will have the funds I need to obtain my cousins' visas."

"I thought you said there was a lottery system?"

He twirled the contents of his glass as another gust created its own mini sand cyclones on the beach beyond them. "It is, but as I said before, the only way to the front of the line is through some

135

persuasion. And hey, money talks. So next week, we'll travel to meet my contact where I'll make the payment, and then we'll honeymoon in Cuba while we wait for him to get the visas. If all goes well, we'll deliver the visas in person and then send my cousins off to the States when we return home."

The bread turned to plaster in her mouth. Her fiancé was not only a witness to murder but also a briber, and he expected her to join him, no questions asked. What happened to his promise to give her as much time as she needed?

"Honeymoon? That means—" She snatched her water to gulp down the blob stuck in her throat. Hands trembling, she returned it to the table and eyed her soup. She had skipped lunch, and her stomach grumbled at its emptiness, but her appetite had fled.

"Yes, I've scheduled a marriage officer to marry us right here on Saturday at sunset, and then we'll leave for our honeymoon the next day." Mario strummed his fingers on the table as if expecting her to respond, but words failed her. He sighed. "Anyway, that is the plan. However, if you return my ring and don't travel with me to Cuba, I won't be able to protect you."

She slapped at her fabric napkin to keep the wind from stealing it. "So, this is essentially a blackmail arrangement?"

Mario chugged the rest of his wine and glared at her. "You are not helping the romance here, Jayna. I am offering you a very good life and protection from what Kevon would do to you. If it doesn't work out after a few years, marriage doesn't have to be forever, but you'll be alive, and we'll have had a fun time of it."

Tears threatened to overflow her lashes, but she furiously blinked them away. She wouldn't marry him now for the world, but she had to be smart if she had a prayer of escaping Kevon.

"Okay, then, may I have a week to give you my answer? I—I just need time to take all this in." She swiped at her eyes. "The sand—the wind got it in my eyes."

"Yes, I think we're going to have to move inside." He picked up the ring and slid it toward her. "I can give you until Saturday morning. We'll have a simple ceremony that night and leave on Sunday by yacht. In the meantime, you wear my ring, and I'll have the maid move your things into my room. You'll join me on all my excursions, and we'll spend some quality time together. I know you were scared, but you can trust me, Jayna. I'm the man for you, and I'll prove it."

Her face heated, but she picked up the ring. Saturday gave her only five days. "I'll wear your ring and go on all your excursions, but I'll sleep in my room. We can tell anyone who asks we're old-fashioned."

Mario's eyes narrowed in frustration.

She slid the ring on her finger and played a coy smile across her lips. "Trust takes time, Mario. But I think you'll win me back."

The first raindrop splattered into her untouched soup. As if on cue, William reappeared with to-go bowls. "I'll pack this up. You two get inside and find a place to sit."

"Please send it to our rooms." Mario glanced down at his shirt. "I need to change before our new guests arrive."

"As you wish."

Jayna's shoulders relaxed. Having the evening to herself would be ...

Mario stepped next to her and lowered his voice. "I'll be expecting you at the front desk at eight. Sharp."

His gaze dropped to her chest. "And look a little more— inviting?"

Her face flamed, but she forced a nod. "I'll be there."

"Don't be late." As if aware that William was observing them, Mario snatched her hand and raised it to his lips. "I'll make up our dinner date when the weather is less savage."

A fresh onslaught of rain drops spared her an answer and provided an excuse to flee from the man who planned to marry her in less than a week's time.

Chapter Twenty-Two

Through the rain-streaked glass, Liam squinted to read a stained wooden sign, edged with painted hibiscus flowers. *Bimini Road's End Resort.* They were here.

The taxi circled through the roundabout and parked close to the steps leading up to a covered porch. The driver popped open Avery's door and offered her an umbrella before retrieving a luggage cart from the porch and returning to the trunk for their bags.

Liam dodged puddles before reaching the porch and then pulled out his wallet to tip the man for his trouble. For two people, they sure did have a lot of bags. That was mostly his fault, due to his cover of being an avid surf fisherman, which wasn't too far from the truth.

The driver traded their bags for the crisp bill, accepted back his umbrella, and then rushed to his idling car.

Above them, a weathered fan made a clicking noise while the fauna in the shrubbery croaked and strummed in the rain. Avery had set her purse in one of the wicker chairs and was scrolling on her phone, probably to pull up their reservation.

Fine by him. He was in no rush to get to the lobby, though the odds of Jayna being there seemed slim, but his stomach flipped at the possibility.

He glanced at Avery, who had dyed her reddish-brown hair bleached blonde and freshly cut to the top of her shoulders. Thanks to his church friend Brittany, his own ginger hair was now black, and he'd lost the beard. His chin felt bare and exposed without it, but even Avery had to squint to recognize him with the change.

Still, what if Jayna saw right through him? Or what if he gave himself away by staring?

He shook his head and pushed the luggage rack toward the

entrance. He was a professional, and this job wasn't his first rodeo. Avery had selected a wardrobe for him that traded his usual clean, simple attire for flamboyant tropical prints and baggy cargo shorts. "You won't even recognize yourself." She had laughed and handed him a gold pair of aviator sunglasses that normally he wouldn't be seen dead in.

"Ready?" Avery shifted her phone to her other hand and retrieved her purse. "I mean, are you ready for some fun, babe?"

He snickered and opened the door for her. "Oh, honey, we're gonna have so much fun."

Avery puckered her lips and blew him a kiss as she sashayed inside the door in her black halter dress.

Liam smirked and followed her. He'd never worked with his boss undercover, and he'd never seen anything but a no-nonsense woman who barely smiled or wore makeup. Now, she sported lash extensions, bare shoulders, and a saucy red smile that almost made him uncomfortable.

But without a doubt, there was at least one Glock strapped beneath her sexy sundress, because their Bahamian contact had supplied them both with approved weapons the moment their plane landed.

Avery might look like a brainless bombshell, but she was anything but. The woman was a lethal workaholic who had no time for relationships, friends, or God. She made the perfect platonic work partner for him, but for her own sake, he hoped that one day, she would discover there was more to life than the job.

Right now, though, he was grateful for her laser focus. She beelined for the front desk while he trailed with their luggage. Playing the quiet, introverted love interest suited him and allowed him to do what he did best—observe.

A few couples loitered near an hors d'oeuvres table that had been set up in the lobby, and another motioned to a server to refill their champagne glasses. Delgado certainly knew how to make guests feel spoiled.

Speak of the devil. There he was.

Liam had just rolled their luggage cart next to Avery as Delgado swept into the room. He wore a plastered-on grin and—

but it didn't matter what he wore. The woman hanging on his arm was all Liam cared about.

The woman wearing a strapless black dress and the saddest smile he'd ever seen.

Jayna.

Liam edged closer to Avery, but in doing so, bumped his long fishing rod case, which toppled onto the hardwood floor.

At least the ridiculous shades he wore helped conceal the heat radiating up his skin. Quickly righting the case, he turned his back on Jayna and everyone now behind him. Maybe no one noticed the klutz who had arrived. Hopefully, Jayna hadn't.

"Thank you so much." Avery accepted their room key and then wrapped an arm around his waist. "Our room is ready, darling, or do you want to get a drink first?"

He planted a kiss on her forehead. "Let's drop off our bags."

Avery nodded, and he followed her gaze past the receptionist's desk to the large front window where the rain had slowed to a drizzle in the fading daylight. "Maybe we can catch the sunset."

The man at the desk jerked up his head. "I think it's still raining."

Avery laughed. "A little rain can't spoil mother nature."

The receptionist frowned. "Well, parts of the beach are closed. I'd recommend waiting 'til morning when the sand has been groomed."

Liam glanced at Avery and pursed his lips to a smile. "Good to know. Thanks."

Did he imagine it, or did the man's shoulders relax?

Avery snatched her purse off the counter as he resumed pushing the luggage cart, careful not to lose the long fishing rod case again. Then, as Avery led the way, he angled his body away from where the other guests mingled and kept his head turned toward Avery.

Still, the hair on his neck stood on end.

Though refusing to look back, he couldn't ignore the sensation that someone was watching him.

Once inside their room, Liam locked the door as Avery strode toward the window. She pulled back the curtains to reveal a full view of the beach and fading daylight.

"So, sunset swim, yes?" She pulled a hair tie off her wrist and tugged her hair into a short ponytail. "Clearly, someone told the clerk to discourage guests from going on the beach."

Liam unzipped his bag and tossed his snorkel and mask onto the bed. "I just need to change into my swimsuit."

"No need." Avery grabbed the mask, along with her compact waterproof camera, and strode toward the door. "I'm already wearing mine under this dress, and you can stand watch on the beach."

He checked his pocket to make sure he still had the room key. "Let's go. There's another beach entrance on the other end of this hallway, so we don't have to go through the main lobby."

Avery breezed past him into the hallway as he tugged the door closed behind them. "I see you read the resort layout I sent you."

He tapped his head. "Memorized."

She winked and led the way to the farthest exit, past some casual seating areas and other rooms. Liam made a mental note of the new carpet smell and bright white baseboards. The place had suffered water damage, but Delgado had efficiently made his repairs while other places on the island still seemed to be in the elementary stages of recovery.

For a small resort owner, his pockets must run deep to get the priority along with the more elite resorts.

Avery didn't wait for him to open the double doors that deposited them onto a small patio that gave way to the beach.

"Darling, let's do this together." Liam reached for her hand. His boss clearly needed the reminder that even though the beach was deserted, they didn't know who could be watching.

She squeezed his hand back. "Yes, thanks, dear." Still, she practically dragged him to the shoreline.

A drizzle continued to fall, and the rain had cooled the evening considerably. His toes sank in the damp, clumping sand as the waves rolled onto shore and swept up to his ankles. The sun hovered right above the horizon.

Avery wasted no time. She tugged her sundress over her head and tossed it to him, revealing a green bikini. Her gaze swept up and down the vacant beach before she waded into the water, pulled the snorkel mask in place, and then dove in head first.

The woman was determined for sure. He balled her sundress under his arm and cast a glance toward the resort lobby. Though it was a short distance away, the evening's light would easily silhouette him on the beach. He took half a dozen steps backward before sitting in the sand. In a seated position, he would be less obvious, and this way, he could keep a close eye on the water where Avery had disappeared.

Only her feet flicking the surface helped him keep tabs on her. She was making a beeline toward the edge of the beach, which was cordoned off, and where in the water, a strand of buoys attempted to keep snorkelers away.

As if they could deter his boss.

Still, he hoped she didn't get tangled up, because he was not wearing his swimsuit, a fact his very wet clothes reminded him of.

Within minutes, the sun dipped below the shoreline, but the rain didn't disappear. Instead, it fell harder. He scanned the water for Avery. He had no excuse to be sitting on the wet sand without a sunset to watch, and Avery had no excuse for swimming at twilight.

She reappeared offshore, and he breathed more easily. He had lost sight of her more than once, but now, she was wading back toward shore.

He rose and strode toward her, brushing off the sand that clung to his soaked pants. She emerged onto the shore with a triumphant tilt to her chin. She'd found something.

Liam tossed her the black sundress and hooked her arm with his. "Good swim?"

Water dripped from the tips of her eyelashes. Even in the dim light, her blue eyes seemed to shine with excitement. "Very good. Let's get back to the room, and then we can talk."

He had no sooner deadbolted the door than Avery ran to the small desk in the room and clicked on the lamp. She tugged the camera leash from her wrist and flipped the mini camera over to browse through her pictures.

Liam grabbed another chair from the corner and set it next to hers. He edged onto it with elbows propped on the back. "So what was past the barricade? I saw you swim over."

"Are you kidding? That barricade is a total joke. I spotted only a handful of debris in the water."

He rubbed his chin—still not used to the absence of his beard. "Then what did you see?"

She paused her browsing and tilted the display screen toward his face. "Crab traps. Lots of neatly placed traps."

"Wonder when the season ends here." He grabbed for his phone, still in his pocket. "Did you happen to see the tag on them?"

"Yep, it's the next picture. Snap a photo of it if you want to run it through the database."

Whether Bahamian crabbers would be in a database he could access was another matter, but he would still try. "Thanks, but it still doesn't make sense for someone to be crabbing on the other side of a barricade."

"No, it does not." Avery retracted her mini camera and resumed browsing through her pictures. "It does make sense, however, if you're trying to hide something."

"You mean—"

She waved her camera back toward his face. "Look familiar?"

Liam squinted to understand what he was seeing. The water was dark, but he could make out the crab trap.

"Let me zoom in," Avery said.

He waited and then studied the close-up detail. There, caught on the edge of the trap, was a piece of fabric or wrapping.

"Recognize those colors?" Avery asked. "I know it's hard to see in the picture, but the wrapping is purple and green. I think it belongs to the same type of brick that seems to be Big Eddie's trademark. It must have torn while being retrieved."

"You think they're using the crab traps as drop-off points?"

She swiveled her chair and rose. "Yep—like the crab traps near Anclote that you and Drew were monitoring. I don't think it's coincidence. I think it's a pattern."

He twisted in his chair and then started for his suitcase and the laptop he'd hidden inside. "I'll see what I can find out about that tag number. If it's not in the database, I'll borrow a golf cart and hunt down a local fisherman tomorrow. There's got to be a place where a guy can talk fishing around here."

"*We'll* borrow a cart," Avery corrected him. "Remember, we're each other's cover. A couple doesn't come to Bimini and then go their separate ways. We'll make excuses for splitting later if we have to, but otherwise, we need to put on a solid front."

He grinned. "Right, sleep in, get a leisurely brunch, and then go exploring."

She snorted. "If by *sleep in* you mean get up early, work on the laptop, but don't leave the room until ten, then yes."

"You read my mind." After retrieving his laptop, he set it on the long couch and glanced at the time. Nine o'clock. He'd like nothing better than to shower off the rain and sand from his skin before diving into work for a few hours before bed. "You want to shower first?"

She glanced up. "Actually, yes. I need to get the salt off before I head back to the lobby for a drink—and maybe a chance to meet this girl of yours."

He returned to grab his suitcase and propped it up on a stand next to the couch where he'd be sleeping the next few days. "She's not my girl."

"Right, but you like her." Avery dug inside her own suitcase in search of dry clothes. "I mean, you knocked over your luggage the minute you spotted her."

He sighed and turned toward Avery. "Really? You have to throw that in my face?"

She held up her palms. "Sorry, but facts are facts. And I want to make sure your head is in the game, because there's a fifty-fifty chance your girl is either in on this operation or runs a risk of becoming collateral damage."

Though his gut denied Jayna could be anything but innocent,

her getting caught in the crossfire was a fear that had already crossed his mind.

"I know," was all he said.

Avery snatched a white dress from her bag. "I'll be five minutes, and then the bathroom is yours."

He didn't care how long she took to shower. He'd need more time than that to forget the achingly beautiful woman with the sad smile who had stolen his breath in the mountains and now in Bimini.

Somehow, he had to find the truth and pray it would allow him to protect her.

Chapter Twenty-Three

Jayna stared into her glass of champagne and watched the contents swirl. She should have said no to a refill. Beside her, Mario chatted with another couple about tomorrow's sunset cruise, but she'd heard the spiel a dozen times already. The only reason she remained put was the ring on her finger—and the solid seat beneath her.

A streak of white in her peripheral pulled her chin up and her gaze back into focus. It was the same woman who had checked in with the clumsy man earlier that evening.

The clumsy man who had reminded her of Ginger Ale.

Ridiculous. They didn't even look alike. But there was something about him that made her instantly bristle toward the blonde diva who now accepted her own glass from William and picked her way to the refreshments table.

Jayna gulped the rest of her glass and whispered to Mario. "Be right back, darling."

He pecked her cheek and continued to focus on the couple as if they were his new best friends. That same razor-sharp attention had charmed her at first. Now, she recognized it wasn't reserved for her and might have resented it had it not allowed her an opportunity to escape.

The floor felt a little woozy. She was only a social drinker, but if she wasn't careful, she wouldn't be in control of herself when Mario walked her to her room.

If he did. He may not yet have forgiven her for her performance at dinner.

Jayna massaged her temple and willed herself to focus. The woman would be gone if she didn't hurry.

But there was no need. William was currently chatting with her beside the refreshment table.

She was truly Jayna's opposite. Blonde and fair, not brunette and bronzed. Slim, not curvy. But the way she held herself suggested either a similar background in modeling—or a natural confidence few were born with.

William's gaze shifted to welcome Jayna to the table. "Ah, my dear, is there something I can get for you?"

Jayna placed her empty glass on the table. "I could use a water. Thank you, William."

"I'll get you a chilled one from the kitchen."

The blonde popped a grape in her mouth, swallowed, and offered a grin. "I'm Amber. Great place here, huh?"

Jayna leaned against the table and nodded. "Yes, it is. I'm Jayna."

Amber picked another grape off a small cluster on her plate. "Did you just arrive too?"

The question was natural enough, but there were so many ways she could answer it. "Actually, my fiancé owns the resort."

Amber's eyes widened, but she popped another grape. "Wow, nice. Is he the gorgeous guy you were sitting next to earlier?"

Jayna's arms felt like lead, but she motioned toward the high-top table where Mario and the other couple still chatted. "Yes, that's him."

"Gurrrrl. Good for you." Amber gave her an approving smirk. "Are you one of those high-school sweetheart stories, or how did you get so lucky?"

To her relief, William reappeared with her water and handed it to her. "Anything else I can get you, Miss Jayna?"

She took a long swig and shook her head. "No, this is perfect. Thank you."

The cooling water had a steadying effect on her. She wanted to learn about Amber, not talk about herself.

"Want to sit?" Jayna motioned to two fabric chairs and slid onto one of them without waiting for Amber's reply.

Amber set her glass on the small table between them and placed her plate on her lap. "The suspense is killing me. I love a good romance story."

Jayna forced a laugh to cover the ache and fidgeted with her

147

water bottle. "Oh, it's pretty simple. I came here for a job, met Mario, and the rest is history, as they say. But what about you? How'd you meet your guy?"

Amber paused to take another sip of her champagne. "Work brought Oliver and me together too. We were both extras on the set of a zombie movie—and both casualties in the same scene. Who knew two people could bond over a blood and gore makeup session? But we did."

Her relationship with Mario had its own share of gore, none of which was filmable. "Wow, so you're an actress."

"Loosely speaking." Amber crunched on the last of her grapes. "I'm really a bartender who gets a few roles, but it's more fun to say I'm an actress who bartends."

"Still a cool story." Jayna risked a glance at Mario. He raised his chin to catch her eye, and she acknowledged him with a nod of her own. At least he would consider her hostess duties fulfilled by entertaining a guest.

Though who was entertaining who at this point was harder to say.

"So, what's your favorite thing to do here—other than, you know, our host." Amber's saucy smile seemed so natural it didn't faze her.

"That's a tough one. All our excursions are great. If you like free diving, the Bimini Road snorkeling trip is fun. My personal favorite is Honeymoon Harbor and swimming with the stingrays. It's really peaceful."

Amber crinkled her nose. "Stingrays? I'm not so sure about that. But if it's a good fishing spot, Oliver will be there."

Fishing. Hadn't Liam liked to fish? Or had she imagined that? "Is that why you guys have such a long skinny luggage case?"

"The one my babe knocked over?" Amber snorted. "Yes, that's for storing his poles, and he had another bag for his tackle. I swear, men can be more high maintenance than we are."

Gauging from Amber's wet hair twisted into a messy bun, her Oliver didn't require her to look like a barbie doll the way Mario expected it of her. But she couldn't dwell on that. "Do you like fishing too?"

"Ugh, no. He took me deep sea fishing once, and I threw up. Seasickness, you know." Amber made a face. "But hey, it's good to get some me time, so I encourage him to fish while I do my thing.

"Speaking of which, what about the town? Oliver wants to chat up some locals about surf fishing spots, so I figure I'll go with and explore. Can we call a taxi from here?"

"You don't need a taxi, and there isn't much of a town. You can reserve one of our golf carts at the front desk for tomorrow and go exploring yourself. The Dolphin House is neat, and I can recommend a great place for conch fritters."

Amber set down her empty plate on the table. "Now you're talking. I'm a total foodie."

Whether it was the wine or the long day, Jayna felt her head getting woozy again. She needed to call it a night. "Just tell the receptionist you want to reserve a golf cart and tell him I sent you."

Her new friend stood and smoothed her dress. "Thanks, I'll do that. It was nice meeting you, Jayna."

"Same." Jayna rose more cautiously. "Oh, and there's a sunset cruise tomorrow night. Those are fun too."

"Thanks, I'll tell Oliver. If I can get him away from his fishing gear, we'll probably be there." Amber offered a small wave and strode toward the lobby desk.

Mario was still thick in conversation with some other guests, and she wasn't about to get pulled into more chit-chat. Retrieving her water, she slipped down the hallway toward her room.

She liked Amber, and her Oliver didn't sound anything like Liam—except for the fishing hobbyist bit. Still, maybe she'd get a chance to observe him on the cruise and see what it was about him that seemed so familiar. Either way, Amber was smart, and right now, Jayna needed smart friends. Maybe befriending these two actors could be her ticket to escaping her paradise prison.

Chapter Twenty-Four

The golf cart hit a pothole, jolting Liam from his seat for a split second before he smacked down on it. "You told her what?"

Beside him, Avery gripped her seat with one hand and her straw hat with the other. "I told her we were actors who met as extras on the set of a zombie movie."

The hibiscus welcome sign for the resort faded in the small rearview mirror, and the receptionist had assured him they would reach the town in no time.

Which was hardly enough time to untangle Avery's conversation with Jayna.

"I don't even like zombie movies. Which one am I supposed to have appeared in?" Liam swerved to avoid another rough patch of road, a reminder of the lingering hurricane damage.

"You pick a recent one. I didn't give her a title."

Liam bit down a sarcastic response. He was here to track down a smuggler and find a way to help Jayna, not figure out the latest zombie blockbuster.

He had to focus. "How was she?"

"Anxious. And unsteady on her feet."

"What?" He glanced at Avery.

"Pot hole." Avery grabbed the wheel and yanked to avoid another rut. "Pay attention."

He grunted and snapped his gaze back to the road. "Just tell me how she was. You could have told me all this last night, you know."

"We were both busy with work e-mails, so I saved this for the ride to town." Avery resumed her grip on the seat. "Anyway, I don't think she's happy with Delgado. Her 'how I met him' story was shorter and less detailed than the one I made up for us on the spot. She also kept glancing his way as if she expected him to be watching her. Maybe that's why she was drinking more than she should."

"Do you think she's in danger?"

"I don't think so, but she did act a little caged."

The visual of Jayna in a cage didn't set well with him. He willed himself to focus on the job. "I wasn't able to find the crab trap ID number in the database, but I did confirm crab season ended in June. So, either we have an illegal crabbing operation—"

"Or something much worse," Avery finished. "I suspect the latter."

"You're such an optimist."

Brightly painted shops in vibrant shades of blue, yellow, and pink appeared on the horizon. The receptionist was right that the island was small.

In that case, everyone should know everyone, and he shouldn't have any issue finding the owner of the tag.

A sign for Joe's Conch Shack popped into view, and Liam swerved toward it. Conch shack and fishermen seemed like a probable combination.

After parking the cart, he hopped out, but Avery remained seated. "You can't be hungry. It's barely eleven o'clock, and we had brunch less than an hour ago."

"Exactly why this place isn't crowded, and it's the perfect time to stop by and chat up the locals." He walked around the cart and held out a hand. "Besides, I hear conch salad is a delicacy in these parts."

She took his hand and scooted out of the cart. "You made your point. I'll let you do the talking since fishing is your thing."

"Great, and you can be eye candy."

Avery glared at him and lowered her voice. "I know we're uh-hem *dating*, but don't ever call me eye candy again."

Liam smirked and led the way to the shack. Undercover with his boss was awkward at times but watching her get riled at compliments made up for the discomfort.

Clear blue ocean water formed the backdrop to the shack, a fitting name for the small structure made from sheets of plywood and wooden beams. He passed a pair of faded picnic tables, unoccupied except for one man who hunched over his smartphone. At the counter, almost every square inch of wood framing was covered with stickers or graffiti left behind by tourists. Clearly, this place was a mecca.

A middle-aged Bahamian man wearing a blue baseball cap and striped tank top held a large chef's knife and was busily dicing up someone else's order. He offered a smile and "be right with ya."

After mixing together what looked to be conch, diced veggies, and peppers, the man called out, "Paul, ya order's ready."

Paul, another Bahamian, uncurled his lanky frame and accepted the plastic bowl, filled to overflowing with his own conch salad. "Thanks, Tony."

Tony then turned to Liam. "What can I get started for ya?"

"Same as him." Liam nodded toward Paul who had returned to the picnic table to devour the food. "I hear you've got the best conch salad in these parts."

"Ya can say that again." Tony grinned and nodded past Liam to where Avery was reading graffiti on a support beam next to the counter. "Do ya want a second for your bey?"

By *bey*, he must mean *girl*. "No, we'll share, but thanks," Liam said.

"She can grab a conch shell if she wants one," Tony pointed at Avery. "There's a mountain of them out back."

"I'll do that." Avery pointed behind the shack and said something about not being long.

"Thanks." Liam paid the man. "You wouldn't happen to know where some good surf fishing spots are on the island?"

"Me and the other boys take the boat out for conchs, but Paul there could tell ya."

Liam nodded his thanks and claimed a seat on the other side of the table across from Paul. The man was so busy with his lunch that he didn't seem to notice him.

He finally cleared his throat. "Hey—uh, Paul—I hear you're an expert on surf fishing in these parts."

Paul jerked his head up at his name and swallowed a bite. "Yeah, ya see."

"Nice, I'm here for a few days and wanted to know if there's

152

any place you recommend."

The Bahamian shrugged as if not wanting to give away any secrets. "If no sign says ya can't surf fish, any beach will do. The best time is before sunset."

Liam already knew that information but nodded. "Thanks, oh, and I was wondering if you could identify a tag for me? I think my—partner—may have accidentally broken someone's crab trap on a dive, and I want to make it right."

"It's off season." Paul scooped the last of his conch salad into his mouth.

"Right, I was just curious if you'd recognize it." Without asking permission, he pulled out his phone and swiped to the picture he'd already made sure to have open. Then, he slid it into Paul's line of vision.

Paul stopped chewing, though his cheeks remained full. Slowly, he swallowed, and he slid the phone back to Liam. "Keep that to yourself." With that, Paul rose, as if the conversation were over.

Liam slid out of the seat to follow him to the trashcan where Paul ditched his empty bowl. "Wait, so do you know the crabber?"

Paul glanced around and then turned to face Liam. "Look, man, ya seem nice. Kevon's a mean one. Forget the trap. It shouldn't be out now anyway."

With that, Paul waved to Tony, hopped on his golf cart, and sped away.

Avery reappeared holding two shells, one in each hand, and grinned at Liam. "I couldn't decide between the two. They're gorgeous—and there's thousands more out back. So cool."

Liam shook his head. Either Avery was a brilliant actress or she had a soft spot for shells. "You can keep them as long as they go home in your luggage."

She made a pouty face. "I was thinking maybe we could put them with your tackle box."

"Ya order's ready," Tony called, interrupting the conversation.

"Already?" Avery placed her two prizes on the second picnic table. "That was fast."

153

"I'll get two spoons." Liam returned to the counter to claim his bowl.

"Hot sauce?" Tony held out a bottle to him.

"No, thanks," Liam said. "I'm already sunburned."

Tony laughed and told him to enjoy. The conch salad already looked spicy enough with its Caribbean seasoning, peppers, and diced onions. But the lime helped offset the spice.

"This is delicious." Avery chewed and scooped another spoonful for her next bite.

It was, but he couldn't enjoy it. If the crabber Kevon was one and the same as the Kevon Rolles on their watch list, he was the same man who had helped steal Jayna away from Beech Mountain.

Maybe some surf fishing tonight at the Bimini Road's End Resort would give him an opportunity to see what was really going on offshore.

Chapter Twenty-Five

Words failed her.

Jayna sat cross-legged on her comforter with her laptop propped on her lap. She had procrastinated as long as she could by eating breakfast, showering, and drying her hair.

She needed to write something—anything—to publish on her blog, something that would suggest to her nosy sister and doting parents that she was enjoying her stay in Bimini.

It was a big fat lie, yet for their safety, she needed to spin a credible story until she could figure out her escape.

She'd already blogged about breakfast more than once and shared more food shots on her gram account than she usually did. Everything in her bedroom had been staged at some point.

But she didn't want to leave it. Her room was the only place she felt she could be herself. The moment she stepped outside, she had to put on a façade for Mario.

Her stomach rumbled, reminding her she had skipped lunch to avoid seeing him. Who was she kidding? If she didn't escape in less than five days, she would never be able to avoid him again.

Her phone buzzed. Texts from Mario now made her stomach churn.

Missed you at lunch, but I'll pick you up for the sunset cruise dinner at 5:30 on the beach. Happy writing until then.

Drat, she'd forgotten about the cruise, but maybe it would provide the inspiration for her next post, which would have to wait. Five thirty was just over an hour away, and she should scrounge up some food so she didn't pass out.

Mario would expect her to help host, which meant there would be no enjoying the food on the cruise. Would Mario use his private yacht for it? She doubted it, not with Kevon's tendency to forget body parts in the freezer. Mario had probably made a deal with a local company to host the event.

Maybe Amber and her boyfriend would be there. That thought made her fold the laptop and swing her legs off the bed. For some reason, the pair of actors seemed like her best chance at allies. But then, she didn't have a record for getting first impressions right.

She squinted into the mirror. Her curly hair was less than immaculate but had a messy beach wave vibe that she hoped would work. As for her T-shirt dress, the only thing Mario would approve about it was its shortness. Whatever. She would change into something nicer after begging for a late lunch from William.

After slipping her feet into a pair of flipflops, she pulled open her door and stepped—directly into another guest in the hallway.

"Oof!" The man plowed right into her but spun her so that he hit the ground first. She landed on top of him with a thud.

Oh, no. It was Amber's boyfriend Oliver. His Aviators hung half off his face, but he quickly adjusted them back onto his nose.

Weird. Who wears sunglasses indoors? There was something else she couldn't put her finger on.

She would have to figure it out when she wasn't sprawled on top of his chest. Face flaming, Jayna rolled off him. "I'm so sorry." She shoved her T-shirt dress back down and jerked her head to the sound of laughter from behind them.

"Bravo! Class act." Amber stood there looking as chill as a cucumber in a short jumper that showed off her long tan legs. A Bimini-branded fabric bag slung over one arm. "I was hoping we'd run into you, but I didn't think it would be such a literal thing."

"I'm sorry." Jayna ran a hand through her tangled curls to give her nervous energy something to do. "I should have looked where I was going."

"No harm done," Amber said.

Oliver nodded and offered a good-natured smile, before mumbling something about needing to charge his phone. Seconds later, he disappeared down the hall.

Her heart squeezed. Had she embarrassed him? But surely, someone who served as an expendable extra in a sci-fi drama wouldn't care about an awkward accident.

"... for the dinner cruise?" Amber was still talking.

Jayna shook her head to concentrate. "Sorry, what were you saying?"

"Oh, I was wondering if you were going on the dinner cruise tonight." Amber pulled a flyer from her bag. "The man at the front desk handed me this when we returned the golf cart keys and asked if we wanted to sign up."

"Yes, I'll be there. I'm heading toward the lobby now if you want me to sign you up." Jayna motioned down the hallway.

Amber adjusted her bag onto her other shoulder. "Sure, that would be great. Amber Bozeman, room 12."

Jayna frowned. "What about Oliver? It's going to be a catered meal, from what I hear, and the sky is clear tonight. It should be a lovely—romantic sunset."

"He's already got fishing plans for this evening, but he committed to the swimming with the stingrays excursion tomorrow, though I'm not sure how romantic that will be." Amber paused to snort-laugh. "With or without him, I'm a sucker for good food and a sunset, so I'll see you there." She waved and then padded down the hallway after Oliver.

Jayna stared after her for a minute. Amber and Oliver were the oddest couple. What guy chose fishing over a romantic date night with a sexy woman on a tropical island? And what girlfriend seemed totally cool with the decision?

Not that she could judge. Her relationship was in shambles. If she could choose between fishing and spending the evening with Mario, she'd choose fishing too.

However, Amber didn't seem like a manipulative Mario. On the bright side, a companionless Amber meant more time for her to get to know the actress on her own terms and more time to determine if she could trust her enough to tell the truth.

Liam released a long breath as he surveyed the resort's beach. Avery and the other guests had long since been ferried to the waiting sunset cruise, and now, the beach was deserted. He'd already confirmed earlier in the day that no signs were posted to prohibit surf fishing, an oversight on Delgado's part if his resort really was a drop spot for illegal drugs.

With a glance back to the resort, he checked that he'd left on the small lamp in their suite. It was the signal to Avery that he was outside. Once he returned safely to their room, he would shut it off. If all went well, he would be back long before she stepped foot on the beach.

He gripped his tackle box in one hand and the rest of his fishing gear in the other. His feet sank a little deeper into the sand with each step until he reached the shoreline where the waves had packed the sand harder. The warm, salty water swirled around his bare feet, tempting him to relax.

Pausing for a moment, he sucked in another deep breath and let it go. But breathing techniques couldn't calm the memory of Jayna in his arms. The rush of her tropical scent and the feel of her smooth skin sent shivers through him even now. The woman would be his undoing if he couldn't clear his head and stay focused. Avery had promised to get close to her tonight on the cruise and see if Jayna wanted to confide in her. But Avery warned him there was still the chance Jayna was a guilty party, though everything inside him wanted to believe that was impossible.

Whispering a prayer, he committed Jayna to God and asked for guidance. Avery might not believe in prayer, but he sure did. If he had any chance of observing offshore activity, it would be tonight. His gut told him that he wasn't the only one who planned to take advantage of the deserted resort.

The waves erased his footsteps behind him, leaving no evidence that he had come this way. He'd reached the end of the moon-shaped beach. In front of him, a narrow peninsula jutted into the ocean, and he planned to surf fish on the other side of it—an area still taped off due to hurricane debris.

Liam had tugged on his water boots in case there was any sharp debris, but from what Avery and he had observed so far, the tape was less to protect people from getting hurt and more to keep them out.

After ducking under the construction tape and squeezing

through some haphazard barricades, he plodded toward the surf in the U-shaped beach. The sun dipped toward the horizon, and already the sky had changed colors into vibrant hues of orange and pink.

He couldn't have asked for a better view for his sunset fishing. Setting down his tackle box in dry sand, he released the PVC sand spike from underneath his armpit and rammed it into the sand until it stood securely on its own. Then he unhooked his rig from where he'd fastened it to the pole. He'd had plenty of time to adjust the rig back in the hotel room, and now, he simply had to hook some of the live shrimp bait he'd purchased in town.

His fingers worked from muscle memory, and his shoulders relaxed. He was blessed to be able to do something he loved while working for something he believed in.

With the shrimp secured to the hook, he cast into the surf and then inserted his pole into the PVC spike. Now, he only had to wait—and observe.

The beach remained clear, and there was no trace of the sunset cruise or any other vessel on the horizon. Liam sat down on the sand. From this spot, he could see the beach on either side of the small peninsula. If the crab traps Avery had found were any indicator, the drug runner's boat would beeline for the other side of the peninsula, giving him an opportunity to creep up from his side and observe.

As the sun continued its descent, Liam's pole jerked, and he retrieved it from the PVC spike. For the next several minutes, he fought what turned out to be a pompano—about a ten pounder. He removed the hook from its mouth and tossed it back. After another pompano catch, followed by a fifteen-pound bonefish, the sun had completely disappeared, and the evening's blue-blackness settled in.

He cast his still-empty hook back into the surf so he could use it for cover if needed, but the time for catching fish was over.

A yacht's lights had flashed on the horizon minutes ago, and the soft humming of the engine now reached his ears. After grabbing his binoculars from his gearbox, he began crawling into position on the peninsula. He pressed his body tightly into the sand bank and peered over the top of the narrow peninsula toward the half-moon bay on the resort side. Some brush and debris remnants obscured his view, but he could detect the dark outline of the approaching vessel.

But he needed evidence, not speculation. His infrared binoculars would help him observe, and if he could get close enough, the water might amplify any conversations so he could hear them—and record them.

The shrubs were too thick for him to climb further onto the narrow peninsula that jutted into the water, so he went the long way around, returning to the roped-off section of the resort's beach. While still hidden, he started a new recording on his smartphone and secured it into a back pocket of his cargo pants.

Leaving behind his gear meant potentially losing it if someone discovered him, but there was no indicator that it belonged to him. He had also left a spare rod and smaller tackle case behind in his room if anyone suspected him.

Crawling as fast as he dared, Liam reached the resort beach and flattened himself to the sand, feet away from the ebbing waves.

Then, with his chin buried in the sand, he raised the binoculars. He counted three bodies moving on the deck. Though the fishing boat's name was faded, he could barely make out the word *Riptide* on the side. They picked up three square objects— the size of crab traps—and tossed them in the water. The captain then spun the fishing boat around and headed for deeper water.

For a second, Liam debated whether to grab his snorkel mask which he'd also shoved into his tackle box. If Avery was here, he would risk it. Something told him the latest shipment had just been deposited and was now waiting the pickup. He couldn't get any harder evidence than a freshly deposited brick.

But instead, he stopped his phone recording and waited. There was no point becoming a dead hero and Avery wondering why her partner disappeared. Though his legs soon fell asleep, and sand gnats made him want to scratch off his exposed skin, he continued to wait with one hand on his phone and the other on the binoculars. It was thirty minutes to nine o'clock, and the dinner cruise was scheduled to return by ten. If no one showed up in the next fifteen minutes, he would retrieve his gear and get back to his room before the other guests returned.

Fifteen minutes passed in silence, and he began shaking the blood flow back into his legs. Then, he bear-crawled back across the stretch of beach that separated the two small bays from each other.

He had just crested the mid-point when he froze. A boat floated offshore where he'd staged his gear, and someone shined a flashlight, illuminating his pole and tackle box.

Liam dropped to his stomach and snatched his binoculars from his belt. The boat was the *Riptide*. It must have circled back and seen his gear. Or had someone else been watching the beach and tipped off the crew?

Either way, he had to get out of here. A spotlight flashed near him, and he ducked again before taking off toward the resort as fast as he could while hunched low.

But now, a light suddenly illuminated the resort's beach, and he hugged the shadows on his way to the side entrance. Someone must have turned on the lights to welcome the guests returning from the sunset cruise. He couldn't get back to his room soon enough.

Fifty meters.

Twenty-five meters.

Liam reached the side door and inserted his room key.

The knob twisted, but the door didn't open more than a few centimeters.

His pulse raced. Someone had locked a swing bolt latch from the inside.

He pushed the door back in place and flattened himself against the wall. He couldn't use the back entrance now, and someone would see him for sure if he went around front.

He was trapped.

Chapter Twenty-Six

The clinking of serving lids being lifted off steaming entrees signaled that dinner would be served soon, yet Jayna hesitated to leave the railing. The fading sunset still lingered on the horizon, and at least Amber seemed to appreciate it as well. She stared out across the water and slowly sipped from her champagne glass—though Jayna had watched her closely enough all evening to know she had requested sparkling cider.

Perhaps the woman was pregnant—or *big up* as they said in the Bahamas. She didn't seem like the type who would refuse a drink when it was on the house.

As if reading her thoughts, Amber turned toward her and nibbled on her painted red lips. "Do you ever feel like you're leading a double life?"

Jayna clutched her own champagne glass to keep from dropping it. "Excuse me?"

"Oh, I don't know." Amber waved a hand at the general luxury of the sunset cruise where couples and a few young families waited for the catered dinner around candle-lit tables and twinkle lights illuminated the dance floor. "This is all so lovely, but it's like we're frauds. We can afford to enjoy this for what—maybe a week?—and then we go back to our real lives."

There were many reasons Jayna felt like a fraud, but enjoying luxury wasn't one of them. "I don't see the harm in that. Everyone wants to escape something—whether it's the daily grind of a job or the demands of family."

Amber caught her gaze and held it. "What do you want to escape?"

A gasp slipped through her lips, and she glanced around the deck for Mario. He was at the bar getting a new glass and too far away to overhear her.

Now was her chance, but did she dare tell this woman, still a virtual stranger, her truth? She swallowed a sip of her drink, choosing her words with care. "Perhaps not every life that has the appearance of a fairy tale really is one."

Amber arched an eyebrow. "Is that code for Prince Charming might not be your happily ever after?"

Jayna's face flamed. Was she that transparent?

Amber held up her hands. "It's none of my business, of course, but if you want to talk to a girl who's had her share of failed relationships, I'm here for you. At least for the next few days while I pretend to play the part of an actress who can afford this type of luxury for a lifetime instead of just a vacation."

Jayna's shoulders relaxed, and she nodded. Amber was right. What did she have to lose in talking to another woman who would go back home in less than a week? Unfortunately, a few moments on the railing weren't enough to untangle the mess she was in.

She bit her lip. "I found out some things about him, but we're engaged. I feel trapped."

"Yuck, I don't like that." Amber's jaw tightened. "There's always a way out. Have you tried giving him back the ring and telling him you need to work through some things first?"

"Yeah, that didn't go well." Jayna glanced over her shoulder again. Mario was making his way toward her. "He plans for us to elope on Saturday, and I'm scared."

Amber's eyes widened, but Mario was now too close for either of them to say more. Straightening, Jayna motioned for Amber to greet Mario in the hopes he wouldn't guess they had been talking about him.

"Hasn't this been a perfect evening?" Jayna reached for Mario's hand and pressed a kiss to his cheek.

"It's more perfect for you being in it." He lifted her hand to his lips.

She hoped her blush made her look flattered. "Mario, I want you to meet Amber. She and I were getting to know each other."

Mario greeted her with a handshake. "It's a pleasure to have you here. Would you and your partner care to join us at our table? Surely, a lovely lady like yourself is not alone."

163

"Ah, thank you." Amber batted her eyes. The woman really was an actress. "My boyfriend stayed behind because he wasn't feeling well, so it's only me tonight."

Jayna dropped her gaze to the now-empty glass in her hand. Hadn't Amber said that Oliver was going fishing tonight? She hadn't mentioned anything about him not feeling well.

"In that case, you must join us." Mario offered them both an arm.

Jayna accepted his right one and let him lead them to a table, but she cast a glance at Amber once they were seated. Amber offered her a subtle smile and took another sip from her glass. "This champagne is delicious."

"Glad you like it," Mario said. "I'm going to tell the waiters we're ready for them to serve the meal. I'll be right back."

Jayna avoided meeting Amber's eyes, a nervous flutter filling her stomach. Amber had lied about drinking champagne and about what her boyfriend was doing tonight.

Maybe they were both leading double lives. She had spilled her secret to Amber, but what was this actress hiding?

"Are you done, miss?" The server motioned to Jayna's empty plate.

"Oh, yes, thanks." Jayna lowered her hands to her lap and sneaked another glance at Amber. The woman was her saving grace, even if she was a liar. Amber had engaged Mario and the other guests at their table in conversation most of the evening, leaving her to relax for the first time since returning to Bimini.

She sure owed this woman.

Another waiter edged between her and Mario and bent toward his ear. "A man who calls himself Kevon arrived on his tender and demands to speak with you. He—he doesn't look like the type of man who will be easily dismissed."

The hair on her neck prickled. What could Kevon want now? Mario's reply was too soft to hear, but she could sense his agitation.

Mario's chair scraped against the deck, and he jerked to his feet. He flashed a smile at their table and bowed. "You'll have to excuse me. But please, take advantage of the dance floor. I believe cheesecake will be served soon as well."

He then leaned toward her and planted a kiss on her cheek. "I'll be back soon, dear." His hot breath made her skin tingle, but she simply nodded in response. For once, she hoped he would come back. If Kevon were here, she wanted to know why.

Beside her, Amber propped her elbows on the table. "Want to stretch? Feels like we've been sitting for hours."

"I don't feel like dancing—"

Amber's snort cut her off. "Not dancing. I was thinking the railing."

"Oh, sure." Was that an invitation to pick up their conversation from where they left off? "I can't go too far in case Mario comes back though."

"We can see him perfectly fine from there." Amber pointed to the railing behind them.

Jayna scooted off her seat and followed her new friend. She leaned against the railing to keep her eyes focused on the back of the boat where Mario had disappeared.

Amber leaned the opposite direction to gaze over the ocean, though only the water right next to the boat was illuminated. The horizon had vanished into the night.

"So, Oliver wasn't feeling well? That's a shame he couldn't go fishing." Jayna broached the question that had been nagging her all evening.

A grin slowly spread its way across Amber's lips. "Oh, that. He's fine. We've just noticed that some people at the resort don't like us being on the beach, so I didn't want to mention surf fishing if it's a touchy subject. We like to live by the 'ask forgiveness instead of permission' policy."

"Ah." Amber had noticed the resort's strict beach clearing policy. But did she suspect something else was off?

Movement to her left drew her focus. Mario was fast-approaching, and the frown on his face didn't promise good news.

"Darling, I have to leave. The emcee will finish hosting the event. I'll check on you later tonight, okay?"

Before Jayna could reply, Amber made a retching noise. Her head disappeared momentarily over the railing, and when she stood back up, her face was white.

"Sorry." She gulped. "I'm really not feeling well. Could I go back to shore with you?"

Jayna blinked. Moments ago, Amber had seemed perfectly composed.

Mario shook his head. "I'm sorry, but the tender is small, and I have business—"

"You don't understand." Amber clutched her stomach. "I'm pregnant. I really need to lie down. Surely, you can understand that. I didn't know the cruise would last this long."

So that explained the sparkling cider. But why had she called it champagne? And why had she shown no symptoms of nausea earlier?

It didn't matter. She wrapped a steadying arm around Amber. "I'll make sure she gets back to her room, Mario. We won't get in the way."

A grimace spread across Mario's face, but he nodded. "All right. But we've got to hurry."

Keeping an arm around Amber's shoulder, she led the staggering woman toward the waiting tender.

Kevon growled when he saw them. "What are they doing here?"

Mario glared back and offered both her and Amber a hand as they stepped down into the tender. "This woman is big up—and feeling sick. Jayna is escorting her to her room. Let's go."

For once, she offered Mario a genuine smile. For all his bad decisions, he did have a heart.

The tender made quick time returning to the beach where the resort's warm lighting from the patio's trellised canopy welcomed them back. For a moment, peace washed over her. Even in her predicament, she could still help people like Amber. If she could help others, maybe someone could help her.

Kevon jumped onto the shore and pulled the tender part way onto the sand. She ignored the hand that he offered her and jumped down by herself. But once her feet hit the sand, Kevon snatched her hand and pulled her toward him. "See that she gets inside."

Jayna jerked away. "That's what I'm here for." She scowled at him.

Still groaning and clutching her stomach, Amber nearly slid over the side of the tender into the surf. Rushing toward her, Jayna steadied the woman. Kevon didn't bother to help but shoved off and hopped back in.

"I'll be back soon," Mario called to her. There was something sincere about his words.

Her heart skipped, and she called back, "Thanks, darling." It was better to keep up appearances since Kevon was in ear-shot. At least, that's what she told herself.

Jayna wrapped an arm around Amber's waist and pointed them toward the patio. "Let's get you to your room."

But Amber seemed to drag her feet as the tender's engine faded. Then suddenly, she straightened and whirled to face Jayna. "We need to hurry."

"Wait, what?" Jayna released her new friend.

Amber shook her head. "I can't explain. I need you to trust me—and trust that I'm here to help you."

"Help—help me?" Jayna frowned at the perfectly composed woman before her.

"Yes, I need you to make sure the side entrance is open—the one that leads outside from the hallway by our rooms. I'll meet you there in five minutes."

"But why?" Jayna crossed her arms. "I'm supposed to be escorting you inside. What are you going to do? What if someone sees you?"

Amber winked. "I'll act." With that, she darted down the beach, looking anything but the pregnant guest she had claimed to be.

Jayna stared after her. Mario would be furious if he knew. But she wasn't exactly loyal to Mario these days. Still, she had no idea what Amber was up to. What if she were trying to rob the place?

That seemed ridiculous, but the last thing Jayna needed was

to get pegged as an accomplice.

Another thought struck her. What if Amber was on to Mario? What if she suspected something illegal was taking place offshore? She had observed how tightly the resort closed the beaches at night.

Helping her was a risk, but if it paid off, she might finally escape her prison.

With a sigh, she jogged toward the patio entrance. She would make sure the side entrance was unlocked. Then, she would get answers.

The inside of the resort seemed eerily silent as most of the staff had the night off. As she passed through the lobby, even the front desk was deserted. At least she didn't have to worry about being questioned.

As she turned the corner to the hallway, she froze. A tall form paced the last stretch of hallway, right in front of the side entrance Amber had asked her to unlock.

Chapter Twenty-Seven

Jayna's hand flew to her throat as the man caught sight of her and spun to face her.

William. Kind, smiling, helpful William stood there with one hand on a handheld radio and the other gripping something inside his belt. The bulge beneath his T-shirt suggested a handgun. Were all of Mario's staff expected to lead double lives, or had Kevon paid him off?

When he saw her, his facial features relaxed, though his brows knit in surprise. "Miss Jayna, what are you doing back early?"

She had to play her cards right. Fluttering her lashes, she clasped her hands in relief. "Oh, I'm so glad I found you. One of the guests is pregnant—*big up* as you say—and Mario had me bring her back to the resort early, but after he dropped us off on the beach, she—collapsed. She's too heavy for me to get inside. I have to get her to her room—but I also have to—pee."

Jayna crossed her legs and motioned to her room. "Meet you on the beach in two minutes?"

William glanced over his shoulder at the door and then nodded. "Yes, I'll help you get her inside. I know the boss wants the beach clear."

Jayna dipped her chin and focused on pulling out her room key. "Exactly."

She pretended to fumble with it while William disappeared. Then, racing to the side door, she unlocked it and hesitated. She had to let Amber know the coast was clear.

Sucking in a deep breath, she cracked it open. As she did, two people darted from the shrubbery toward her.

Amber's face appeared in the partial opening first. She tugged the door the rest of the way. "Good work."

"No, you have to get to the beach." Jayna pushed her back outside. "The only way I could distract the guard was to tell him you had collapsed on the beach. I'll meet you there in a minute."

The other shadow took form, and Jayna gasped. Though his hair was the color of the night and his beard was missing, the face could belong to only one man.

"Liam?" She staggered backward into the hallway. "Liam is Oliver?"

Amber growled and shoved him inside. "We don't have time for this now. I'll meet you on the beach, Jayna, and you can help me to my room."

With that, Amber raced toward the beach, and Liam silently closed the door behind her and locked it.

Jayna's feet wouldn't move, and her tongue didn't do much better. "How—what—I don't—"

He placed a hand on her shoulder. "Go. We'll talk later."

Amber. The beach. If she didn't appear, William would suspect her.

Liam nudged her again. Sucking another breath, she turned and ran down the hallway.

She ignored the questions screaming in her mind. The how of it all would have to wait. One thing was for sure—Liam had been keeping his own secrets in Beech Mountain.

When she reached the back patio again, she spotted only one shadow on the beach. Where was Amber?

Ignoring a pinch in her side, she jogged toward the shadowy figure, and William's lanky form took shape. He was bending over something, someone.

Amber. She had made it to the beach in time.

"Let's get you inside." William scooped her into his arms.

Amber covered her mouth. "I don't feel so good."

Oh no. What if Amber played drunk instead of pregnant? Was she even pregnant, or was everything an act?

Jayna matched William's strides and grabbed one of Amber's dangling hands. "Don't worry. I'll make you some hot tea, and hopefully your sickness will subside."

Amber closed her eyes and moved her other hand over her

abdomen. This girl didn't miss a cue.

"Thank you. I—I just need some rest. Oh, and I'm in room 12."

Jayna hurried ahead of William to open the resort's door and then led the way down the hallway. When they reached her room, Amber motioned for William to put her down. "I think I can stand now. Thank you for your help."

"You're welcome." William's gaze traveled beyond them to the side door. Thank goodness Liam had thought to lock it again. Static on William's radio preceded a cold voice. "What's your status?" Kevon's voice made her jump, and Amber dropped her key on the ground.

Jayna bent over for it. "I got it, William. I'll make her some tea and see that she's comfortable."

"Good." He nodded and reached for the pocketed radio. "Good night, ladies."

To her relief, he spun and hurried down the hallway, probably eager to increase the space between them before responding to Kevon.

But why was he answering to Kevon? Didn't William work for Mario?

Too many questions. Jayna focused on inserting the key into the lock. With a twist, she swung the door open for Amber.

The room was dark, but light from the hallway showed the bedsheets were rumpled, and the shower was running.

Her face flamed. Liam was Amber's boyfriend, yet he had made her believe he was single in the mountains. He'd even showed her special attention.

Were all men liars?

Jayna stepped out of the way so Amber could enter the room. "I'll be back in a few minutes with that tea."

"Yes, perfect." With that, Amber closed the door.

She'd better keep her word, because Jayna needed answers.

Ear to the inside of the bathroom door, Liam relaxed his stance

171

when Amber clicked the door shut.

Jayna's ice-cold words played over in his memory. *I'll be back in a few minutes with that tea.*

What must she think of him? Liam returned his handgun to the holster hidden inside his belt and moved to turn off the shower. He could use a shower, but it would have to wait. No way was he missing a chance to see Jayna.

He popped open the door as Avery collapsed into the swivel chair by the desk. "You okay?"

Her lips twisted in a frown. "That was too close."

"Tell me about it." He checked the peephole. The hallway remained clear for now.

"So what happened? When I saw the light still on in our room, I knew you were in trouble."

"I watched a boat drop fresh—presumably full—crab traps, and I was waiting for the pickup. It was getting late, and I went back for my gear. That's when I spotted the same boat, *Riptide*, just offshore of my gear. Someone must have seen it or reported it. Anyway, I ran back to the hotel and discovered someone had locked the door. I hid out by the beach chair storage until you returned. Man, I'm glad you did."

"Busy night," Avery said, "but no hard proof."

"Right." He stretched his back. "If they think someone was watching them, they'll be extra careful for a while. By tomorrow morning, those traps will for sure be empty."

Avery groaned and ran a hand over her face. "Yeah, and now I've gambled that Jayna is an innocent party. If she's not, this investigation is toast."

Liam leaned against the wall and brushed off the remaining sand that stuck to his shorts. "She's innocent. Why else would she help us tonight?"

Avery crossed her arms. "She's scared. Mario plans for them to elope on Saturday, and she doesn't see a way out."

"What?" He shook his head. No, that couldn't be right.

A tap sounded on their door, and Avery motioned for him to answer. "Remember," she whispered, "that scared and innocent don't always go together."

He disagreed with Avery, but a glance through the peephole assured him of one thing. Jayna might be scared, but she was also angry. Her brow knit between her eyebrows, and her lips puckered together in a determined line.

With a deep breath, he cracked open the door and offered a tight smile of his own. "Come in?"

Her dark brown eyes gazed hard at him before she stepped past him. "I brought your tea, Amber."

Amber motioned toward the couch, but Jayna shook her head. "I can't stay long, but I need to know who you really are." She turned her head to stare at him again. "And what you're doing here."

Liam locked the door and then moved to lean against the desk by Amber. "Remember how I told you I was a cop?" It had been simpler than telling her he was a private investigator.

Jayna crossed her arms. "Yeah, but most cops don't disguise themselves and show up with pregnant girlfriends at my fiancé's resort."

She might as well have gut punched him. "What? Who's pregnant? And I thought you broke up with Mario?"

Jayna's jaw clenched. "You don't know your own girlfriend is pregnant? Then what business do you have asking about my relationship status?"

"Whoa, time out." Avery jumped to her feet and moved between them. "First things first. We want to know you're okay. From what you told me on the sunset cruise, you're scared. Maybe we can help."

His gut twisted. "Are you being held against your will?"

As she opened her mouth to respond, his cell phone vibrated on the desk behind him. Jayna's gaze darted to the screen. "Reef? Why is he calling you?"

Liam glanced at the caller ID. "I don't know."

Jayna took a step backward. "Is he a cop too? Are none of you who you said you were?"

He poised his finger to cancel the call. It could wait. "No, Reef's just Reef. He's my friend, not a cop."

She crossed her arms. "Then take it."

From her seat, Avery shrugged, and he slid his thumb to accept the call. "Hey, man, you'll never guess what Jake called to tell me." Reef spoke fast, skipping any introduction.

"What's up? And who's Jake?" Liam held the phone to his ear, though Jayna could probably hear every word.

"Oh, sorry, Jake is Sam's and my assistant. Anyway, he was diving with his last scallop group and came upon some crab traps, even though it's off season. The odd part is that there was a piece of fabric caught in one of the traps. Does a purple, green, and black wrapping mean anything to you?"

Jayna took another two steps toward the door, and her eyes narrowed. "You said he was just your friend. Sounds like he's making a report."

"Hold on a sec, Reef." Liam set the phone down on the desk. "He is my friend. He was just—"

She held up one hand and reached for the door knob with the other. "You know what? Never mind. You're as big a liar as Mario. I was a fool to think you were different."

Avery rose from her chair. "Wait, Jayna—"

"Hope you like your tea." Jayna jerked the door open. "Whatever weird business you have going on here, don't expect me to stick my neck out for you again." Then, she ran, leaving the door gaping wide.

While Avery rushed to close the door, Liam retrieved the phone. "Sorry, Reef. I'll call you back. Thanks for the call."

He squeezed the phone and resisted the urge to throw it at the wall.

"That went well." Avery massaged her neck and eyed the bathroom. "On the bright side, she doesn't know why we're here. We can still investigate, with caution."

"Yeah, but what if she tells Delgado about tonight–and why on earth did you tell her you were pregnant?"

Avery waved a hand. "I needed an excuse to fake being sick. I don't think she'll tell Mario about us, at least not right now. She doesn't know who to trust."

Her words stung. How could he help Jayna now?

174

Chapter Twenty-Eight

Jayna slammed the door to her room and threw herself onto her bed. Swiping away angry tears, she pummeled the closest pillow.

Nothing in this life was real. Everything she'd ever known was a sham.

Her successful modeling career? Scarred by abuse.

Every man in her life? A liar.

Her tears slid faster onto the pillow she now hugged to her chest. Knowing Liam and Reef were frauds hurt in a deep place. Maybe because they had claimed to be different, claimed to follow the God her sister had told her about.

If God was a sham, there was no hope for her.

Deep breaths.

Hyperventilating was not going to help her cause. She needed a level head more than ever now that she couldn't hope for any help from Amber.

She took another steadying breath.

No, that wasn't right. Hadn't Amber said she wanted to help her? If that was the case, what was she doing with Liam? Were they both undercover cops?

It couldn't be a coincidence that they arrived in Bimini shortly after she left Beech Mountain. Had Liam gone looking for her? Why the disguise?

She laugh-cried into the pillow. He looked ridiculous without his ginger hair and beard. Had he done that—for her?

Why had he stayed behind on the beach tonight, and how had he gotten locked out? Was he investigating Mario?

Are you being held against your will?

His words echoed in her memory. Did he care? Had she thrown away her one chance for help because she was upset that he had lied to her?

She rolled onto her back and groaned. She had too many questions and no answers, but none of them mattered. No one could save her from Mario.

Someone knocked on her door. "Jayna?"

Speak of the devil. No, Kevon was the devil. Mario was his underling.

"Just a minute." Jayna bolted from her bed and ran to the bathroom to splash her face free of tears.

When she answered the door, he helped himself inside and closed it behind him.

She didn't relish being alone with him, but his jittery movements indicated he wouldn't be staying. "Everything okay?"

He kissed her cheek. "It will be. Something came up. I'm going to be out late but wanted to make sure you made it to your room okay and that our guest is safely in her room."

Jayna fidgeted with her hair. "Yes, she's resting now."

"Good." He turned toward the door. "I'll see you in the morning."

"Wait." She hesitated. If he would tell her what was going on, could she help Amber and Liam—or somehow help herself? But would leading Mario on have dangerous consequences?

She pulled a pouty lip. "Where do you have to run off to tonight?"

Mario's eyes lit up. He strode back toward her and wrapped her in his arms. "You miss me?"

Instead of answering, she tugged his head down and brushed his lips with hers. "You were such a great host tonight," she whispered.

He kissed her harder as if he might devour her. Then he backed her onto the bed.

Panic rushed through her, even while her body urged her to give in to desire. This wasn't what she wanted. She wanted information.

She pulled back and sucked a deep breath. "What's so important that you can't stay?"

Please don't stay. God, please don't let him stay. I'm not strong enough to stop.

176

Mario's lips traced down her neck, but he jerked away when his phone vibrated.

"Stupid *Sapona*." He released her and plunged a hand inside his pocket.

"*Sapona*?" She sat up. "Another night dive?"

He nibbled her ear. "Nothing for you to worry about. I'd rather stay with you."

If she kissed him back, she'd completely lose herself, and he'd forget all about the *Sapona* shipwreck dive.

"Then can I come? I've never done a night dive."

Mario shook his head and pushed himself off the bed. "No, love, it's not that kind of excursion. The good news is we won't have to worry about Kevon after Sunday, at least for a while. Then, you and I will never be parted again."

He blew her a kiss and then let himself out.

Jayna collapsed onto her pillow, her body trembling. That was too close, and now, Mario thought she wanted him.

Her body did. Her heart didn't.

At least he'd left. She was safe, for now.

Had God heard her prayer?

"If You are there, thank You," she mumbled into her pillow. "I could sure use some guidance for what I'm supposed to do next."

The room remained silent.

Maybe not all of God's answers were audible.

When Jayna woke up, her mouth was dry, her hair was in her face, and she was still wearing her dress from the night before. At least she'd slept uninterrupted.

Tumbling off the bed, she made quick work of showering and changing into a comfortable maxi dress. After tying her damp hair into a braid, she slipped into some flip flops and padded toward the dining area.

For almost ten in the morning, it was surprisingly empty. Most of the guests had been on the sunset cruise and were probably sporting hangovers this morning.

The usually sun-streaked glass windows were coated in rain, and Bimini's blue skies seemed to be on vacation. Did that mean Mario's activities today would be canceled? If he had nothing else to do, he might be knocking on her door again soon. Her stomach knotted at the thought.

To her relief, her fiancé wasn't in the dining area, but William was. He offered to make her a custom omelet, but his tone lacked its usual levity, and he seemed to search her face as if looking for something.

Perhaps it was her imagination, or perhaps he suspected her deceit last night. She had never imagined kind William being involved with Kevon—but now she couldn't be too careful around him.

She spun toward the coffee station, grateful for a steaming pot. The liquid warmed her mug and helped calm the shiver racing across her skin. Gripping her mug, she settled into an arm chair while she waited for the omelet she would take back to her room. There was no need to stare out drizzle-coated windows for a view today.

It would be a good day for writing, if her thoughts weren't so tied up with a particular ginger who was impersonating a brunette.

As if Liam could read her thoughts, he appeared at the entrance to the dining room. He wore cargo shorts and a gold-colored shirt with a blue crab centered on it. Below were the words, "Got the blues."

She dipped her nose into her mug to hide a nervous chuckle. She couldn't decide what was funnier–his awkward fashion sense or the fact that his dyed hair made him look more like a ghost than ever.

The fluttering in her stomach caught her off guard. She chanced a second glance, and now, his blue eyes settled on her.

Those eyes. They were piercing but kind, sad but determined. Her breath hitched, and she willed herself to look away.

"Your omelet, Miss Jayna."

She jumped as William placed her plate on the end table beside her.

"Th-thank you," she said, trying to ignore Liam who had claimed the chair adjacent to hers.

William's eyes darted between the two of them. She had to get back to her room before Liam said anything that might suggest they knew each other.

Thunder boomed in the distance, and she hoped it masked the hammering of her own heart. Liam seemed oblivious to the danger and ordered something for breakfast. William disappeared once more to fulfill it, but he wouldn't be gone long.

"Guess even paradise has its off days." Liam's voice pulled her attention to him like a fly to sugar water.

"Yes." He was staring at her with those eyes again. Could he see her black soul?

Liam took a sip of his orange juice and then leaned forward. "How are you?"

She bristled. There were a million ways to answer that question. She bit into her omelet and swallowed. "I don't like surprises."

"Ouch, guess I deserved that one." He rubbed his naked chin. Did he miss his beard as much as she did?

Focus, girl. You don't even find vanilla men attractive.

But she did. Now, apparently. White chicken skin and all, the man beside her had gotten under her skin and somehow breached the boundaries around her heart with his genuine smile and seemingly sincere concern for her.

What was wrong with her? He owed her an explanation—and the truth.

"Are you going on the excursion tomorrow?" she blurted. Maybe they could talk there—where there would be enough other noise to cancel out listening ears.

"Are you?"

"Mario has asked me to accompany him on all guest excursions this week."

He glanced around as two other couples entered the dining area. "Where can I sign up?"

"Front desk." She rose, careful not to spill her mug. William would be back any minute.

179

"Will you let me talk to you if I do?" His eyes searched her face. Was that regret or worry she read in his expression?

"Yes." Somehow, she'd find a moment away from Mario. Despite what she'd said last night, she did want to know what Liam was doing here, but she couldn't let Mario find out.

Liam raised his orange juice glass toward her. "Tomorrow then."

Chapter Twenty-Nine

The next morning, the resort's catamaran moored offshore the stretch of beach that Delgado introduced as Honeymoon Harbor. The water was pristine and the purest shade of blue but paled in beauty next to the woman who hung on their host's arm.

Liam fidgeted with his GoPro wrist mount and snapped a picture. Maybe he'd run Delgado's image through the system again and try for matches. Or maybe he'd torture himself thinking about Jayna. She was more than just a lovely face. She was intelligent. She was big-hearted. If she cared only for herself, she wouldn't have come back with Delgado. No, she must be trying to protect her family.

Avery nudged him and passed him a snorkel mask. "Stop staring. If she said she'll find you, she'll find you."

Maybe. Or maybe he was all wrong about Jayna. She looked at home tucked into Delgado's side.

He looked away. This case was not putting him in a good headspace. Yesterday had been a wash with the weather, and he and Avery needed a lead. They hadn't seen Delgado at the resort yesterday, which either meant he'd been busy helping Kevon with a shipment or—

No, he refused to think he'd been wrapped up in Jayna's arms. The way he looked at her now was enough to make Liam gag. The man was obsessed with Jayna.

If only he could blame him.

"C'mon, let's snorkel." Avery dove off the boat's edge and into the sparkling waters. He followed her lead and immersed into an underwater world where the visibility below the surface was as clear as above.

Smooth white sand blanketed the bottom. Avery tapped his shoulder and pointed about ten feet ahead where a stingray hovered above the ocean floor. Their presence didn't bother the creature who swam past them moments later.

A flash of red to his right drew Liam's attention. Jayna dove in behind them and now made her way toward the shallow waters near the shoreline. A few guests already sat in the sand, feeding the stingrays.

He pointed toward shore and followed Jayna's lead. She had promised to talk with him, and now might be his chance. So far, he hadn't spotted Delgado in the water. Perhaps he had to stay on board the catamaran.

Avery stood and then froze in the shallow water. "There's one right next to me."

"They're harmless as long as you don't step on them," Jayna called to her. "Come join me, and you can feed them."

Liam choked down a laugh at Avery's discomfort. His boss was the most fearless woman he knew. It was refreshing to find something that made her squirm a little.

Jayna settled onto the sandy bottom in about five inches of water. Her back was to the catamaran where Delgado hung with his legs dangling off the side of the craft. An older couple chatted with him, but his gaze drifted their way.

At least with Avery here, Delgado might not suspect him.

Avery stiffly shuffled next to Jayna, and he chose a spot across from her where he could keep tabs on Delgado.

"Aren't they magical?" Jayna grabbed some chum from a bag tied to her wrist and placed her hand below the surface as a stingray swam toward the food.

Avery grimaced. "Not sure I'd call them magical."

"But they're so graceful, and they only hurt people who hurt them. People hurt each other for no reason." Jayna's gaze remained focused on the stingrays swimming around her.

"It doesn't have to be that way," Avery said. "People can help each other."

"In a perfect world, I suppose."

Liam kept his head low, as if studying the ocean life, but fixed his focus on Jayna's features. She seemed relaxed, yet this was hardly the conversation he expected to have with her today.

"Did you enjoy your time in North Carolina?" he asked.

Jayna jerked to look at him, and the stingray next to her swam off. "I did."

"We were worried when you left."

"I texted Kaley."

He sighed. At this rate, they could play a game of twenty questions, and he still wouldn't be any closer to answers. Jayna either did or didn't want to tell him what was really going on here. "Do you want to tell us why you came back here?"

Jayna glanced at him with her rich, dark, sad eyes. "I was told it would be safer for my family."

Avery shifted in the sand beside her as another large ray approached. "You must have found something on your first trip that wasn't a souvenir."

Jayna arched an eyebrow. "Something like that."

"Anything you want to show us?"

Liam frowned. Avery was pushing hard. Would she scare Jayna off like the last ray that had tried to swim toward her?

But Jayna only pulled another piece of chum from her bag and tossed it near Avery. "There's nothing left to show." She lowered her voice and tapped the bag on her wrist. "What I found probably chummed a lot of water."

A body.

Liam whispered a silent prayer. "Dear God, please don't let her become another casualty. Show her that she can trust us and show us how to help her."

Two of the rays competed for the last piece Jayna had flung in the water, their wings flapping against each other.

Liam glanced from her to Avery whose jaw was tight—and maybe not just because of the closeness of the rays. "Let us help you, Jayna. We have connections."

Help. Jayna wanted it more than they could ever know, but was it even an option for her? She lowered her voice and nodded toward the catamaran behind them. "And you think he doesn't have connections too?"

Avery frowned. "Protecting people is our job. Tell us how we can help."

"By being honest with me."

"Jayna." Liam's tone was kind, probably kinder than she deserved. Still, she deserved the truth too.

"Sometimes, the people who care about you care so much that they don't tell you everything," Liam said. "You know my job is to uphold the law and protect people like you. Let me do that, and one day, maybe I can explain more."

My job is to uphold the law. Her heart thudded to her flippered feet. She was only a job to him. Why did that disappoint her so?

But what did it matter if he were offering to help her out of the mess that she had created for herself?

She would tell them, everything she knew. Swallowing hard, she took a deep breath. "Okay, Mario is—"

As if he could read her thoughts, Mario shouted from somewhere behind her. "Jayna!"

Her face flamed. Did he suspect her? She shoved off against the sand. "We've talked too long. I don't want to see you get hurt."

"Wait—" Liam whispered.

"I'll be on tomorrow's excursion as well." Maybe she could find a quiet moment to talk with them some more?

Unlikely.

Jayna swam back to the deeper water. She had made her choice to trust Liam and Amber too late. Now, she couldn't risk getting them killed because of her.

Liam tossed and turned most of the night. What did Jayna know? What could she tell them? The next morning brought no relief to the questions nagging his mind. But maybe the excursion today would change that.

"I still don't think you should go." Avery towel dried her hair while skimming her e-mails. The woman was nothing if not a multitasker.

"We have no other leads." Liam tossed sunblock and a towel in his dry bag. "Jayna is the only possible clue we have."

"And she's a wildcard." Avery frowned. "She disappeared after the excursion yesterday. If she wanted our help, she could make a way to talk to us. I wanted to believe she was innocent, but now, I'm not so sure."

"She said she doesn't want to see us get hurt. Maybe she's protecting us."

Avery wadded up her hair towel and tossed it in a corner. "Nonsense. She knows you're a cop and has to suspect I'm more than your girlfriend. At this point, there is only help us or not help us. Avoiding us falls into the second category."

Liam added his snorkel to the bag. "She invited us to the excursion today. I have to find out why."

"If she's working for Delgado, you could play right into a trap. I think you'd be better off going through these financials with me." She tapped her laptop screen. "If I can find the money trail, we can bring Delgado in for questioning."

He grabbed the strap on his dry bag and headed toward the door. "You don't need me looking over your shoulder. We're better off dividing and conquering. We've only got two more days before we go home—and Jayna disappears for good."

"Fine, but don't be a hero. Stay with the other guests if something feels off. I doubt Delgado is willing to risk the reputation of his resort."

"Roger that." After closing the door behind him, Liam strode down the hallway and out the side entrance for the beach. A few other guests were already milling around the beachfront where Delgado's catamaran moored offshore.

A tender pulled up to the shoreline, and Kevon Rolles uncurled his muscular, lean frame and jumped out to offer a woman a hand.

Liam's blood heated. What was Rolles doing here? He'd never interacted with guests this way before.

Avery's warning rang in his ears, but he shoved it aside. If Jayna wanted to tell him something, she would find a way.

A retired couple remained on the beach, and he struck up a conversation with them. He had written off Jayna as already being on board the catamaran when she appeared in his peripheral.

She'd just left the resort's large patio and started toward him, her short black coverup blowing in the breeze. In one hand, she clutched a small bag, and in the other, a canteen.

He shifted his gaze back to the tender, which was already returning for him and the couple. Once again, Rolles hopped out and offered the wife a hand, but his focus was beyond them on the lovely woman who was approaching.

"What's your favorite dive so far?" the man asked Liam. "Everyone keeps talking about the *Sapona*."

"I haven't done that one yet either, but I'd like to," Liam said.

The man's fuzzy eyebrows shot up. "That's the shipwreck, right? Did you know that back in the 1920s, it was used to store Prohibition liquor?"

The wife rolled her eyes. "Honey, not everyone cares about history the way you do."

The fuzzy eyebrows scrunched. "History is better than those docudramas you watch. But whatever. I also read that a group of divers found a solo diver dead at the *Sapona* last month. Poor guy must have gotten trapped and run out of air. Is that more your speed, dear?"

The woman glared at her husband, moved to the seat across from them, turned her back, and started scrolling on her phone.

The man sighed and muttered to Liam. "Sorry, but when you've been married thirty years, you know each other's buttons. And sometimes, you make the poor choice and push them."

Liam patted the man's shoulder. "Well, thirty years is an accomplishment. Truth is, I should have done more research before my trip. What do you know about today's dive at the Bimini Road? Is it really the lost location of Atlantis?"

The man perked up and rattled off all the theories he'd read, but Liam was only half listening. Jayna had reached the tender, and Rolles whispered something to her. She jerked away and splashed toward the side of the tender, stepping over the side without his help.

Liam jumped to his feet and extended a hand. "Here, let me help you."

Jayna's round eyes seemed full of fear. She shook her head and claimed a seat next to the man's wife.

Rolles scowled and started the engine.

What the man was doing on this excursion made him pause. Delgado worked for Rolles, not the other way around. Right?

When they reached the catamaran, about a dozen other guests were settling in for the cruise. Jayna beelined for Delgado, and Liam settled onto an empty seat. If she didn't plan to talk to him, this trip would be a waste of taxpayer dollars.

Not that he wouldn't enjoy the chance to snorkel, but he'd rather go exploring on his own time with his friends. Reef would dig a dive like this one.

He had called his friend back after Jayna's accusation the other night, and he'd connected Reef with his partner Drew. Sure enough, the torn brick Jake had found matched the others. If their suspicions were correct, Big Eddie's network was selling hard and fast right now, using natural covers.

Florida was in its peak scalloping season, where boaters took to the water like shoppers to a mall. Sometimes, the boats were so thick they nearly formed their own island. The Fish and Wildlife Conservation agents were stretched thin keeping tabs on the regular problems like wake zone violations, expired registrations, and disorderly conduct.

It would be too easy to miss a convenient handoff between boats that were parked nearly on top of each other.

His gaze flitted toward Rolles who was securing the tender. Using organic covers for tradeoffs was brilliant. Was that why the man was here today? Were they going to use an excursion for a cover?

Rolles took over the wheel, freeing up Delgado to address the guests. "It's a beautiful morning to snorkel at the Bimini Road, which is only about half a mile offshore. Since it won't take us long to get there, I want to make sure everyone has their gear and safety instructions before we get to the location."

Jayna moved into an empty seat two spots over from him but

didn't even glance his way. Her eyes seemed glued to Delgado, but she sat rigidly straight.

"First, safety." Delgado motioned to four large bins. He opened the first one and pulled out a mask and snorkel. "When we arrive, you will each take a mask and snorkel. We've already sprayed the masks with an antifog, but if your mask fogs up, don't panic. Simply come back to the boat, and we'll spray it again. Your mask should fit tightly and snugly, and ladies, try to keep your hair tied back so you don't mess with the seal."

He placed the snorkel mask back in the bin and retrieved a bright yellow vest from the next bin. "This is a snorkel vest. Regardless of how good a swimmer you are, everyone must wear one. You can inflate and deflate the vest with the valve here. You simply press down on the valve to deflate and blow into it to inflate. Make sense?"

As Delgado moved on to explain how to adjust the fins for sizing, two men toward the back of the catamaran caught Liam's attention. They were hauling what looked like scuba gear bags. But he had asked if scuba rentals were an option for this dive and had been told no.

So what was in the bags?

"… rock formations are eighteen feet below the surface," Delgado was saying. "It's possible with free diving, but don't feel like you have to go all the way down. The visibility is clear, and you might even see a dolphin or two. Relax, enjoy the water, take pictures on your underwater cameras, and then come back to the boat anytime you get tired. Understand?"

A woman in a red rash guard raised her hand. "Is it true that the Bimini Road is part of the lost city of Atlantis?"

Delgado flashed a tour-guide worthy smile. "It depends who you ask. We like to think so. You tell me what you think at the end of the day."

From the captain's seat, Rolles tapped his wrist as if reminding Delgado of the time.

Their host cleared his throat. "One more thing. A film crew has asked to join us today for a videography project. If you see anyone in the water with bags and equipment, give them space to work. Also, there may be a few other boats on the site, so make sure you stay close to ours. That's it for now. Hold on to your hats 'til we get there."

Liam looked back to where the alleged film crew secured a last duffle-sized bag. So far, he had yet to see an actual video camera. One of the men had a GoPro strapped to his forehead, but that hardly qualified as a video crew. Liam wouldn't even consider himself an amateur photographer, and he had his own GoPro. Almost every diver did.

Delgado waved toward Rolles, who began accelerating. The catamaran generated its own breeze, and a woman to his left lost her straw hat to the sea.

Liam tightened his GoPro wrist strap and secured the camera onto the mount. His gut told him the videography crew was a sham, and he planned to get some footage of his own to prove what was really going down today.

Chapter Thirty

She should never have suggested that Liam join the excursion today. With her shades drawn over her eyes, Jayna glanced to where Mario had gone to the back to check on "the videography crew."

Right, the crew that owned as much video equipment as an amateur photographer. Some of it probably didn't even work, and no one would care if it didn't. They weren't here to record a documentary on an alleged Atlantis location.

Mario had only told her about the transaction during their hasty breakfast together. In one sense, she was relieved he had been too busy to spend any time with her the last two days. On the other, she knew he wasn't telling her what had kept him so busy all of Wednesday and most of Thursday. Other than the excursion to Honeymoon Harbor yesterday, she'd seen next to nothing of him.

"What about the guests?" She had nearly choked on her breakfast banana. "What if they get in the way of the—exchange?"

"They won't." He had pecked her cheek. "You can help me keep an eye on everyone and make sure they don't get too close to the other boat. And make sure you don't get too close to anyone either."

She had frowned. "I wouldn't dream of going near the exchange."

"Not the exchange. Kevon suspects someone at the resort—whoever was behind that surf fishing stint. Keep your eyes open. But I'm sure everything will be fine. I gotta go get the catamaran ready. See you soon."

Now, as she scanned the faces of the unsuspecting guests, she hoped he was right. Kevon and his men might look casual enough in their hibiscus resort shirts, but they had no social skills.

Moments earlier, a guest who had asked about their equipment met with a gruff bark and was told to find a seat. She didn't want to imagine what might happen if someone actually got in their way.

Her gaze settled on Liam who was busy fastening a GoPro on his wrist. If he were investigating Mario, he would be outnumbered today. Where was Avery? She would have to find a way to warn him without giving Mario a reason to think she was flirting with a guest.

As the catamaran slowed to a stop, she had an idea. Jumping to her feet, she moved to the edge of the swim platform where guests would be entering the water. There, she could offer pointers to anyone who had gear trouble, help guests with questions, and position herself so Liam would have to get close to her.

She waved at Mario who was distributing gear, and he gave her a thumb's up. Perfect. He thought she was helping him.

"How do I get in the water with these fins?" A woman gripped the railing next to her. "I can't walk down the ladder."

"Take a giant stride," Jayna said. "Make sure the person in front of you has cleared the water, then look at the horizon, and take a big step."

"What about my mask?"

"Go ahead and put it on now. Hold it in place so it doesn't dislodge when you hit the water."

"That's good advice." Liam appeared from behind her. "I've been diving a lot of years, and the giant stride entry is a solid approach."

The woman still looked unconvinced. "You go first then."

Jayna's stomach knotted. She couldn't whisper to Liam with the woman right here. "Tell you what," she said. "He can go first, then you, and I'll be right behind you. Okay?"

Liam offered a small smile, and she hoped that meant he would wait for her to get in the water.

Jayna hurried back to her seat where she deposited her hat, sunglasses, and coverup. Then, grateful that Mario was talking with another guest, she helped herself to a snorkel, vest, and fins and hurried back to the swim platform where Liam was perched on the edge.

"Do what I do." He tugged his mask in place, pressed one hand against it, and then, with his fin pointed slightly upward, stepped off. He landed vertically in the water and gave the woman a thumb's up.

"Well, that looks easy," she muttered. Though slightly off balance, she entered the water successfully as well.

Jayna tightened down her fins and pulled on her vest and mask. Without looking back to see if Mario were watching, she stepped off the platform.

The turquoise water was the perfect temperature against her skin, warm but just cool enough to be refreshing.

"It's right below us." The woman gasped and then stuck her head back under the water.

Now was Jayna's chance. She turned toward Liam. "Listen, Liam, you've got to be careful. There's an exchange happening today, and I think Kevon suspects you. Stay with the other guests, and you'll be safe."

He removed his mask and spit into it. She wrinkled her nose. What was that supposed to mean?

"Poor man's antifog." He rubbed his spit in the mask. "And thanks for the warning, but safety isn't part of my job description. I would like to make sure you're safe though."

His eyes seemed even bluer offset against the tropical waters, and she removed the snorkel from her mouth to suck a full breath. "You can't help me if you're dead."

He grinned. "Then I'll plan to stay undead. What can you tell me?"

Jayna hesitated. She still wanted answers from Liam—and the truth about him and Avery. But there was no time for that now. She either had to help him or not.

She swallowed. "I don't know much, only that the videography crew is a cover for Kevon's exchange. There's supposed to be another boat—"

The woman surfaced a few feet away. "Are you guys coming or not? This is so cool."

"Right behind you." Jayna waved before the woman dived again.

But Liam was looking the opposite direction. "Another boat like that one?"

Jayna swung her head around. Sure enough, a small craft hovered over the dive site and raised its dive flag as well. The videography crew had just entered the water from the swim platform, each man holding his gear and accompanied by a floating, black bag.

Kevon and the two other men were swimming straight for the other boat.

"Forget them. Come explore the Bimini Road with me." She adjusted her mask and then plunged in for her own look.

The sight awaiting her did look too intentional to be a natural formation, though many people believed that it was. Massive blocks, spaced tightly together, formed what resembled a sunken road. It continued out of sight.

Her imagination started to spin. Where did it lead? What more was there for her to see?

What did Liam think of it all? She turned, expecting to find him behind her, but when the bubbles from kicking her fins cleared, the space around her proved empty.

Surfacing, she pulled off her mask and scanned the water. Several hi-vis yellow vests belonging to other excursion guests dotted the nearby water.

But one vest had separated from the others and was making a beeline toward the adjacent boat.

No, Liam! Why hadn't he listened to her?

Her heart rate doubled. She should never have told him about the other craft. If anything happened to him—

She changed direction and propelled herself toward the boat as well. She would have to make sure nothing did.

He needed a plan. Preferably, one that didn't get him killed.

Liam chanced a sideways look at the boat while keeping most of his face submerged in the water. He hated the bright yellow vest that prevented subtlety, and yet, the vest was his best cover.

The "videography" crew had swum to the yacht's stern, probably to unload their bags using the swim platform, and he angled himself toward the bow. Perhaps he would get lucky and overhear the conversation. In the meantime, he raised his wrist and snapped a few pictures of the yacht with the faded name *Weekend Warrior* on the side.

Judging by its modest size and signs of wear, the exchange today would be on the smaller side. If he had to guess, some tourists with cash wanted a good time. The expansive waters of the Bahamas made the perfect place for tradeoffs among both tourists and cartels. Today's buyers seemed more like the small fries.

Someone had set several rods and reels, and he frowned. There was no reef below them, only the rectangular rocks forming the Bimini Road. He hadn't spotted any fish yet. This place was a busy dive site, not ideal for fishing, so maybe the rods were for show.

He hugged the hull near the bow of the boat and held his breath as footsteps announced the crew was onboard. Small tradeoff or not, he was taking a risk with no backup. Muffled voices echoed within earshot.

"You got the cash?"

"You got the kilos?"

"Yeah."

"Per our agreement."

Bubbles appeared in the water to his right, and he flattened himself about the hull. Was there a diver in the water?

A snorkel and mask appeared right in front of him.

Jayna.

"What are you doing here?" he whispered.

"Trying to keep you from getting yourself killed."

"I'm doing fine, but you could give me away." Though as he spoke, he realized she'd shed her snorkel vest before joining him. Her black one piece was much more discreet than the blazing vest on his chest.

Though there was nothing truly discreet about this brave woman.

She grabbed his hand. "We need to get out of here. Please."

194

He nodded and tightened his mask. He'd overheard enough, and no amount of evidence was worth risking her safety.

As they descended below the yacht, Jayna came to a jerking stop, and her mask muffled her cry underwater.

She struggled against something that was tugging at her.

Oh no. A hook had caught her swimsuit. Those stupid reels!

He motioned for her not to resist. The moment someone on board detected the rod tug, they would start investigating.

Holding his breath, he reached her and focused on removing the hook. Though his lungs burned, he didn't dare risk surfacing and being seen.

There, she was free. But with his waning oxygen, he had failed to toss the hook far enough away from him. Now, it snagged his vest.

A yank on the rod warned him that he no longer had the element of surprise.

Chapter Thirty-One

Dear God, no.

Whether she believed in God was iffy, but if He was real, He shouldn't be letting this happen.

The hook and line yanked Liam toward the side of the yacht where several men had now gathered.

In a split second, she made up her mind. She kicked her fins to surface and began waving her arms. "Stop! He's hurt."

Kevon's scowling face came into focus, but he grumbled to the man at the rod to stop reeling in the line.

Adrenaline surging through her, she finned toward Liam who had removed his mask and was gulping in fresh breaths. Fingers trembling, she reached for his vest and the hook that had already ripped a large gash.

"Just play along," she muttered and ripped it free.

Concern flashed in his eyes. "Are you all right?"

She'd forgotten all about the tear in her swimsuit and the cut which now burned with salt water. "It's minor. I'm fine."

Forcing an extra-large smile, she waved at the men onboard. "All clear. Thanks for your help."

"You said he was hurt." Kevon glared over the edge. He mumbled something to one of the other men and then waved her toward the swim platform. "Get up here. Both of you."

Her heart sank, but she nodded. "Thanks, it would be good to catch my breath."

Liam swam close beside her, and for a split second, he grabbed her hand and squeezed it. Was this his way of assuring her they would be okay?

It didn't work. The moment she reached the platform, one of Kevon's men grabbed her arm and pulled her aboard. She tripped over her fins and collided with the deck. Her forearms burned from the impact, but she pulled herself up to a sitting position.

"Hey, watch it!" Liam's voice called from behind her. "She could have hurt herself."

But another man grabbed him by the vest and dragged him onto the deck as well. Kevon stood over them both, arms crossed. "What are you doing here?"

Liam pulled off his mask and ran a hand through his hair. "I got turned around at the dive site and thought this was our boat. Then I saw that a woman had gotten caught on one of your lines and tried to help. I ended up hooking myself instead."

Kevon grunted. "You expect me to believe that?"

Jayna wobbled to her feet. The sooner she could get off this boat, the better. "The current is stronger than it looks. Your boat isn't far from Mario's. I'm sorry to bother you. I know you're busy with your *recording* project."

If looks could kill, she'd be dead. Kevon took a step toward her, and his breath came hot on her face. "Do you know this diver?"

She shook her head. Maybe too quickly. "No, but I've seen him and his girlfriend at our resort. They're tourists. It was an honest mistake."

Someone behind her cleared his throat. "I hate to interrupt, but we're on a schedule."

Kevon whirled to face the man. "Shut it. I call the shots."

Liam pushed himself to his feet and turned around in his fins so he could walk backward toward the swim platform. "Sorry to bother you, man. We'll get out of your way."

Kevon grabbed his wrist. "Nice GoPro."

"Uh, thanks." Liam tried to pull free, but Kevon didn't let go. Instead, he snapped off the wrist mount with the camera. "Bet you've got some nice shots on this."

Jayna held her breath. Why did Liam's face seem to pale?

He shrugged it off. "A few, maybe."

The camera beeped on, and Kevon pressed the screen. His body stiffened. "There's a picture of the boat."

Liam held up his hands. "What can I say? I'm not a great shot. I probably bumped the camera."

Kevon narrowed his eyes. "You spying on us?"

"No man, it's a new GoPro. My girlfriend got it for me before our trip, and I'm not very good with it yet."

"Is that so? Then why do you also have a picture of Delgado and her?" He thumbed toward Jayna.

Her face flamed. Liam had taken a picture of them? Why?

Even Liam seemed to blush. "Thanks for giving away my crush. Can't a man admire a beautiful woman?"

"Liar." Kevon squeezed the camera in his fist. "You don't have pictures of anything but the hottie, Delgado, and this boat. Who are you?"

"She told you. I'm staying at her resort."

"Who are you?"

Liam sighed. "Listen, I'm an actor, okay? If you need an extra for your videos, I could give you a hand. Maybe make up for wasting your time."

"We don't need a lousy extra." The Bahamian to Kevon's left pushed Liam closer to the platform. "Lose them, and let's get back to work."

"No, wait." Kevon reached for Liam and clutched his vest. "The extra wants some action. Let's give it to him." He yanked Liam backward. To avoid tripping in his fins, Liam toppled onto a seat.

Jayna's throat squeezed, but she managed to growl at Kevon. "Stop it."

Kevon whirled back toward her and clutched her arm. "Get out of here, princess. I'll deal with you later."

"He's our guest—"

"He's an extra, and he volunteered to help with our filming." Kevon's lips curled into a sneer.

She swallowed and yanked away, her arm smarting from his grip. "He'd better be back on our boat by the time we leave."

Jayna chanced one last look at Liam. He offered a thumb's up, but he wasn't fooling her. Leaving him was a betrayal.

Her heart squeezed, but what choice did she have? Taking a giant step, she reentered the water, leaving Liam to Kevon's mercy.

She already knew the man had none.

Her fins felt like dead weights as she swam for the catamaran. *Coward. You're a coward.*

One thought gave her hope. If Mario lost a resort guest, it would destroy his reputation. He could take the tender back for Liam before Kevon could do too much damage.

Adrenaline pumped new strength into her limbs, and she paddled faster. When she reached the swim ladder, she was gasping for breath.

"Darling, are you all right?" Mario appeared above her. His straw hat shadowed his face, but his voice seemed genuinely concerned.

She yanked off her fins and tossed them onto the platform. "No, I'm not."

"What's wrong?" He offered her a hand, and she accepted.

"It's Kevon. He's mistreating one of our guests." The solid platform now beneath her feet seemed to steady her pounding heart. "We've got to do something."

Mario placed an arm around her shoulder. "Whoa, back up. What happened?"

"I saw one of our guests swimming toward the other boat. Obviously, he was turned around, so I went to redirect him. But then I got caught on one of the boat's fishing lines, and when the man tried to help me, he got hooked instead. That's when Kevon reeled him in. He was shoving him around and making accusations. He didn't let him leave with me."

"A hook caught your suit?" Mario moved his hand from her shoulder to her waist. "Here?"

Jayna winced and pulled away. "It's just a scratch."

Concern—and something else—flitted across his face. "Then let's take you below deck so I can clean it."

She shrank against the closest seat. The last thing she wanted was to give Mario an excuse to strip off her swimsuit. "No—I'm fine. But our guest might not be. And if Kevon gets in one of his rages and hurts him, the reputation of our resort will be on the line."

"Our resort?" Mario leaned over her, a smile tugging at his

lips. "You made up your mind then?"

She gulped. Precious time was wasting, and all Mario wanted to do was make her agree to marry him?

"Of course, I'm not going anywhere." *At the moment.*

Mario kissed her softly on the lips. "That's the best news of the day. We'll take care of our guests, and then I'm going to take care of you, okay?"

She trembled at his meaning and hoped he didn't notice. "Okay."

"Now, let's see about that guest."

Jayna shoved off the seat and spun on the deck. "He's right over there—" But she stopped short. The space where the boat had been minutes before was empty. In the distance, a speeding craft faded from view.

"No," she whispered. "Kevon can't just kidnap Li—like that. We've got to stop him."

A frown crossed Mario's face, and he reached for a radio on his waist. "Get a head count on our other guests. I'll call Kevon."

She nodded and gripped the railing, willing her eyes to focus on the yellow vests bobbing in the surrounding water.

But her gaze wandered to the boat vanishing in the distance, and tears blurred her vision. This was all her fault. She should never have left Liam behind, and now, her gut told her she'd never see him again.

Chapter Thirty-Two

Mario glanced between the radio and the woman who seemed too distracted to get an accurate head count.

Jayna knew better than to annoy Kevon.

Maybe this was his own fault. He'd told her to help him keep an eye on the guests. Either way, he was responsible for their safety. Kevon had crossed a line.

"This is Catamaran, calling Riptide. Come in, Riptide."

Mario hadn't noticed the name of the boat Kevon had boarded, so using Kevon's own boat name seemed the best option.

There was no response.

He tried again. "This is Catamaran, calling Riptide. We have a missing guest. Over."

His lips twitched in anticipation. Kevon hated when he nagged him, but the man wasn't getting rid of him so easily today.

"This is Catamaran—"

"Shut it!" Kevon's growl rang through the speaker.

"Riptide, we're missing a guest. I hear you have him."

"Is that what your slut told you?" The sneer in Kevon's voice was unmistakable. "Did she also tell you they were both snooping around the boat?"

Snooping? Mario looked back at Jayna who must have finished her head count, because she had turned toward him.

He cleared his throat. "She said the guest was confused, and she went to help him. I don't like that she ended up with a hook in her side."

"She'll end up with more than that if she interferes again."

Mario ground his teeth. Jayna wasn't interfering—or was she? He studied her as she returned to his side. Her eyebrows knit together, and she opened her lips as if to ask a question, but he held up a hand.

He sighed into the radio. "Listen, return my guest, and you can get back to your business. I can't leave the dive site without him."

"No can do. Your guest needed—medical attention. I'll see that he gets it."

Jayna's hand flew to her mouth. Surely, she didn't have feelings for the man. No, she was just concerned for one of their guests.

She tugged on his rash guard and mouthed. "We've got to notify his girlfriend."

He nodded in relief. The man had a girlfriend, and Jayna was simply being concerned for this couple. "Where are you taking him? I'll meet you there and get him off your hands."

Kevon paused for only a moment. "There's only one place for nosy divers to find rest."

Mario caught his breath. Kevon couldn't be serious. His resort would never survive allegations of negligence if a guest was found dead on a dive site—especially when it was different than the one that he had last been seen on.

He slammed his thumb back into the press-to-talk button. "Say again? I need to notify his girlfriend. Are you taking him to the North Bimini Medical Clinic?"

Another long pause ensued. Surely, Kevon couldn't ignore a girlfriend. The man would be too easily missed.

The radio crackled. "Tell her that her boyfriend volunteered to be an extra on a documentary. We're going to film at a couple sites, so he'll be—late."

Jayna tugged on his sleeve again. "Kevon's a liar. What about medical attention?"

He patted Jayna's hand. "I'll ask. Is the girlfriend in our group today?"

"No. I haven't seen her. She's the pregnant guest I helped the other night, so maybe she isn't feeling well enough to dive."

Mario cocked his head. "You mean the one that joined our table at the dinner cruise?"

Jayna nodded. "She's pregnant, Mario. We can't let Kevon—"

Another guest appeared at the ladder and called out about

having dropped his mask. "Go help our guest. I'll handle this."

A flash of doubt crossed her features. Surely, she didn't doubt him, but her mention of the pregnant guest raised the hairs on his neck. That woman had acted strangely and been clingy with Jayna throughout the night. Did they know each other, or were they just instant friends? Who was this couple she had latched onto?

He'd detangle those questions later. "Come in, Riptide. What about medical treatment? The girlfriend will want to know."

A string of expletives rang out, and he muffled them in his shirt. Something had gotten Kevon riled, and it had to be more than this conversation.

When Kevon spoke again, his voice was so low Mario could barely make out the words. "Change the story. No medical treatment needed. He's filming with us. Out."

"Then when can his girlfriend expect him back at the resort?"

The silence answered for him.

The tender ride from the catamaran back to the beach seemed endless. Perhaps it was because Jayna had to listen to other guests gossiping about the "lucky" one who was picked to participate in the documentary. Perhaps it was because Mario kept sending searching glances her way. Perhaps it was because she could never forgive herself if Liam died.

If he wasn't already dead. Mario had made her swear to stick to the story about the documentary film, but she couldn't unhear what Kevon had said about the guest needing medical treatment.

Why would Kevon hurt him? Didn't he realize the liability a guest's body would be?

Her mind darted back to the last moments on the yacht. Kevon had been perusing Liam's pictures. That must have set him off. Maybe he suspected Liam was the undercover cop that he was.

The tender reached the shoreline, and she was the first to climb out.

"Jayna!" Mario's voice commanded her to answer him.

She splashed to drier sand and then spun back around. "Yes?"

"I'll take care of things, but it might be a late night."

Relief washed over her. A late night meant he would try to get Liam back. A late night meant he wouldn't have time to come to her room.

"Thanks, babe." She blew him a kiss for the benefit of the watching guests and then darted toward the resort.

"Everything okay, Miss Jayna?" William greeted her on the porch.

She slowed to a walk and tried to steady her heartrate. William had been in the hallway—with a gun—and she no longer knew if she could trust him. "Yes, I—I just really need to wash the salt from my hair."

William chuckled and opened the door for her. "Then don't let me detain you."

"Sorry—thanks." She was sorry for lying, but she wasn't about to tell him they'd lost a guest. After slipping past him, she hurried down the hallway. At least Amber's room was close to hers.

She thumped on the door and waited. What if Amber wasn't here? If she was, how could she tell Jayna that Liam had been kidnapped?

The door cracked open, and Amber appeared with her hair wrapped up in a towel. "Sorry, just got out of the shower. Everything okay?"

Jayna glanced down the hallway, which was still empty. "Can I come in?"

Amber's eyebrows rose. "Uh, sure. Did you get back from that excursion with—Oliver?"

"Yes—but he didn't come back."

Amber waved her inside and closed the door in one swift motion. "Where is he? Is he okay?"

Jayna collapsed onto the edge of the bed. "I don't know." She braced herself for an outburst, tears, something.

Instead, Amber dropped into the desk chair, flipped open her laptop, and spun to look at her. "Tell me what happened. From the beginning. As quickly as possible."

No pregnant woman's hormonal outburst? "Are you really his girlfriend?"

Amber tapped her fingers together. "Let's circle back to that later. Right now, I need to know what happened so I can get help."

"But I need to know if I can trust you," Jayna blurted. "Kevon would kill me if he knew I told you—and Mario wouldn't be happy either."

"Fine." Amber sighed. "I'm not pregnant, and I'm not his girlfriend. I'm his boss. We're undercover agents investigating a drug running operation and its mastermind we haven't been able to track."

"Amber, are you serious?"

"Yes, and my name isn't Amber, but for your own sake, keep calling me that."

Jayna's head whirled. Liam and Amber had better be good, because they didn't know what they were up against. For that matter, she didn't either, but underestimating Kevon was something she'd never do.

She took a deep breath. "Okay, I hope that—whoever you are—you can save him. Here's what happened."

As she replayed the day's events, Amber appeared to record the conversation on her phone while simultaneously typing on her laptop.

Jayna finished the story with a sigh. "Mario said he was going to take care of things, and I think he will try to help Liam if he can. But Kevon calls the shots, and Mario won't risk his own safety or jeopardize his payment."

"Kevon pays Mario—for what?"

"I guess for using his property." Jayna shuddered to think Mario might actually do dirty work for Kevon.

"Anything else?" Amber's voice was kind.

"I—I really don't know. I know Mario disappears sometimes, but he doesn't tell me anything about that. He did tell me that the money from these payments is going to help him—" Jayna paused. Did Amber need to know about his family situation? Mario might not be the man she wanted to marry, but he had tried to protect her from Kevon. He didn't deserve her ratting him out.

"Help him with what?" Amber said.

"Help him with some family affairs."

Amber frowned. "Interesting. We can revisit Mario more later, but where do you think Kevon might take Liam?"

Jayna closed her eyes, trying to remember what she'd overheard of Mario's radio call to Kevon. "I overheard Kevon on the radio. He said Liam needed medical help but then changed his story."

"That Liam had volunteered to be an extra on the documentary they were filming?"

"Right, total rubbish," Jayna said. "He also said something about there being only one place for nosy divers to rest."

Amber stiffened. "Any idea where that might be?"

"I don't know for sure. But the other night, Mario said something about the *Sapona* being the reason he had to leave. It's a popular dive spot. Maybe they use it as a meet-up."

"It's a start. Where can I rent a boat around here?"

If only it was that easy. "I mean, you could call around to see who has excursions to the *Sapona*, but chances are, the earliest you could book would be for tomorrow."

Amber's eyes darted back and forth as if running through possible options. "You came to Bimini by boat with Mario and Kevon, right?"

"Yes."

"How long was the ride from Miami?"

"Maybe two hours," Jayna said. "It felt longer though."

Amber nodded and then made a call. "Ugh, voicemail." She tried another number. Someone answered this time, and Amber rattled off the basic details of the situation.

But Jayna wasn't listening. Where was Liam right now? Could anyone get there in time? A conversation surfaced in her memory. She had been in Beech Mountain in the kitchen and had overheard Reef and Kaley who were sitting outside. They'd said something about a boat show in Miami this weekend to pick up a new craft.

Amber ended her call and turned toward her. "Okay, my team is contacting our Coast Guard and the Royal Bahamas Defense Force. Hopefully, they can cut through the red tape fast and coordinate a search."

"I think we'd have a better chance if—."

Amber's phone rang. "Sorry, I've got to take this."

Jayna rose. "I've got to get back before I'm missed. If I hear something from Mario, I'll let you know."

"Hold just a sec, please," Amber said into her phone. She grabbed the notepad on the desk and scribbled on it. "Here's my number. Let me know if you hear anything."

Jayna accepted the paper, let herself out, and scurried to the privacy of her room. There was someone she needed to call.

Chapter Thirty-Three

Jayna's thumb hovered above the phone icon next to Kaley's name. She hadn't answered any of Kaley's texts or calls since returning to Bimini. Would her new friend even want to talk to her now—let alone agree to her crazy idea?

Yes, it was crazy, but Amber's suggestion to leave Liam's search and rescue to the Coast Guard didn't sit well with her. Kevon was smart. If he even suspected someone had notified officials, he'd disappear and Liam along with him.

Liam's best hope was Mario, but her fiancé wouldn't stick his neck out for a stranger. That left her—but she needed a boat.

She pressed dial and closed her eyes. Maybe Kaley wouldn't answer, and she'd forget about the whole idea.

Even so, she couldn't forget about Liam. He didn't deserve to be stuffed in a freezer like the last body she'd found.

"Jayna?" Kaley picked up on the fourth ring.

"Hey."

"Oh, my goodness, how are you?" Background voices made hearing Kaley difficult.

"I'm okay. Where are you?"

"We're loading up at the boat show. This place is a zoo, but Reef and Sam's new yacht for fishing excursions is gorgeous. You'll have to come out with us sometime."

"Thanks, but it's kind of about the boat that I'm calling. And about Liam."

A pause. "What do you mean?"

Jayna closed her eyes and sucked a deep breath. There was no easy way to have this conversation. "Is Reef there? Could you put me on speaker?"

Instead of answering, Kaley spoke away from the speaker. "Hey, babe, it's Jayna. She wants to talk to us both."

"Sam, can you drive?" Reef's voice echoed in the background. "I'm going to hop in the back with Kaley."

More muffled voices.

"Okay, we're here," Kaley said. "I put you on speaker."

"Hey, Jayna." Reef's voice held a smile. "What's up?"

"There's no easy way to say this, so I'm just going to say it." The words rushed out before she had time to process. "Liam is in trouble. He's investigating drug running around my fiancé's resort here in Bimini, and he got taken today."

"Got taken? What does that mean?" The smile vanished from Reef's voice.

Jayna pressed her eyes together to hold back her own tears. "I—let me tell you what I know."

When she finished, she held her breath. They probably hated her.

"What can we do?" It was Reef. His tone was calm, even kind.

"I—I know this is crazy, but I heard you say you'd be in Miami this weekend. It's only two hours to Bimini from there. Liam's girlfriend—or partner—or whatever she is—told me she'd contact the Coast Guard and RBDF, but I can't help but think a show of force will drive Kevon into hiding. Plus, she doesn't know how long it will take to cut through the red tape. It's already the afternoon, and the earliest I could book a rental would be tomorrow. I don't want to wait that long."

Liam doesn't have that long.

"Let me talk to Sam. We'd need to work out some details and drop Kaley off with Sam's Aunt—"

"Oh no, I'm going with you," Kaley said. "Liam came after me when I was in trouble. You're not leaving me behind."

"Kaley." Reef's voice was tight. "We're talking drug runners who make people disappear."

"Then you need all hands on deck."

Reef cleared his throat. "I'll call you back. Is this number good?"

"Yes, thanks. I'll cover the entry fee. I just—I need people I can trust."

The call disconnected, and she collapsed onto her bed. She couldn't trust Mario. He said he'd take care of things, but his choices always reflected his interests, not others.

Was she any different? She was using and perhaps endangering Liam's own friends, but she believed in them. They were different. Whether or not she agreed with all their ideas about God, they were genuine.

Minutes later, her phone buzzed.

"Yes?"

"We're coming," Reef said. "Sam has been to Bimini before for a fishing trip and knows the ropes. He said to ask if you're on the North Island or South Island?"

"North," Jayna said.

A pause.

"Perfect, that's where Sam went before. He said to meet us at the Big Game Club. I'll text you our ETA when we're in the water. Can you meet us there?"

"Yes." Even if she had to walk.

"We're praying for Liam—and you. I'll be in touch."

She blinked back the moisture forming behind her lashes. They were praying. Though God had no reason to listen to her, maybe he would listen to them.

"Hang in there, Liam," she whispered.

Something cool but hard pressed into his face. Liam blinked a few times, but the world was out of focus, and his lip felt as though it were bloated and about to explode.

Dirt crusted the faded lines of the surface that once perhaps had a pattern but had faded to yellow. Maybe it was linoleum. It didn't matter. He was on a floor that hadn't seen a mop in a good long while.

Now he picked up on the subtle rocking motion, and something pinched in his memory. He had been on the excursion. Jayna had been there. They'd gotten hooked and boarded the other boat.

Kevon had told Jayna to leave but made him stay. And then—
He moistened his cracked lip and flexed his jaw. Nothing felt
broken, but everything hurt. Whatever they had used to tie his feet
was cutting into his ankles, and his arms had gone numb from
being bound behind his back.

A flash. They had taken his picture—then interrogated him.
But why the picture? Did they have their own database? Or worse,
could they hack every agency's protected files?

He hadn't talked but hadn't tried to play tough. He'd cried.
He'd begged for them to let his girlfriend send money.

Rolles must not have bought his soft-boy tourist cover, but at
least he was alive. For now.

He craned his neck to glance around the musty interior. At
some point, they must have changed boats. This cabin was larger,
complete with a table and some bunk beds, but he had no sense of
how long he'd been unconscious or when they had ditched the
smaller boat.

"Where is he?" A man's voice filled the stale air. It tickled
something in his brain. Was that Delgado?

"You think you can just march onto my boat?"

Liam winced. Rolles. That man's fist was a hammer.

"Where is he? You think you can just steal one of my guests?"

Definitely Delgado. Liam might have his bones to pick with
the man, but at least he was standing up for him.

Heavy foot falls indicated Rolles had blocked Delgado's
path. "You can't go down there. Your guest is a spy."

"You're paranoid."

Rolles didn't respond right away. "What about this mug
shot?"

A pause. "Who's Liam Bracken? The hair is all wrong."

How did Rolles get my picture?

"The hair is dyed," Rolles said. "It's the same dude. He's a
narc."

Silence.

"This could still ruin my resort."

"I'll take care of the narc," Rolles said. "He won't be with us
for long."

"What do I tell his girlfriend?"

Liam's breath hitched. What was Avery thinking? Was she safe?

"My man found out the Coast Guard and RBDF are looking for him," Rolles said.

Delgado cursed. "Then we're ruined."

"No, my man deleted the advisory. The new word is the narc has gone dark on purpose. To investigate."

Liam groaned as he rolled on his bruised ribs. Great. Rolles had an insider somewhere. If the insider made his disappearance look like a false alarm, he would have to escape on his own.

Not easy when his hands and feet were tied.

"So then what? I don't tell the girlfriend anything? What happens when he doesn't show—permanently?"

"Not your problem. By then, the dish won't be at your resort, and you'll be on your honeymoon."

Jayna. She couldn't marry Mario. The man was a doormat for this dealer.

"I hope you're right," Delgado said.

"See that she goes with you. Otherwise, I'll knock her off too. She's too nosy."

"Leave Jayna out of this. She was trying to help."

Rolles snorted. "Yeah, help a narc."

Delgado hesitated. "She didn't know."

"You buy that? Just do your part and see she doesn't interfere."

Jayna must have tried to help him. Was that why Delgado was here? Had she talked him into this?

The sound of a small engine signaled Delgado's surrender and retreat. If Avery didn't realize her advisory had been canceled, she might be sitting tight. There was no one left to advocate for him.

Except Jayna.

His stomach churned and not only because breakfast felt like days ago. If Rolles suspected her, she might be in danger, and he was helpless to stop him.

Footfalls sounded on the steps, and he smelled the

Bahamian's cigarette before he saw him.

The man's dark, bare feet stopped inches from him, and Liam braced himself for a kick in the face or gut.

"I ought to kill you right now."

Liam nibbled on his tender lip. He wasn't in a position to antagonize the man.

"But unlucky for you, I won't."

Unlucky? How was that unlucky?

"C'mon, man, please." His whine sounded authentic, like the ones he'd heard dozens of times when apprehending a novice dealer who never thought he'd get caught. "You got the wrong guy."

"Shut it." Rolles' foot collided with his stomach, and Liam coughed in pain. "I know you're a narc, Bracken. Theatrics aren't going to save you."

Liam didn't have the breath to argue.

"You've got one chance." Rolles cackled and padded away.

Long shot this chance would amount to anything.

The fisherman paused at the steps leading to the deck and called over his shoulder. "Better hope you're part fish or can hold your breath."

Chapter Thirty-Four

Her palms slipped off the golf cart's steering wheel, revealing beads of sweat on the black rim. The late afternoon heat wasn't helping her nerves. Jayna wiped her hands on her swimsuit coverup and glanced toward the front entrance for the dozenth time.

Maybe Amber wouldn't come. She was probably busy making all her phone calls or whatever it was she had to do.

The resources of the Coast Guard and RBDF certainly made Jayna's plan seem like child's play.

Her phone read two minutes to six. Reef had texted to meet them at the Big Game Club at half past six, the time he estimated their fishing boat would take to clear customs. But on the chance the paperwork took less time, she would be early.

The front door slammed, and Amber skipped down the porch stairs toward her waiting golf cart. She wore black shorts, and her matching bikini peeked out from under a green tank top.

Jayna cleared her throat. "Didn't think you were coming."

Amber grabbed the frame and swung onto the passenger seat. "I came to talk you—and your friends—out of this."

Jayna jerked the gear shift to drive. This woman didn't understand who she was up against. "I'm not asking you to go. I'm telling you where you can find me."

"And I'm telling you to leave Liam in the capable hands that are searching for him."

The golf cart jolted forward, and Jayna eased off the touchy gas pedal. Or maybe the pedal was fine, and she was just annoyed.

"Listen, Jayna, I get that you're worried about Liam, but don't you have other problems you need to work out? Why don't you let me help you get off this island and get safely away from Mario? You'd like that, right?"

She swallowed. "You'd do that?"

"Yes, we can take this golf cart to the airport, and I can get you on the next flight. I can even work out protective services for you."

Could it be that easy? Could Amber give back her freedom? Jayna's instinct said to say yes, that no one would watch out for her if she didn't help herself.

Deep down, she knew that wasn't true. Her sister would do anything for her. Reef and Kaley, with their crazy faith and drop-everything-for-you attitude, had listened to her. They would do anything to help Liam.

Something told her they would do the same for her.

She couldn't leave until they found Liam—whatever that might look like.

Jayna cleared her throat. "That's really good of you, Amber, but Mario returned empty-handed. He said that Liam would be tied up with the documentary for a while."

Amber jerked left in her seat to face her. "He knows where Liam is?"

"Maybe. He wouldn't tell me. In fact, he told me that Kevon would handle the situation, and I should forget about it."

A grin lifted the corners of Amber's lips. "Is this afternoon's plan you forgetting about it?"

"Yep." Even though her heart hurt, her spirits lifted. She was doing something, what little she could. "Mario said he had a job with Kevon tonight, and in the past, he hinted it happens at the *Sapona*—another reason I think we might find Liam there. Anyway, I didn't want him to suspect anything, so I told him I'd like to take one of the golf carts into town to do some last-minute shopping for our honeymoon. He said that was a great idea."

Amber chuckled. "You might be undercover material yourself one day."

"Fat chance of that."

"Never know. We get back home when this is all over, and we can chat about your past, present, and future. You need a better gig than making resort owners fall in love with you."

Amber was right about that. But the idea of her being brave

215

like Amber and Liam seemed ridiculous. Still, it tickled the hope that maybe she did have a future that didn't involve being coerced into marrying someone she didn't love.

If her plan worked.

Jayna squeezed the golf cart among several others outside the Big Game Club. She hoped she'd be able to retrieve her gear and bag from Mario's resort at some point, but if not, she'd backed up all her work online and cleaned any personal details off her laptop.

Those were the least of her problems. As she and Amber strode down the walkway toward the Big Game Club's docks, her stomach somersaulted. Just ahead of her, Reef spoke with a customs officer.

What would he say to her? She deserved a lecture after her hasty departure from Beech Mountain. Plus, she was partly to blame for Liam's disappearance.

Maybe this was a bad idea. Maybe they would hate her.

The officer nodded to Reef, who gave him a thumb's up. Then, Kaley's fiancé stuffed a paper in his pocket and turned toward the dock, but paused midway. He must have seen them.

She offered a low wave. He cleared the space between them in seconds and greeted her with a side hug. "Jayna! We got here as fast as we could."

"Thanks for that. It means—everything."

He nodded and turned toward Amber. "Avery Reynolds? I didn't know you were here. Good to have some real muscle on our side."

Jayna frowned and glanced between Reef and Amber. "Avery? No, this is—"

Amber held up a hand. "No, I really am Avery. You can still call me Amber if you like. That's my undercover name."

Reef arched an eyebrow. "Well, you two can fill us in on the way. The others are waiting on the boat until I cleared customs, but we're all set now. Sam already has the coordinates plugged in the GPS for this *Sapona* you mentioned."

Amber—Avery—fell into step beside Reef while she trailed behind. "I'm sorry you made the trip all the way here, but as I was telling Jayna earlier, you need to leave the search and rescue to the professionals. My team has notified the Coast Guard and RBDF. If anyone has a chance of finding Liam, it's them—not some independent contractors, no offense intended."

"None taken." Reef pointed left. "We're moored on the D Dock, this way."

"Then you understand why we need to leave this to the professionals."

Reef scratched his neck. "Yes and no. Jayna said a large show of force will send the dealer into hiding. Is that right?" He looked at Jayna.

"Yes." Her voice sounded like a squeak to her own ears.

Avery sighed and reached for the phone stuck in her back pocket. "I get that you want to help. I respect that a lot, but I'll show you—"

A squeal cut Avery off midsentence. "Jayna!"

She jerked her head toward the voice and the woman jumping up and down and waving from a boat at the end of the dock. With one hand holding down her straw hat, Kaley called out, "Can I get off the boat now?"

Reef laughed and called back. "Yes, we're all clear with customs."

Jayna felt her face flush. How could Kaley be this excited to see her—after she disappeared the way she had?

She didn't have time to untangle that thought before her petite friend hopped onto the deck. A gust of wind blew Kaley's hat farther down the dock, leaving her bronze-blonde hair to hang loose in waves around her face. Kaley ignored the hat and raced toward her.

Jayna had no choice but to accept her bear hug. "It is so good to see you. How are you?"

"I'm okay." Jayna cleared her throat, suddenly tight. "Thanks for coming."

Kaley stepped back and then blinked. "Avery? Oh wow, I had no idea you were here."

217

Jayna retrieved Kaley's hat and passed it to her. How did everyone else seem to know who Avery was?

"Colbert, you're looking well." Avery pressed her lips into a thin line and frowned at Reef. "What were you thinking bringing her here? The men we're dealing with are ruthless. I've already got Jayna to watch out for."

Now what did *that* mean? If this were a beauty contest, Avery might as well include herself. Did the woman not realize how attractive she was, or did she simply think she could take care of herself?

She probably could, but even Avery was no match for Kevon's brute muscle.

Kaley reached for Reef's hand. "I wanted to help, and I promised Reef I'd stay on the boat. I learned all about how to captain her on our way over—though from the looks of this wind, I'll be getting some more practice in choppy seas."

Avery shook her head. "It doesn't matter. You all need to turn around and go back home—though you might want to wait for the storm to pass. This is no place for—"

A vibrating sound cut her off mid-sentence, and she glanced at the phone in her hand. "Excuse me." With that, Avery spun and walked away as she took the call.

Jayna tried to stuff her hands into her pockets—but her coverup didn't have pockets. Instead, she picked at the floral-printed fabric. "I'm sorry you came all this way for Avery to tell you to get lost."

Reef waved away her words. "Don't apologize. This is a free country. We're cleared to explore whatever waters we want. Avery can tell us to get lost, but she doesn't have to come with us."

"You mean—"

"We came to help Liam any way we can, and that's what we're going to do. A little wind and rain don't make any difference to us. Sam and I have seen much worse."

Jayna glanced at the graying clouds. Weather was one thing. Kevon was another.

Reef steadied Kaley as she climbed back into the yacht, and then he extended a hand to help Jayna as well. Hope surged in her chest as she boarded the "gently used" craft, named *Meridian*.

Reef rambled on about it being a thirty-five-foot center console fishing boat that would help them expand their deep-sea-fishing excursions, but all she really heard is that they cared so much about Liam that they would drop everything to come help him.

Kaley offered her a seat as Reef introduced Sam Winfrey, the third member of their party and his colleague at his water excursion company. The lanky captain wore a backward baseball cap on his sun-bleached head and seemed a man of few words.

Jayna sunk onto the tan leather bench seat and let her gaze drift toward Avery who paced on the dock. She must be on an important call.

Hope surged in her chest. Maybe someone had found Liam. Maybe they could all go home.

Home. What home? Her parents or sister would give her a place to stay, but she didn't really belong anywhere, a side effect of her travel blogging. In the past, the no-strings career seemed like freedom. Now, it reminded her of the one thing she craved—a place where she belonged.

"Looking at the maps, it's a few miles to the *Sapona* from our location," Reef said. "Do you think we need to wait for Reynolds? It doesn't sound like she wants to come."

"We should wait," Jayna said. "Maybe the call is about Liam. Or maybe she's right, and this search is too risky for us. But I can't help but think Liam needs us. If I were the one out there, he'd be searching for me."

A lump formed in her throat. Why Liam even noticed her made no sense. He had always been kind to her, been watching out for her. No man had ever done that before. They had always wanted something in return.

He had never treated her with anything but respect. Was it possible he liked her for being herself?

"Permission to board?" Avery called from the edge of the dock.

"Of course." Reef extended a hand to her, but she climbed aboard without any help.

219

Now, Avery stood squarely in the middle of the boat's deck. "I've got bad news. The search advisory for Liam has been discontinued."

We're too late. The thought came unbidden. *I'm too late.*

"No." Kaley's hand went to her mouth.

"It's not what you think," Avery hurried to continue. "No one has found his body, but this news isn't good either."

"I don't understand," Reef said.

"Someone changed the advisory to say that Bracken went dark on purpose and not to follow him. But I never authorized that change, and no one is owning up to it."

Sam snorted. "You have a rat?"

"Possibly. I don't know. But the time it's going to take to get to the bottom of this isn't time we have to spare."

Reef tapped his fingers on the railing. "So, what I'm hearing is that no one is out looking for Liam."

"That's right."

Reef nodded to Sam, who stepped back behind the wheel. "We're here to change that."

Avery fidgeted with her phone. It was the first time Jayna had seen her nervous. "Mind if I join? I can work on your boat as well as anywhere."

Reef held out a hand. "We're glad to have you on board."

This time, Avery took it. "Let's find Liam."

Chapter Thirty-Five

The fishing boat floor rolled and Liam's stomach along with it. Either they had moved to high seas or a storm was coming.

His wrists were raw from trying to escape the fishing wire, which only seemed to dig deeper into his skin. How had he allowed Rolles to string him up like this?

Jayna. He could have escaped, but she had been hooked. Watching her get hurt was something he couldn't bear.

What was it about her that made him put everything on the line? Sure, he had a job to do, but when it came to Jayna, his protective instincts went on overdrive.

But she wasn't free for him to care about in any way except on a professional level. Her choices didn't reveal that a relationship with God was a priority to her, and the woman he dated—one day, married—had to share his faith.

Was it his imagination, or had Jayna leaned in—really listened with interest—when Reef had shared that devotion in Beech Mountain? Could he help her find God and in finding Him, find freedom from her past?

Even if he could, she still belonged to Mario, a man who was not worthy of her.

She deserved better. She deserved a chance to make her own choices, not to be coerced into an elopement.

He couldn't help her from here. He had to escape. Somehow.

There had to be something sharp in this space, something he could use to saw his way to freedom. He inch-wormed until his feet were against the wall. Then he crunched his way to a kneeling position. His head started spinning, and he took several steadying breaths. At least if he could stand, he could see what options the cabin offered.

Legs trembling and feet bound, he shoved his way up against

the wall. This must be what a bowling pin felt like—ready to topple at any moment.

Aside from the table and sloppily made bunks on one wall, the cabin was bare.

But the opposing wall that led to the steps wasn't. Old frames displayed fishing licenses, but it wasn't the frames that caught his attention.

It was the jagged fishing hooks someone had used to hang them.

If he could get across the room, he could maybe reach the hook and use it to slice off the layers of fishing wire that entangled his wrists.

He slid back down to the floor and resumed his inch-worm routine. His knees and elbows scratched against the dirty, uneven floors, but he gritted his teeth. Freedom would be worth it.

The boat lurched, throwing him off balance. He rolled and collided with the base of the bunk bed.

Liam shut his eyes and sucked in several deep breaths. Who was he kidding? In his current condition, he was no match for these men, even if he did manage to get free.

I could use some help, God. Why was he just thinking to pray now? His own efforts had proved futile.

Sorry, Lord. He knew prayer made a difference and that God would never abandon him, but he hadn't been acting like it.

Show me what I should do. And keep Jayna safe.

He blinked the room back into focus. Even if he couldn't escape, he could at least work to regain feeling in his hands.

When he reached the adjacent wall, sweat soaked his shirt. But he forced himself to inch up the wall toward the picture frame and hook. One was low enough that he could reach it, even with his hands tied behind his back.

He bumped the frame, and it fell, shattering on the floor. Someone might have heard, though perhaps the wind that whistled down the stairs masked the noise.

Liam swung his wrists over the hook and began to slowly move back and forth. If he pulled the hook from the wall, he'd have to retrieve it, which would only take more time.

Back and forth. Back and forth.

His arms ached, but one of the lines finally snapped. How many more to go?

Boots thudded on the stairs, and before he could even react, a man he didn't recognize appeared at the cabin entrance.

The dark Bahamian glanced from him to the shattered frame and stalked toward him. Then, he pulled out a knife.

Liam braced himself, but the man slid the knife between his wrists and then sliced through the wire that bound his ankles.

Grunting, the man replaced his knife in his belt sheath and jerked open a storage closet.

As blood rushed into his feet, Liam tried to shake life back into his hands. He couldn't feel his fingers. What was this man doing?

The tall islander yanked a wetsuit from the closet and threw it at him. "Put it on. We'll be there in ten."

With that, he retraced his steps and disappeared onto the boat's deck.

Relief and dread washed over him as he slid to the floor and reached for the wet suit, inches away. The man had freed him.

Was this relief temporary? Regardless, he was grateful for it.

But why did he need a wet suit?

The wind whipped through Jayna's hair as the *Sapona* wreckage came into view. The location was a popular diving site for photographers and travel influencers—like herself.

But today, there seemed something ominous about the rusted shell of the cargo steamer that had run aground in the 1920s. Where the framing had peeled off, the sides left gaping holes that resembled mouths locked in a scream.

She shivered. The darkening clouds forming the backdrop behind the wreckage didn't help her mood. Though the sun hadn't set, the only clue to its presence was the eerie yellow-blue light that filtered through the storm clouds. This late in the evening, that light would soon vanish entirely.

As they cruised closer to the location, only two other boats dotted the nearby seascape. One was a dinghy, and its few divers were climbing back inside. They'd probably seen the approaching storm and decided to head to shore.

The other looked like an ordinary fishing boat, but it sent her heart racing. Jayna scooted down on her seat as her pulse picked up like the ever-increasing wind.

Kaley, who lounged in the seat next to her, shot her a concerned look. "What is it?"

Jayna swallowed. "It's him. The *Riptide* is Kevon's boat." She looked between Kaley and Avery, both seated with her at the helm, and focused on Avery. "You should get out of sight too. Kevon could recognize you."

Kaley popped up from her seat and held out her hat to Avery. "Here, wear this. Jayna already has one. It will help hide your blonde hair."

"Thanks." Avery popped it on her head. "But we need a plan."

Kaley waved at Reef and Sam through the glass window that shielded the helm from the wind. She gave them a thumb's down, which Jayna guessed meant to slow down.

Avery moved across the deck to join Jayna. "Do you think Liam is with Kevon?"

Jayna hugged her waist. "If he's alive, he might be, but at some point, Kevon changed boats. He was on a smaller craft at the Bimini Road dive site. I think that boat was buying from him. The owners seemed nervous about taking us on board."

"If Liam's on board, we'll get him back," Avery said.

"He might not be. A lot of time has elapsed. Kevon could have—" Jayna couldn't say the words out loud. The idea of Kevon dumping Liam's body somewhere before his nightly run made her want to vomit.

The *Meridian* slowed to an idle, and the three of them rose to join Sam and Reef by the wheel.

"What's up?" Reef moved toward Kaley and wrapped an arm around her shoulder.

Kaley motioned beyond the *Sapona*. "Jayna recognized that

fishing boat."

Sam kept a firm hand on the wheel. "Should we get closer? We could inflate the tender."

"I think inflating the tender is a good idea," Avery said. "Once it's dark, they would be less likely to notice it."

Jayna was only half listening. Her gaze was focused on the *Riptide* and the ant-sized figures who were entering the water from it.

"Guys, do you have binoculars?" she asked. "Someone's getting in the water."

"Yeah." Reef reached into a watertight compartment by the wheel and retrieved a pair. "Here you go."

"Thanks." Jayna pressed them to her face and steadied herself against the railing. She had to adjust her angle a few times before finding the boat through the lenses and then shifting down toward the water.

Three men had entered the water in full scuba gear. Their masks concealed their faces, but two were dark Bahamians and the other had pale skin. Could it be Liam?

Before she could study him further, the divers disappeared beneath the surface.

She lowered the binoculars and turned toward the others. "Three men are in the water. I couldn't make out their faces, but one had light skin. It might be Liam, but I couldn't tell."

"Do you have scuba gear?" Avery asked. "We need to get in the water."

Reef had taken the wheel so Sam could retrieve the deflated tender from the cabin. "Yes, we have three sets—one for Sam, Kaley, and me."

"You can use mine," Kaley said. "I can wait with Jayna and the boat."

Jayna's skin prickled. "I'm not waiting here when Liam could be down there."

Avery crossed her arms. "Are you scuba certified?"

Her cheeks flamed. "No, but I'm a good swimmer."

Kaley touched her arm. "We have extra snorkels and masks. You could use one of them."

Hope filled her heart at Kaley's warm touch. "Thank you."

It was Reef's turn to frown. "I don't like the idea of you being left on the boat by yourself."

Kaley lightly punched him in the arm. "Come on, babe. We need only one person to babysit the boat. I know to steer clear of trouble."

"All right," Reef said. "Kaley, let Sam know we need to get our gear. You can inflate the tender while we gear up."

"On it." Kaley turned to Avery. "You can help us carry the equipment from the cabin."

The two disappeared inside while Reef stayed at the wheel. Jayna retrieved the binoculars and scanned the waters for any sign of the divers.

They must have gone to the wreck, but why?

The horizon seemed eerily empty of any other boats. Didn't Kevon usually make exchanges here?

If he wasn't making a sale, there only seemed one other reason for him to be in the water: to hide any evidence.

And if Liam was the evidence, they couldn't get in the water fast enough.

Chapter Thirty-Six

Hold your breath.

That's what Kevon had told Liam. Right now, though, Liam's regulator was working fine, and his tank had air.

Even so, he had no illusions that Kevon planned to feature him in a documentary film—unless it was about the latest diving accident at the *Sapona*.

If only Kevon and the other man would give him some space. But they kept their spear guns trained on him. Though the spear guns were illegal to use for fishing, something told him these two wouldn't blink about using them on him.

The only other boats on the dive site were too far away for him to reach. Perhaps once they were closer to the wreckage, he could use it as a shield and get far enough ahead of them that their spear guns couldn't reach him. Once he surfaced, he would give the distress signal and pray one of those boats noticed him.

It was a weak plan, but it was the best he had.

The sunken bow loomed ahead, a dark scar on the ocean floor. It rose to the surface where the unsubmerged wreckage sometimes served as a diving board for adrenaline junkies, whose footage he had watched on YouTube.

Not today. The storm above must be growing closer as little light filtered through the surface. No other divers were in view, which only added to his growing concerns. If the storm chased the other boats away, he had no hope of escape.

Rolles waved his spear gun and motioned for him to enter the wreckage. What remained of the frame appeared like exposed ribs picked clean of any siding. The inside of the ship resembled a rib cage of a prehistoric animal.

As a diver, it would be a dream to explore. As a captive, it could become a watery grave.

A school of bait fish darted past them, engulfing the three men in a flurry of fins. Liam backed away from the other two men. Maybe the fish could offer some cover for an escape, but Rolles once more closed the distance between them. Yanking Liam's arm, he pulled him toward one of the darkening beams. A hole gaped below them, perhaps an even deeper level of the boat concealed by debris.

It was now or never. Liam jerked free and shoved off against Rolles, knocking the man sideways. He kicked hard to propel himself forward, but the gap to any cover was too far away.

Something razer-sharp sliced through his calf, and he reeled at the pain. Rolles's partner collided into him seconds later and dragged him back toward Rolles, whose spear gun was now empty.

Gritting his teeth, Liam caught sight of the spear protruding from his calf. Rolles was either a lousy shot or hadn't tried to hit him in a vital spot. He must plan to leave that to the sharks. This much blood would be a calling card for them.

The other man cable-tied his hands together but not behind his back. Rolles went for his feet and did the same.

Resisting them was futile and would only lead to more blood loss. His only chance now was to escape once they left—which didn't take long. Neither one wanted to stick around a bleeding diver.

Their fins had no sooner disappeared from his cave-like tomb than he began the maneuver he'd learned in training to break out of cable ties.

But the trick of forming a fist and pulling back toward his chest didn't work as well underwater where the water prevented fast movement. Still, maybe he could break down the strength of the ties over time by repeating the move.

A shadow above him signaled at least one shark had already arrived. He had to get his hands free, and then he could defend himself with the spear still protruding from his calf.

If he didn't run out of oxygen first.

Goosebumps prickled Jayna's skin as their tender buzzed toward the wreckage. At least the wind and fresh rain masked the sound of the small motor. Kevon's boat *Riptide* still anchored on the other side of the wreckage, but for how long, she didn't know.

With the binoculars, she had kept checking in on the boat while Reef, Sam, and Avery donned their gear. When only two divers had returned to the *Riptide*, her chest had squeezed.

Now, she half sat on Avery's lap since the tender, designed for two, transported the four of them while Kaley stayed behind on the *Meridian*. They had agreed taking the tender would be faster than swimming the whole way, and if Liam were trapped in the wreckage, time was not on their side.

Sam tossed an anchor overboard and passed out pole spears for each of them. They also had enough headlamps for everyone, and Jayna secured hers. "Should I turn it on?"

"Wait 'til you get in the water," Reef said. "Sam and I will go first to make sure the coast is clear."

She gulped and watched as they slid off the small boat's edge into the dark waters. Although some people preferred night diving, she dreaded the idea of not being able to see beyond her headlamp.

Sam surfaced moments later. "Just to warn you, there are a lot of sharks. They should mind their own business, but don't freak out."

Avery grunted. "I'm good, but you can stay in the boat if you want, Jayna."

Jayna's pulse pounded. The last thing she wanted was to get out of the boat. She couldn't stay under like the others and would have to surface frequently.

"The tide is low, so you can still stay with us for the most part," Sam said. "But it's your choice. Reef is already exploring the wreckage."

Liam wouldn't hesitate—hadn't hesitated to help her when she'd been hooked. She couldn't turn coward on him.

"I—I'm coming." She scooted off the edge following Avery. Mario had told her attacks were rare, and she hoped he was right.

God, I don't want to get eaten.

Did pleas for self-preservation count as prayer? Did she even believe in Liam's God? He must be real for a strong, smart man like Liam to believe in Him. But whether He heard her prayers or not was a different matter.

Sam motioned for her to swim close to him, and she did. The man was so tall and thick that, surely, someone like him wouldn't look like dinner to a shark. As for Avery, she looked like an appetizer, and Jayna probably did too.

Two mid-size sharks darted past them inside the cavernous walls of the sunken ship, and she bumped into Sam. He gave her a thumb's up, but he wasn't fooling her. What was drawing so many sharks? She hadn't seen a school of fish yet.

Thanks to the low tide, she could still surface for air inside the wreckage. That's when she saw it—a wad of chum someone had chucked inside the ship's remains. The fish meat was wadded into a thin plastic bag that the sharks were attacking.

Her gut twisted, but the bag was only the size of a mid-size trash bag. Liam couldn't be inside it.

Sam tapped her arm and pointed to a part of the wreckage not submerged in the low tide. He wanted her to climb onto it? She was only too eager to get out of the water and hauled herself onto the ledge, followed by Avery and Sam.

Avery yanked off her mask. "This is crazy. Someone's drawing the sharks here."

"Has anyone seen Reef?" Jayna couldn't hide the tremble from her voice.

"No, but there's a lot of ship to cover. Reef can take care of himself," Sam said, but his brows were tight. "Jayna, I think you should go back to the boat. You don't have a tank if you got cornered by a shark. I wouldn't be concerned except that chum has started them on a feeding frenzy."

Avery tightened her pony tail. "I'll go with her and then rejoin you."

"Sounds like a plan." Sam was about to secure his mask back in place when he jerked right. "Look!"

Jayna followed his pointing hand. There, on the far side of the wreck, Reef was waving his arms.

"That's a distress signal," Avery said, "but he looks fine.

Maybe he's found Liam."

"I'll go help him. You get out of here." Sam eased back into the water.

Jayna followed his example, careful not to make a splash that might attract sharks. Avery motioned that she would go first, and Jayna stayed close to her.

Leaving the cover of the wreckage made her feel vulnerable, but it was only a short swim to the tender. They would—

But her heart stuttered as a long, thick shark bumped into her. It had to be at least eight feet long.

She froze. It was as if the creature were summing her up before starting its dinner.

Where had Avery gone? Jayna was at the surface and could feel the cool rain on her scalp, but she didn't take her eyes off the shark. Instead, gripping her pole spear, she thrust it toward the creature who remained dangerously close. It jerked and snapped at her pole, breaking it in half.

The stub that remained in her hand was too short to do any good. Terror raced down her spine.

Dear God, if You're there—

Something splashed on the other side of the shark, and it spun, its tail mere inches from her face.

Hands grabbed her shoulders. "Get in!" Avery cried as she hauled Jayna over the side of the tender.

Jayna collapsed onto the floor of the tender, gasping for air. She was intact. She was alive. "Wh—what did you throw to distract the shark?"

Avery dropped into the seat by the engine. "What do you mean? I didn't throw anything."

"But the splash—"

"What splash?"

Jayna hugged her arms around herself. The splash was real, the only reason the shark turned around from devouring her. Maybe Avery hadn't noticed it. Or maybe—

Thank You, God.

It didn't matter. The old Jayna would call it luck. Today, she knew beyond a doubt that God had heard her, seen her, saved her.

I don't know much about You, God, but I want to learn. If You'll have me.

Her limbs still quaked from the close encounter, but she felt strangely safe.

It was a feeling she never wanted to forget or lose. Now, something told her she wouldn't have to.

Avery revved the engine. "We're getting out of here. This boat isn't much bigger than that bull shark."

Jayna pulled herself up to a seated position on the floor. "What about Reef and Sam?"

"We'll have Kaley move the *Meridian* right next to the wreckage." Avery steered for the waiting craft.

Another sound made Jayna look around. "Wait, what's that?"

"Sounds like another boat."

Avery had no sooner said the words than Jayna's headlamp revealed the yacht. It was heading straight for the *Meridian* as well.

"Turn off your headlamp," Avery hissed.

Jayna fumbled with the switch, but not before she made out the name on the yacht's side: *Seaduction.*

Mario was here.

Chapter Thirty-Seven

Half way there. Though his wrists were raw, Liam had finally snapped the cable tie. This next step he dreaded. The spear was embedded in the back of his calf and had to come out if he were to have any way to cut the cable ties on his feet.

He also needed the spear to defend himself. A shark bumped against the top of the opening above him. This caved-in section of the hull was turning out to be a blessing, providing limited coverage from the predators.

Not for long. Sooner or later, one would thrust its way through the opening.

Gritting his teeth, he gripped the end of the spear and yanked. The pain choked him, and the salt water burned through the three-pronged gash on his leg. Blood gushed through his scuba suit. That wouldn't help conceal his location.

Stars played across his vision, and he squeezed his head with his hands. He had to stay awake. Passing out meant game over.

Sucking deep breaths, he reoriented himself. Now, he had to get his feet free. Bending over, he prepared to slip the trident-shaped spear between the cable tie.

The hairs on his neck prickled, and he spun as a smaller bull shark dove toward the entrance of the cave-in. He thrust the spear at his throat, slicing at the skin. The shark snapped at the spear, and he shoved it into its throat.

The spear lodged into its upper jaw, and the shark retreated.

Now, his weapon was gone, and he had no way to break the ties on his ankles.

Could he swim for it? If he were a merman like in Atlantis legends, he could, but without his feet, he didn't stand a chance of outmaneuvering the sharks that were drawn to his blood.

He glanced at his gauge, and his heart sank deeper. He was running on fumes. It was either try to swim or drown right here.

Another shadow appeared above him.

I'm Yours, Lord. He prayed and spun to face his fate.

This business was getting out of hand. His honeymoon could not start soon enough.

Mario threw the handheld radio against the dashboard of his yacht's steering wheel and accelerated in the direction of the *Sapona*.

How had this business relationship spiraled out of control? All he was supposed to do was clear the beach. Now, he had to do whatever dirty work Kevon tossed his way.

He was sick of it, sick of being the dealer's dog, at his every beck and call.

But the gnawing inside his gut warned him he was also scared. Scared that he would be in the next body bag.

There's a boat hovering by the Sapona. Get rid of it.

That's what Kevon had said. Mario understood the dealer didn't want any other boats witnessing his next exchange, but exactly how he thought Mario would "get rid of it" was unclear.

One thing was for sure. Mario didn't plan to kill anyone.

The fishing boat's sidelights glowed just ahead. He hoped the crew was sober. The last thing he wanted was to convince drunken tourists to leave, though thanks to his resort, he certainly had enough experience.

Mario slowed his yacht and squinted. A tender had pulled alongside the boat, and two figures were climbing out of it.

One was petite with a bright patch of yellow-blonde hair. The other was curvy with an hourglass figure he would recognize anywhere.

Jayna. What on earth was she doing here?

He snapped his jaw together. She had lied to him. Lied about shopping for their honeymoon. What else had she lied about?

Another woman on board aimed a spotlight on him. "Ahoy there!"

He cursed under his breath. He had to keep his cool to get to the bottom of this—and send this trio of females packing.

A thought lit a small surge of hope. Maybe she had gone on a girls' pleasure cruise with that guest from the resort, like a bachelorette party. But it couldn't be pure coincidence they were close enough to witness Kevon's next deal.

Either way, it gave him an angle for conversation.

"Ahoy!" He called as he steered next to the fishing boat and shifted to idle. Jayna seemed to freeze midstride at his voice.

She turned and locked eyes with him. Was that guilt? Fear?

"Hey, babe. Looks like you chose a bad night for a pleasure cruise."

The spotlighting cast dark shadows under her eyes, making her appear ghostly and not like the vibrant beauty she was. It wasn't a good look.

"Wh—what are you doing here?"

He plastered on a grin. "Sorry to cut your pleasure cruise short, but if you haven't noticed, that storm is getting worse."

"How did you know I was here?"

Her tone nettled him. She was in no position to be questioning him. "I finished with a private group and happened to be passing by. There aren't many boats crazy enough to stay out in this storm, and I thought you might be out of gas or something. I didn't know it was you."

There. That should appease her.

Jayna lifted her chin. "What about Kevon's boat? Are you worried about him in a storm?"

A growl surged up his throat, but he swallowed it. "What? Kevon's here too? Is there something I need to know about you two?"

Jayna scowled. "Absolutely not. Since you're here, I would like to know what happened to our resort guest."

"I told you. He's filming with the documentary."

"And I'm Taylor Swift."

Mario swore under his breath and tried to keep his voice from shaking. "Look, I hope you've had your fun tonight, but we need to get back to the resort and rest. Our ceremony is tomorrow—if you haven't forgotten."

The two women on deck exchanged glances, and Jayna crossed her arms. "We can pack later. Show me you're the kind of man who doesn't leave someone behind. That's the kind of man I want to marry."

"Jayna, I'm trying to—"

"That's all I ask. Then I'll marry you."

Although the rain had momentarily stopped, a sudden blast of wind kicked him in the gut. Couldn't Jayna see he was trying to keep her safe, trying to protect the fragile future they had together? Why did she have to be so difficult?

Despite the wind, he leaned over the railing to be closer to her. The determined tilt to her chin and the intensity of her eyes both aroused and angered him.

"You don't understand. You have to leave—all of you—or Kevon will have it out for me."

There, maybe she would stop thinking about their guest and recognize the danger he was in if he let Kevon down.

"So, you're helping him with his deals now? Is that it?" Was that a tremor in her chin?

"It's not like that, Jayna. He just asked me to do this one last thing—"

"And that will lead to something else and then to something else. Don't you see? He has you on a leash. He could easily turn around and pin your guest's death on you. You've got to stand up to him."

Foolish woman. She'd seen the body bag and the fragments of the man inside.

"I'll go with you." She swung her leg over the side and reached out a hand toward him. "We'll face him together."

"Jayna, wait." The blonde woman grabbed her waist. "This is crazy. We need a plan."

"The plan is to find out if your boyfriend is on Kevon's boat or not."

Mario studied the blonde woman harder. It was the same one from his resort. His heart raced. She must be worried sick.

She also wasn't swallowing the documentary story Kevon had fed them.

Maybe he could pacify these women—and then get them all safely out of harm's way.

"Fine, we'll go, but you have to tell that woman to take her fishing boat and leave. I have to do my job of clearing the area."

The woman by the spotlight shook her head. "No, we can't—"

"Yes, go back to the Big Game Resort. The storm is too fierce to stay out any longer. Besides, our rental time is almost over," the blonde said, a little too loudly.

Maybe she was trying to talk over the wind.

"I'm coming with you two," the blonde continued. "It's my boyfriend who is missing, after all."

"Now wait a minute." Mario extended a hand to steady Jayna as she crawled over the railing but couldn't prevent the blonde from jumping onto his yacht too.

"I'll call you later." Jayna called back to the woman on the boat. The spotlight died, and Mario rushed back to the steering wheel. They had to get out of here and fast.

To his relief, the fishing boat took off in the other direction. At least her disappearance would pacify Kevon.

The two women crowded around him at the helm as he shifted to cruising speed. "We'll talk with Kevon tomorrow. It's not smart to interrupt him when he's busy."

The blonde whipped something out from the small of her back. A handgun? What—

"We'll visit him now, if you please." She stepped back and aimed at him.

Of all the nerve. "Who are you?"

"Private investigator. If you cooperate, I can help you negotiate a deal."

He jerked to face Jayna. "You knew? All along?"

"I had no idea until recently, but these people can help us—can help you. We need to cooperate."

This couldn't be happening. He'd worked so hard to rebuild, to rescue his cousins. He couldn't do jail time. Forget about jail time. Kevon would kill them all first.

"Look, your boyfriend—or whoever he is—was on Kevon's boat. By now, he's probably dead. We will be too if we try to board Kevon's boat uninvited."

Jayna gasped, and her hand flew to her throat. "How could you let him?"

"I tried to talk to him—I really did. He told me to leave the narc to him and ran me off."

"You're sure he's dead?" The blonde frowned at Jayna. "If that wasn't him you saw in the water, maybe he is still on the boat."

Mario didn't know what she was talking about, but holding on to false hope wouldn't help their cause. "Kevon isn't the long-speech type. Yeah, he's dead by now."

Jayna's voice shook. "You don't know that. You didn't see him. He could still be on the boat."

He reached for her. "Darling—"

She jerked away. "Don't *darling* me. If there's even the smallest chance that he's alive, we've got to find out."

Mario balled his hands into fists and slammed them on the steering wheel. "Then what? Kevon will kill all of us."

They had rounded the *Sapona* now, and the *Riptide* was in full view. Another boat idled about fifty yards away.

"It must be the deal," Mario muttered. "We need to leave. Now."

"Kill your lights," Avery said.

"What?"

"Just do it. This thing got a tender?"

"Yeah, but—"

"There's a tender moving from Kevon's boat to the other one. We board the *Riptide*, get in, and get out before he gets back. If Liam's there, we'll find him."

"You're crazy," Mario spat. *But her plan could work.*

If he cooperated, it would also put him in good standing with this investigator. Maybe he could still recover and get the money to Cuba.

He killed the lights and glanced at Jayna. "Okay, we do this your way, but if we die, don't say I didn't warn you."

She actually smiled. This woman was mad. He would dump her after this. He didn't deserve a woman who lied and kept secrets from him.

Yes, he'd dump her. Maybe after one last fling.

She would owe him big time after this. Assuming they survived.

Chapter Thirty-Eight

Liam's heart stuttered. From lack of oxygen or a surge of hope, he couldn't tell.

Above him, Reef gave a thumb's up in question. Liam gave a thumb's down and pointed to his tied feet. Reef held up a finger and disappeared.

What was his friend doing here? Didn't he realize the danger?

Moments later, Reef reappeared with another man. Liam's eyes wouldn't focus well enough to identify him.

A choking sensation gripped his lungs, but he tried to kick toward Reef. His friend grabbed his shoulder, and Liam jerked a thumb toward his oxygen gauge. Reef's eyes widened inside his mask.

Reef motioned toward the surface, and the other man nodded. He gripped something long and lead the way.

They stopped. Why?

The tie binding his feet gave way, providing a temporary relief, but something was wrong. His eyes wouldn't focus, and his chest convulsed. He was out of air. Reef still held on to him. His friend wasn't letting go.

Someone knocked the regulator from his mouth and replaced it. He gulped the fresh air greedily. Reef had given him his octopus, or spare regulator. Though dots still played across his vision, their surroundings slowly came into focus.

Half a dozen sharks circled like vultures above them. Most were longer than even Reef.

His friend pushed him between the other man, who he now saw was Sam, and himself. Both held pole spears, which would be helpful for only so long.

Close their mouths, Lord.

Grouped together, they looked almost as big as the largest bull shark that eyed them. Though he swam but feet away from them, he didn't bump at them, and the other sharks left them alone as well.

The Daniel-in-the-lions-den moment felt much longer than the minute it took to surface.

"Where's the boat?" The second diver asked. Liam recognized him as Reef's work partner, though he couldn't remember his name.

"I don't know." Reef's face tensed. "Oh, God, watch over Kaley."

"Kaley's here?"

Reef didn't answer him but motioned toward the *Sapona's* skeletal frame. "Quick, let's scale this and get out of the shark's nest."

Reef kicked upward to reach the lowest rung, about three feet out of the water. He did a pull-up and swung his legs over both sides. "Give me your hand."

His partner helped shove Liam toward Reef's outstretched arm. The loss of blood and lack of oxygen had weakened him more than he realized.

"I've got you." Reef latched onto his hand and pulled him up.

Liam managed to scoot on his stomach onto the beam as Reef helped his partner scale the frame as well.

Reef pulled off his snorkel mask and scanned the dark waters. "Sam, do you see the boat anywhere?"

"No, but there's two behind us."

Removing his own mask, Liam followed his rescuers' gaze. *Riptide* remained moored in place, and another boat had moved close to it.

"No, there's three," he whispered. "See the one that's all dark just past the bow of the wreckage?"

"Is it Kaley?" The worry in Reef's voice was not lost on him.

He'd be worried too if his fiancé was mixed up in this mess.

"Can't tell," Sam said. "I see movement in the water. Might be a tender."

Reef tore his gaze from the horizon and turned back to Liam. "I have so many questions about what's going on here. First, are you okay?"

He offered a tight smile. "Been better. Thanks to you, I'm alive."

"What happened to your leg?"

"The guys that dumped me shot me with a spear gun. I pulled it out to fight a shark. Afraid I'm a little wobbly from all the blood loss."

"If you feel like you're falling, let me know."

"I'm good for now, but how did you get here?"

Reef nodded at Sam. "Sam and I were in Miami to buy a new fishing boat for our company. We got a call from Jayna that you were in trouble and came as fast as we could."

"Jayna called you?"

"Yeah, sounds like that girl's in trouble up to the gills. You're not far behind."

The thought of Jayna drowning in trouble made even his sluggish pulse quicken. "When did you last hear from her? Is she okay?"

"Dude, she was supposed to meet Kaley back at the boat. She came diving with us, but with all the sharks, we told her and your gal Avery to go back to the boat."

"You don't think—"

"The tender is gone. That means they made it back without getting swallowed by a shark. Where they are now, I don't know."

"Psst, you guys should see this," Sam said.

Liam swung his head to peer through the skeletal hull to the other side. The sidelights from *Riptide* revealed a small tender had pulled up alongside it.

"How many are there?"

"Two women, one man," Sam counted. "I think it's Avery and Jayna and some dude."

"Where's Kaley?" Reef's tone was agony.

Liam closed his eyes for a moment. They still weren't focusing great, but his ears had picked up a faint noise. "Listen."

"Might be a boat idling. Maybe Kaley isn't far," Sam said.

Reef gripped the rotting frame. "I'll watch for Kaley from this side. You monitor the situation on the port side."

Liam continued to balance on the frame. Falling off meant almost certain death, though he was less worried about the sharks below than the evil inside the *Riptide*.

The same God that closed the sharks' mouths could protect

241

Jayna and Avery from Rolles's cruelty.

He knew that truth in his head, but his heart feared the worst.

Avery killed the dinghy's engine and let its momentum take them the rest of the way. Jayna squeezed the thin cushion on her bench seat and gulped as Mario reached for the boat ladder. She'd never been on *Riptide*. Its crusted sides and discolored paint didn't exactly shout welcome-aboard.

It was much larger than Mario's private yacht, but whereas Mario's offered luxury and class, the *Riptide* offered a crude, but functional fishing vessel.

It was the perfect cover for Kevon's drug dealings and dirty work.

Mario hesitated at the ladder. "This is our last chance to head back. Even if Kevon and his men went to the other boat, they could have left someone behind. Every last one of Kevon's men is as mean as him."

"Lead the way." Avery motioned him forward. "Try anything, and I'll shoot you."

Jayna's eyes widened. Mario had his faults, but she didn't want to see him hurt—least of all by her new friend.

Maybe Avery was bluffing, but the hard line of her lips suggested otherwise. Liam was her partner, and she wasn't messing around.

Jayna stood and stepped behind Mario. "I'm right behind you." She gave his free hand a squeeze.

Though he had done her wrong in forcing her back here, he had kept her safe from Kevon until this point. He deserved credit for that.

Mario knocked her hand away. "Our funeral." His attempt at sarcasm failed. The fear in his eyes was tangible.

They climbed in silence. The deck was empty, and Mario hunched toward the cabin entrance. Avery cleared the deck and motioned for him to proceed.

He wouldn't look at Jayna, though she followed right on his heels. Perhaps he thought this situation was her fault. Maybe they were both to blame, but couldn't he recognize how his poor choices with Kevon had led them to this place? He couldn't let a man die because intervening was inconvenient for him.

The end did not justify the means. He had to see that, but the scowl on his face as they slinked down the stairs made her wonder if he wouldn't just trade her in for his ticket out if they were caught.

How could she have ever thought herself in love with this man?

Mario paused at the base of the stairs and scanned the cabin. His shoulders relaxed, and he waved her forward. "See? Empty. Now let's get out of here before that changes."

Jayna glanced over her shoulder, but Avery wasn't there. She must still be scanning the deck.

"Let me take a quick look." Jayna strode around him and popped open a cabinet. "You said he was here."

"Yes, in that corner, but he's gone now. It's too late for him, and it will be for us if we don't leave now."

"Mario." Jayna grabbed his arm. "Listen, I'm scared too, but we have to make the right choice, even if it's hard."

He jerked away. "The right choice is staying alive—and I thought it was loving you, though I guess I was wrong."

Her lip trembled. "Yes, we were wrong about each other. But I still want the best for you."

His brows furrowed as if he didn't believe her but wanted to.

She took another breath. "You have the makings of a good man, Mario, but taking shortcuts with the likes of Kevon is ruining you."

Mario opened his mouth to respond, but a thud interrupted him. Avery's unconscious body tumbled down the steps.

He backed away from the stairs as footfalls signaled Kevon or his men had returned.

Jayna's gaze darted to Avery. She was out cold, an ugly gash on her head, but the soft rise and fall of her ribcage indicated she was still alive.

Mario pulled Jayna to his side. "Let me do the talking."

Her throat tightened. A lot of good talking would do right now. They were trapped.

243

Chapter Thirty-Nine

"You."

Two of Kevon's men filled the base of the stairs, and his right-hand man, Raoul, pointed a finger at Mario. "I knew we couldn't trust you."

He threw up his hands. "I had no choice. That agent forced me to board." *At gunpoint,* he thought to himself. Where was her gun now? Had they already disarmed her?

Raoul crossed his arms. "Why?"

"She wanted to find the male agent and thought he might be here. I told her it was a stupid idea, but she wouldn't listen."

"And what about her?" He jerked a thumb at Jayna.

Mario hesitated. He could throw her under the bus or paint her as another helpless victim. "She—"

"I chose to come." Jayna stepped forward. "It's wrong to hurt innocent people."

A sneer cut across Raoul's features as he snatched Jayna by the arm. "Tell that to Kevon. A narc ain't innocent."

Mario swallowed. He hated to see Jayna get hurt, but she was a fool. She'd made her choice. He wasn't responsible for her.

But the pain on her face as Raoul yanked her up the stairs made his gut twist. She was beautiful and brave and about to get herself killed.

The rain fell again, and an occasional gust whipped across the deck. The other man motioned for him to move forward and didn't shove him. Maybe he believed him. Whether he could still get out of this mess alive was another story.

Then he saw him. Kevon handed another man bag after bag over the edge of the boat. He must be helping a crew member load the shipment. That meant he'd gotten the cash he wanted for the deal. Maybe that would put him in a better mood.

Then again, maybe not. When the dealer spotted Mario, his face was darker than the stormy night. "You crossing me?"

"No, man. I didn't have a choice."

"You always have a choice." Kevon's words sent chills through him, though not because his tone was ice.

Jayna had told him the same thing. Raoul still gripped her arm, but she stood straight. The rain pelted her face and dripped from the ends of her hair, but she had never looked more beautiful, more alive.

Right now, all he felt was dead inside, and he was the only one with a shot of getting off this boat without a bullet to his head.

Kevon jerked toward Raoul. "What's she doing here?"

"The agent who forced Mario to search for the narc is out cold in the cabin. This one claims that she came on her own, because she wanted to tell you something." He snorted. "Go ahead, darling. Tell him what you told me."

Mario's chest tightened. *Don't say anything stupid, Jayna. Beg for mercy.*

She stuck out her chin. "Kevon, what you're doing here is wrong. You're hurting innocent people. This has to stop."

Kevon roared with laughter. "Wrong?" He stuffed a hand in his pocket and flipped out a wad of cash. "You call this wrong? I'm bringing industry to a recovering island. I'm giving people what they want. You're interfering."

He narrowed his eyes at Mario. "You. What do you have to say for your fiancé?"

Mario glanced at Jayna. "She's not my fiancé anymore. I could never marry a woman who goes behind my back."

The words were true, so why did speaking them feel like a knife to his heart?

"Looks like you finally got a backbone. Let's see you prove it." Kevon stuffed the money in one pocket and pulled a handgun from his belt. He strode toward Mario and held out the butt of the gun. "Shoot her."

The stock felt like a dagger in his hand. Kevon stepped back and motioned to Raoul to release Jayna. "Kill him if he tries anything."

Raoul seemed more than pleased to train his own gun on Mario.

His world zeroed on Jayna. She didn't even move. She only

stared at him, her eyes pleading. "Don't do this, Mario. You've made mistakes, but you can be forgiven like I was."

Mario swallowed. "You want me to forgive you?"

"No, I'm not talking about human forgiveness. I'm talking about God's forgiveness. He's real, Mario. What's more amazing is that He wants to save us forever. All we have to do is ask Him and believe He will."

"It's no good, Jayna," Mario said. "You can believe what you want, but we've crossed too many lines for God—if there is one—to want anything to do with us."

"The nature of God is doing impossible things. Nothing is too hard for Him."

Kevon growled from where he'd returned to loading the last of the bags. "Just shoot her. If you're man enough."

If he didn't shoot now, Raoul would shoot them both. Maybe he could graze her—but then Raoul would finish her off. He might be brutal about it.

The nature of God is doing impossible things.

Until the last few weeks, Mario wouldn't have considered himself a bad man, but he couldn't deny some of the despicable work he'd done for Kevon. What if Jayna was right, and the end didn't justify the means? Where did that leave him?

Forgiveness from God seemed like crazy talk, yet Jayna's face had a peace about it he didn't understand. But he wanted to.

He fired.

"Kaley!" Reef's voice pulled Liam from his half-awake stupor. The blood loss was taking its toll, but the hope in his friend's tone sent a shot of energy through him.

"Where?" He adjusted his grip around the beam and squinted into the dark. The rain only made the visibility worse.

Then he heard the idling of an engine. It sounded right below them.

Reef jumped and fist-bumped the air. "She's right here."

Liam blinked, willing his eyes to focus. Sure enough, the

shadowy outline of the fishing boat appeared right next to the side of the wreckage.

"Can you jump from there?" Kaley called. "Jayna and Avery said the sharks were awful."

"Sam, wait here with Liam, okay?"

"Sure, man."

Seconds later, Reef propelled himself onto the back of the boat.

Sam chuckled. "That's the second time I've seen him do that for her."

Liam smiled, recalling the crazy story he'd heard about Reef rescuing Kaley in the Gasparilla boat parade last winter. His friend would do anything for the girl he loved.

Although Liam didn't know Jayna well enough to love her the way Reef did Kaley, he couldn't deny that he had come to care for Jayna, despite the red flags that littered her path. He prayed for a chance to get to know her more and show her what God's love looked like.

He jerked his gaze toward where the *Riptide* moored. The empty dinghy still bumped against the side.

Was Jayna safe? Could he get off this wreckage in one piece and make sure she stayed that way?

"How are your arms?" Sam tapped his shoulder with one hand while holding onto a rope Reef had tossed him with the other.

"Fine—It's my leg that's hurt."

"Okay." He wrapped the rope around a beam, and Liam's gaze followed the other end back to where Reef stood on the boat's bow.

"Think you can shimmy down the rope toward Reef?"

The distance wasn't far, but if he fell, there was no going back. Good thing he kept up with his physical training.

"I can do it. What about you?"

"I'll jump once you're on board," Sam said.

Liam understood. If it weren't for his leg, jumping would probably be easier.

Don't overthink. Just do. Taking a deep breath, he rose and grasped the rope. The full body wet suit would help. He wrapped an elbow around the rope and then secured that arm with his other hand. Here went nothing.

He focused on the boat and leapt off. The rope burned through his wet suit sleeves, but it was better than his bare hands. With gravity on his side, he reached the bow shortly.

Reef caught him at the landing and slid him onto one of the seats. "Welcome aboard, man."

His chest hitched at the pain shooting through his leg, but he forced a grin. "Good to be here, captain. Now let's go get those girls back."

"Are you sure that's a good idea?" Reef asked as Sam swung himself on board. "You could use a hospital."

"My leg can wait. That dealer is deadly. Avery doesn't know what she's walking into."

Kaley rushed up to the three men holding a first aid kit. "Liam, I'm so glad you're okay, but I heard your leg is a mess. Maybe you can use something here before we get you to a hospital."

Liam opened the kit in search of something to wrap the wound. "Thanks, but we're not going to a hospital."

Reef nodded toward the wreckage. "We're going to get Avery and Jayna. But I want you below deck in case things go south."

Kaley reached for his hand. "Okay, but I'm here if you need me."

"I do need you, sweetheart." Reef pulled her into his side for a hug. "Right now, I need you to get the weapons from the safe and load the spare mags. I'll be down in a minute to help."

She nodded and disappeared.

"Weapons?" Liam asked. "How did you—"

"I cleared them with customs," Reef said. "Private boats often carry a gun, but it has to remain locked up at all times."

"We have one for each of us," Sam said and then moved to take over the wheel. Reef excused himself to go below to help Kaley.

Liam propped up his leg and wrapped the gauze around the gash. Maybe if he wrapped it enough, the blood would stop staining through. After tightening it as much as he could tolerate, he tied it off and then popped four pain killers.

He lowered himself flat onto the seat bench as Sam idled toward the *Riptide*. Reef joined him minutes later and passed him a handgun. It looked like an older Glock, but even the old models were deadly dependable.

"There's ten in the cartridge and one in the chamber," Reef said.

"Thanks." Out of habit, Liam pulled back the slide to confirm the bullet in the chamber.

Reef made a slashing motion across his neck, and Sam killed the engine. "We'll take the tender from here. Sam, you stay with Kaley."

Liam swung off the bench seat and grunted at the pain.

Reef frowned. "Maybe you should stay too."

"I'm coming." Liam gritted his teeth as he put pressure on his leg for the first time. He could stand, he could walk, and he could shoot.

As if realizing further argument was pointless, Reef motioned for Liam to get into the tender first. He did, but not before he heard Reef whisper to Sam, "If this goes south, get Kaley safe."

Guilt traced through Liam. He hated to put his friends in danger. "You should stay, Reef. I'll be fine."

Reef snorted. "Nice try. Friends don't let friends go alone."

"But Kaley—"

"God's got us." Reef shoved off, jumped into the tender, and then started the engine. The latest downpour provided the perfect cover for the engine, and now, the *Riptide* loomed just ahead.

They were so close—

Shouting rang out above them. Reef killed the engine and exchanged a glance with Liam. His friend would have his back, no matter what happened.

Liam reached for the first rung of the metal boat ladder and pulled himself up. Pain shot through his calf, but he ignored it and climbed the next rung.

Rain and sweat poured down his face as he grasped the final rung.

A shot rang out, followed instantly by another, then another. The blasts echoed through his mind, and his chest constricted.

I'm too late.

Chapter Forty

"No!" Jayna screamed as Mario crumpled to the deck. Her ears still rang from the back-to-back gunshots.

Mario had shot Kevon instead of her, sending the dealer over the railing into the dark waters below. Raoul had opened fire on Mario, but shots from behind Jayna sent Raoul staggering to his knees. Moments later, he face-planted in front of her.

Not moving. Not breathing.

Jayna forced her limbs into action, and she whirled to see who had shot Raoul. Avery stepped out from the stairway shadows. She swept the deck with her handgun, but there was no one else left. The third man must have jumped into the dinghy loaded with drugs. He was either searching for Kevon or making a run for it. She suspected the latter. Searching for Kevon's body would be futile in these shark-filled waters.

Dried blood caked one side of Avery's hair, and she settled her gaze on Jayna. "You okay?"

But Jayna didn't answer. Instead, she rushed to where Mario had fallen and pulled him into her chest. How many times had he been shot?

He gasped for breath and gripped his chest. "Ja—Jayna."

"I'm here." Tears poured down her cheeks. She may not want to marry Mario, but she also didn't want to watch him die.

"I—I'm sorry."

"Shh, it's okay. We'll get you out of here."

"No, listen. My—cousins. Have to help them."

Something thudded on the deck behind her, and she tore her gaze off Mario to see who they had to fight next.

Her heart flip-flopped. Liam? He limped onto the deck and had a wad of gauze wrapped around one of his legs. Her heart constricted. What had happened? She wanted to run over and hug him, but she couldn't leave Mario like this.

Reef climbed over the railing behind him. What were they doing here? Avery rushed over to greet them.

Liam looked past Avery to her. He searched her face as if memorizing every feature, as if wanting to know she were okay, but then his face went blank. He must have seen Mario—and the way she was holding him.

No, it wasn't like that. He had to understand.

"Help's coming," she told Mario. "Hold on."

He coughed up blood and wiped his mouth. "I don't need saving. They do."

"Of course, you need saving. We all need saving."

"Jayna." He breathed her name like a kiss and then closed his eyes. "Made. Peace. With God."

Jayna sobbed with relief. Could it really be true? Only Mario and God knew.

"Somebody, please!" Jayna scanned the deck and spotted Avery a few yards away. "Please help me!"

Avery rushed over and dropped to her knees. "He's gone, Jayna."

"No—No, I still feel a pulse. See?" Jayna pressed Avery's hand to Mario's palm.

The next second, Mario's eyelashes fluttered open, and his gaze locked on Avery's. "Help them. Promise me."

Avery frowned, but to her credit, didn't pull away from the dying man. "What's he talking about?"

"His cousins." The words caught in her throat. "The reason he did all this was to save enough money to buy their freedom."

Avery patted his hand. "I'm sorry."

"Help them." Mario gasped, his lips fixed in a determined line. "July 25th."

"What?" Avery asked.

Jayna closed her eyes. "That's this Sunday, the day we were supposed to leave on our honeymoon with the money for his cousins."

Mario nodded. "Promise? Help them?"

Jayna closed her eyes. The pleading in Mario's gaze was

unbearable. She didn't have the resources to make right the situation with his cousins. Only God could do that now.

"I'll do my best."

Avery's words made Jayna blink. She didn't know about Cuba, what such a promise would involve. But maybe with her connections, Avery could help.

"Now, rest. We'll get you out of here as soon as we can." Avery passed his hand to Jayna. "I've got to help Reef and Liam secure the boat."

"Thank you." Jayna inserted her hand into Mario's. "I'm still here."

He locked his gaze on her. "Sorry. Jayna." And then his eyes glazed over.

Jayna bowed her head. Their love had been so selfish, even sinful. *Rest in God's love now.*

She lowered his head to the ground and closed his eyes with her fingers.

"I'm sorry I was too late."

With the rain and the roaring in her ears, she hadn't heard Liam return. He favored his right leg and reached a hand toward her.

She placed her hand in his and rose. "You're here now. That's what matters."

"Are you okay?"

Jayna nodded and swiped away more tears threatening to fall. "You're hurt."

Liam's smile looked forced. "I'll be fine."

The space between them seemed far too wide. "What happened?"

"I'll tell you another time. Avery has called in the RBDF and will wait for them while Reef and Sam take us to the hospital."

"I don't need a hospital."

He leaned forward and brushed a strand of hair from her face. "I am so glad for that."

Then he faltered and fell to one knee. A grimace tore through his features.

She dropped beside him and wrapped her arms around his

shoulders. "You really are hurt. Lean on me."

"Thanks." But he didn't meet her eyes. "I'm sorry about your fiancé. I—I see you cared for him."

Mario? Why was he talking about Mario when he needed a hospital?

"I am sorry about Mario too, but not because he was my fiancé. He even said he'd been wrong about me—about us. We would never have worked out."

"He must have loved you. He took a bullet for you."

She paused to choose her words. "Yes, he did, but I think it was because he finally realized he needed to do the right thing."

He relaxed against her shoulder and sighed. "I'm proud of him for making that choice."

They sat in a quiet silence, interrupted moments later by a boat's engine. Help was arriving.

She might not have any time alone with Liam again, and she couldn't begin to say everything that he meant to her.

"Liam?"

"Hmm?"

Her throat tightened. "I just want to say how much it means that you didn't give up on me."

"I'd never give up on you." His voice cracked. "You are worthy of—being treated as worthy." He fumbled over the words. "I hope you know that."

For once, she was thankful for the rain and dark night. Liam was so awkward at saying how he felt. Yet his words filled her with hope. "I'm learning to believe that God makes me worthy."

Liam shifted to face her. "You mean—"

"Yes, I don't understand it all, but I believe in God now."

"I want to hear more about that later."

"I'd like to tell you about it."

He hesitated. "And Jayna, I'd like to be part of—your journey. If you'll let me."

Jayna wrapped her arms around him and whispered. "Oh, Liam, you already are."

253

Chapter Forty-One

Jayna stepped onto the cool, pre-dawn sand and shivered. Though last night's gale had passed, a lingering breeze remained. A new day was about to be born, and she had a front row seat to the event.

Was it possible that less than twelve hours had passed since the *Sapona* nightmare? Most of the evening had been a blur—taking Liam to the hospital for outpatient care, contacting Mario's surviving parent, alerting the staff, giving statements, and trying not to collapse from an adrenaline aftermath.

Somewhere in the flurry, she asked Liam to meet her on the beach for sunrise. There had been no time last night to say all the things she wanted to tell him. He had said yes, though a glance around the beachfront showed she was alone.

Dear man. With the blood loss and abuse he had suffered, she wouldn't blame him for sleeping through his alarm. Kaley and Avery had been still asleep in her room when she tiptoed out the door, and no doubt Reef and Liam were just as exhausted.

Strangely, she wasn't. The emotional rollercoaster and lack of sleep would hit her later in the week. But right now, she felt more at peace than she ever had.

She was free in more ways than one. She wasn't bound to marry someone she didn't love. Thanks to Jesus, she wasn't bound by the wrongs she'd done or that others had done to her, but Liam still needed to know the truth. She was done with lies. A relationship had to begin with honesty.

At least, friendship did. She couldn't deny the attraction she felt toward Liam, but she needed to follow Beatriz's wisdom for once and go slow. She wanted her friendship with Liam to begin with trust so that if it budded into something more, she wouldn't have regrets.

A door behind her thudded, and she spun to see him gimping

across the patio toward the beach with the cane Reef had made for him. It was less a cane and more of a tree branch, but it served the same purpose.

Retracing her steps, she reached him at the edge of the patio. "I didn't think you were coming, but I'm glad you did."

"I wouldn't miss my first sunrise with you." Despite the bags under his eyes, his blue eyes shone. He had a day's growth of reddish blond beard on his chin, a humorous contrast to his dyed hair. What a fool she had been to judge a man based on her silly profiling.

She chuckled as they sauntered toward the shoreline.

"What is it?" Liam searched her face. "What's so funny?"

Jayna covered her mouth to hold back a laugh. "Us."

"Come again?"

The navy horizon turned a pale blue, foreshadowing the first rays of sunlight.

"Sit with me?" She motioned to the sand just out of reach from where the waves teased the shore.

"Sure." He lowered onto his good knee and then reclined onto the sand. "Now what's so funny about us?"

She stole a glance at him. His eyes crinkled in amusement. Or was that concern?

"I mean, look at us. You're a private investigator, and I'm the ex-fiancé of the man you were sent to investigate."

"You were a victim, Jayna, and I have you to thank for saving my life." He held out his hand, but she hesitated at the word *victim*.

She had to set the record straight. "All my life, I have been a victim because I allowed myself to become one."

"Now, Jayna—"

"No, let me finish. You need to know what kind of woman I really am." Her face burned as a flood of memories returned, reminding her of her past.

"You're a woman Jesus has redeemed." His voice was full of quiet conviction. "He has removed your sins as far as the east is from the west."

Salty tears pricked at her eyes, but she blinked them back. "Thank you, Liam. But I still want you to know."

He folded his hands and nodded. "I'm listening."

"I—I started doing nude modeling in high school, because my manager told me it would help my career. I knew it was wrong—hated it—but I didn't say no. Then I let myself get taken advantage of by my agent, and that only led to me looking for love in all the wrong places. Mario was one of many men I thought—I thought would really love me."

She gasped for air. Her chest felt lighter, but the shame of confessing out loud was overpowering. Liam would surely walk out of her life now. A godly man like him wouldn't want to deal with this kind of baggage.

Instead, he reached for her hand again. "Look at me, Jayna. Please."

Guilt weighed down her eyelids, but she pressed through the discomfort to meet his gaze, though she wouldn't let herself take his hand.

His eyes were moist with tears. "None of that makes a difference to me. Jesus doesn't love you any less. You do believe He loves you?"

Her face warmed, but not with shame this time. "Yes, but I'm only beginning to understand what real love is, Liam."

He leaned forward as if promising to keep her secrets safe. "I know, and I know you have a lot of healing to do. You don't have to be alone in that process. Our friend Kaley is a Christian trauma therapist, and she can help you, if you're interested."

Jayna hugged herself and focused on the horizon. Detoxing from her past would take time, yet her heart craved affection—this wonderful man's affection. She cleared her throat. "I would like to talk with her." *I would like so much more I can't let myself have right now.*

They sat in silence as the waves teased their toes and the sun climbed past the horizon to debut a new day.

It promised a new beginning for her but also an abundance of unknowns.

As the sun rose higher, Liam didn't reach for her hand again. Maybe he was starting to understand the temptation a man's touch held over her—or perhaps he no longer wanted to hold her hand after everything she'd shared.

Instead, he reached for his cane and began to stand. She blinked back the disappointment that their time together was over.

She would stay right here and savor the remnants of the sunrise, savor how fleeting but precious their time together had been.

"Are you—"

"I'm going to stay right here," she blubbered through unwanted tears.

"The sunrise is over." His voice was so gentle.

She sniffed back a sob. "I know."

"You know what's so wonderful about sunrises, don't you?"

Jayna shook her head, refusing to take her gaze off the horizon.

Liam touched her shoulder. "We get a new one every day God gives us here on earth."

"It's not just the sunrise. It's who shares it with you. After this, you're going to be so busy with your work—"

And forget about me. She choked on the words she couldn't bring herself to say.

"Oh, Jayna. You've got that wrong." With a sigh and a grunt, he fell onto the sand beside her again.

She wiped her eyes with the back of her hand and dared to look at him. His mouth was cracked in a ridiculous grin.

"I'm not going anywhere, Jayna. You can't bottle this sunrise, and you don't need to. It's just the first of many sunrises I plan to share with you."

Her breath hitched. She dipped her toe forward to touch the wave, to assure herself this moment was real.

"Now can you give me a hand to get back up?" He started laughing. "Because my leg is killing me."

Jayna jumped to her feet. "I'm so sorry. Here, let me help you."

He grasped her hand and shoved off the ground with his branch-cane. "No worries. One sunset down the road, it will be my turn to pick you up." He winked and offered her an arm. "Let's get some breakfast. I pulled a few strings, and the kitchen has all the ingredients I need to make you those Pioneer Woman cinnamon rolls I promised you back in Beech Mountain."

He remembered that? She slipped her hand onto his arm and grinned at him. "Let's see if you can top those Pillsbury ones."

"Oh, these will be better." His tone softened from teasing to serious. "In time, lots of things will be better because we'll get to share them together."

His words held a promise. She glanced over her shoulder at the sky filled with sunlight and dared to believe that tomorrow's sunrise might be even more beautiful.

Epilogue

Howard Park Beach, three months later

Jayna spread a picnic blanket across a patch of sand that should give them the perfect sunset view. A family with two children splashed nearby, while some teenagers picked their way across a pile of rocks to claim their own sunset spot. Behind her, some couples started a game of volleyball she hoped wouldn't land in her dessert.

Howard Park, Florida was a much different scene than Bimini, Bahamas—and she preferred it that way.

She cast a glance over her shoulder toward the parking lot. Still no sign of Liam's green pickup truck.

Like that day three months ago while she waited for the sunrise, she wasn't sure if he would arrive in time for this sunset. An hour ago, he texted that Avery had sunken her teeth into a new lead on the crime-boss case, and he might be late.

Unlike that day, she would enjoy the sunset regardless. The peace surrounding her heart today was like nothing she'd ever known. Kaley had been helping her address the layers of hurt in her life and find freedom in her new-found identity in Christ and what His Word said about her. She had also plugged into a Crossroads Church Bible study for women that was taking her through the whole Bible in bite-size bits. It was amazing to see how God used so many broken people in His redemptive plan.

Then, there was Liam. Unless he was called away on a case, she saw him every week at church, at least once a week when he made an excuse to visit the bakery where she now worked, and almost every Friday for date night.

Well, it was date night to her. Even if they weren't *official*, Liam was purposefully pursuing her and taking his time about it—

and she was savoring the chance to get to know him.

More noise from the parking lot made her look again, and her heart skipped as the green truck she'd recognize anywhere pulled into a space.

Five minutes at best was all that remained till sunset. Jayna tripled checked her cooler to make sure her carrot cake was staying cool. This year's October was on the warm side.

Then, she jumped to her feet and waved as Liam jogged onto the beach in dark-washed jeans and a gray polo. He must have come straight from the office.

"So sorry I'm late." Liam greeted her with a kiss on the cheek. "This evening hasn't gone anything like I'd planned."

"That's okay." She motioned to the picnic blanket and sat down. "You made it for the sunset, and I brought two big slices of fresh carrot cake." Unzipping her cooler, she handed him a container with cake and a fork.

Liam moaned and patted his stomach. "Thanks to you, I have to visit the gym more than I used to."

Jayna pulled the container away and grinned. "Fine, I can eat cake all by myself."

He tugged it back. "No—friends don't let friends eat cake alone."

Friends. Yes, they were the best of friends, but surely soon they might be more?

Liam poked one piece of cake and set his fork down as if something were stuck in his throat. "This is delicious, but I wanted to ask you something."

Her pulse picked up, and she set down her cake. "Yes?"

"You know Kaley and Reef's wedding is this coming weekend. Ugh, I haven't even started packing." He ran a hand through his hair, now thankfully his normal ginger color.

Jayna clapped her hands. "I can't wait. Did you remind Avery she's welcome to drive with us?"

"I—uh—I'll need to double check with her." Liam tugged at his collar. "She's razor-focused on this new lead on Big Eddie. You know how frustrated she was with the dead end—literally— that Kevon's death proved to be with the drug trafficking angle."

Jayna nodded. Only after talking with Kaley did she understand the bigger picture of the web she'd almost been trapped in.

"But that's not what I want to talk to you about. Sorry, I'm making a mess of this." He reached for her hands and held them. "What I am hoping is that when we get to Beech Mountain for the wedding that I can tell anyone we meet that you're my girlfriend. Will you be my girlfriend?"

Her heart surged with joy, but before she could answer, Liam hurried on.

"I have loved getting to know you, watching you grow in your walk with God, and I'm so proud of what you've overcome and are overcoming. You've probably been wondering what's taken me so long to ask you, but I wanted to give you space. We'll still take our time getting to know each other, but yeah, I really want to call you my girlfriend."

He laughed, and his pale skin turned several shades of pink. "That probably sounded a lot like a nervous schoolboy."

Jayna grinned. "Yes, it did, and I loved everything about it."

"That's the other thing." He squeezed her hands, and she edged closer to him. "I've been very careful the last few months and haven't told you in so many words—though I hope my actions have spoken for me—but Jayna, I love you. I don't want you to say the words until you're ready, and you can take all the time you need, but I can't sleep at night wondering if you're wondering—"

She leaned in and kissed him.

He pulled back to search her face. "Jayna—"

"Shh." She put a finger to his lips. "Your turn to listen. You are the kindest, most selfless man I've ever met, and I've wanted to love you since that sunrise on the beach in Bimini. I knew I didn't have the right to love you then, and so, I've been learning what real love means. It's so much richer and more wonderful than what I've experienced in the past, and I can honestly say now that I love you too."

Liam wrapped an arm around her shoulder and tugged her in for another kiss. When he released her, he glanced at the shoreline with a sheepish grin. "Looks like we missed the sunset."

"A wise man once told me that we get a new sunrise every day God gives us here on earth." Jayna leaned her head on his arm. "I suppose the same is true of sunsets."

He rested his head on hers. "Yes, it is."

She nuzzled closer into his side. "Then I believe the best is yet to come."

Author's Note

Emily Dickinson wrote, "There is no frigate like a book to take us lands away…"

Writing and reading have never been so dear as during the pandemic. In 2020, my husband and I had hoped to travel to Europe together before starting a family, and then Covid struck. At that point, simply traveling to the grocery store felt like a vacation.

In that context, I wrote *Hold Your Breath*. Although I have been to the Bahamas before, I have not visited Bimini specifically and kept hoping for a chance to go. Although there is no substitute for visiting in person, I resorted to books, websites, and YouTube for my research—and hope the result makes you feel as close to Bimini as writing these pages did for me.

The pandemic is "over" as I type these words, but traveling with a baby is a whole new adventure for my husband and me. We did introduce our son to Beech Mountain, North Carolina when he was seven months old though. In hindsight, I do not recommend eleven-hour road trips with babies that age, but we all lived to tell about it, and our boy now shares his mother's love for that beautiful place. (Okay, he might not remember his first time seeing snow there, but his dad and I will never forget it.)

I do look forward to this setting coming alive for him as he grows older—even as it gave Jayna a new appreciation for beauty and chance to hope for change.

Whether you are a beach person or a mountain lover, this book spans both. Perhaps these settings will inspire your own adventures. Regardless, I hope the story itself transports you like the "frigate" that books can be for us—and touches your life in a special way. If it does, I would love to hear from you. You can connect with me at KristenHogrefeParnell.com.

Happy travels of both the imaginary and literal kind!

~ Kristen

Sign up for Kristen's monthly newsletter at
KristenHogrefeParnell.com and receive a free story.

Romantic Suspense by Kristen:

Crossroads Suspense
Take My Hand
Hold Your Breath

Young Adult Fiction by Kristen, published under her maiden
name Kristen Hogrefe, includes:

The Rogues Trilogy
The Revisionary
The Revolutionary
The Reactionary

Discussion Questions

1. Liam wants to find the woman who is right for him and one that he will also be good for. If you are in a dating relationship, have you considered both sides of this coin? Are you good for your significant other, and is he good for you?

2. *Second chances* is a favorite trope in romance or romantic suspense books, perhaps because it offers not only hope, but also a priceless reminder of a biblical truth. Do you remember the harlot Rahab in Joshua 2? She helped the Jewish spies hide and escape Jericho in exchange for her family's lives. Not only did she help God's people, but she also turned away from her X-rated occupation to marry a Jewish man named Salmon. If that name isn't familiar, let's follow her family tree a little further. Rahab and Salmon had a baby named Boaz, who had a baby named Jesse, who had a baby named David ... King David, who is in the lineage of Christ. Wow! Rahab got a second chance. Jayna got a second chance. And so can you. What "second chance" can you pray about—for yourself or someone else?

3. At one point, Liam reflects on the truth that although God doesn't always answer his prayers the way he wants—Kaley is proof of that—but God always knows what is best for his children. When have you experienced the blessing of unanswered prayer in your own life?

4. The opening song Jayna's first night at church talks about God leaving the ninety-nine for the lost one.
   a. If you related to Jayna's character, how does it make you feel to know God leaves the obedient ninety-nine in search of the one that has strayed?
   b. If not, ask yourself if you are too quick to judge the lost, like Jayna, and their sinful behavior instead of seeing their real need the way God does?

5. At one point in the story, Liam stowed his own relational disappointments to celebrate at Reef's side. We all have times in our lives when we find others receiving something we personally want. The Bible says to "rejoice with those who rejoice, and weep with those who weep" (Romans 12:15). How can we be sincere in joining their celebration instead of feeling sorry for ourselves or seething with jealousy?

6. In that moment, Liam reflected: "God knew what each of them needed and when they needed it. He had to remember that." Have you ever thought God somehow forgot about you? But the truth is, God's timing is never early and never late. When have you experienced God's best timing in the past, and how can that reminder encourage you for the prayer requests you're waiting on God to answer?

7. Jayna discovers that the Crossroads church group prays over everything. When was the last time you talked to God? I challenge you to think of prayer as a daily conversation, something as natural as breathing, and something that lets you have immediate access to God's "throne of grace" (Hebrews 4:16).

8. For anyone recovering from addiction, you know what your triggers are. Jayna reminds herself that overeating could cause guilt from her past purging days to resurface and trigger her. If you have recovered from an eating disorder, how might your story be just what someone else needs to hear? If you're struggling with a secret eating disorder, please do not isolate but reach out to a trusted friend or family member for help.

9. Jayna thinks Kaley's life is perfect, only to find out about Kaley's own harrowing experiences (recorded in *Take My Hand*, Crossroads Suspense Book 1). Have you ever

judged someone based on appearances without getting to know them first? How might realizing that everyone has a deeper story than we see on the surface help you avoid comparing yourself to others?

10. When Kaley reflects on her past, she tells Jayna: "In our most painful moments, He is most present." Her words give Jayna something to think about. Have you experienced this truth—that God is most present even in your hurt? What did you learn?

Made in United States
Orlando, FL
30 October 2023

38395024R00152